Quite before he knew what he was doing, and certainly without conscious thought, Jem stopped right there in the middle of the rose garden, drew Olivia into his arms, and kissed her thoroughly and passionately.

Lost to all reason, he kissed, and kissed, and kissed her again. When he came around, as if from a dream, he found that they had moved to sit on a curved stone bench and that Olivia was cradled on his lap. Her hands were on his back, pressing him closer, and her mouth sought his as if she were dying from the same hunger that afflicted him. Heart pounding, he returned her kiss, losing all reason again as he succumbed to the miracle that was unfolding between them.

Eventually, they paused to look at each other and smile, then kiss again, this time softly, gently, tentatively.

"Olivia!" he murmured against her mouth, feeling her smile in response.

"Jem," she returned softly. "You are kissing me."

"Yes, I am. Is that a difficulty for you?"

"Not at all! In fact, it is an exceedingly pleasant experience."

"For me, too. Shall we, then, do it again?"

For answer, she took his face in both hands, swooping on his mouth with a confidence and enthusiasm that both exhilarated and thrilled him.

Author Note

This is the final book in my series The Chadcombe Marriages. While the books are stand-alone, this story takes place after *Waltzing with the Earl* and *The Captain's Disgraced Lady*. Lady Olivia is the younger sister of Adam and Harry.

My own children are now grown up, and my husband and I have loved watching them grow from wonderful* children to remarkable* young adults. It got me wondering how that journey might have gone for Olivia. I do hope you enjoy it.

I've included a childbirth scene in *The Makings of a Lady*. In Regency times, death in childbirth was not uncommon, with infection, fits and bleeding the most common causes. The discovery of ergot was a breakthrough in preventing some of these women from dying. Now, as then, good midwives and the skilled doctors who work with them understand the importance of supporting the woman so that her body can do its amazing work, and they also know to step in if needed. Doing too much too soon can cause harm, as can doing too little, too late. As we continue to learn more about childbirth, we hope that the numbers of women dying worldwide will continue to fall.

My next series will feature a trio of governesses— all occupying that unusual role in a Regency household. Governesses were not part of the family, but were not quite servants, either. How will my three heroines respond to the challenges that come their way?

*absolutely no bias whatsoever

CATHERINE TINLEY

—

*The Makings
of a Lady*

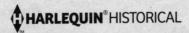

Recycling programs
for this product may
not exist in your area.

ISBN-13: 978-1-335-52294-8

The Makings of a Lady

Copyright © 2018 by Catherine Tinley

This edition published by arrangement with Harlequin Books S.A.

For questions and comments about the quality of this book, please contact us at CustomerService@Harlequin.com.

® and TM are trademarks of Harlequin Enterprises Limited or its corporate affiliates. Trademarks indicated with ® are registered in the United States Patent and Trademark Office, the Canadian Intellectual Property Office and in other countries.

Printed in U.S.A.

www.Harlequin.com

Catherine Tinley has loved reading and writing since childhood, and has a particular fondness for love, romance and happy endings. She lives in Ireland with her husband, children, dog and kitten, and can be reached at catherinetinley.com, as well as through Facebook and on Twitter, @catherinetinley.

Books by Catherine Tinley

Harlequin Historical

The Chadcombe Marriages

Waltzing with the Earl
The Captain's Disgraced Lady
The Makings of a Lady

Visit the Author Profile page at Harlequin.com.

For all my McCoy, Talbot, Sloan, Ferris, Tinnelly and Hemingway relatives—it's a privilege to be part of this big, warm, supportive, close family. Love you all.

And for all midwives—co-mothers, wise women, mothers of light. You who protect the gateway to life hold two lives in your hands, and stand or sit or kneel With Women. We mothers salute you.

Prologue

London—September 1815

'Will you marry me?'

Olivia said the words aloud, thrilled by the way they flowed. She tried it a different way. 'Lady Olivia, will you marry me?'

Oh, that sounds wonderful! She grinned at herself in the bedroom mirror, glad no one was present to witness her giddy foolishness.

Perhaps he would kiss her instead. She dearly hoped so. Thoughts of kissing him had been uppermost in her mind for many weeks. Her heart skipped as she imagined the sensation of his strong, handsome face approaching hers, his lips on her lips, his arms wrapped around her. She closed her eyes, savouring the image. Oh, how wonderful it would be! Could it happen? Perhaps all this time he had been developing warm feelings for her, too. He might say 'Lady Olivia, I love you. Ardently, truly, deeply. Will you marry me?'

And she would reply *Yes*. Of course she would. She wanted nothing more than to be his wife. Now, should she offer a shy yes, or an enthusiastic one, or perhaps a coquettish one?

Honestly, at this point, she cared not. The important thing was that she adored him and he had said it was important that he speak with her. He had said so, in that solemn way of his, and so she had agreed to meet him in the garden after nuncheon.

Quite when she had fallen in love with Jem Ford, she was not certain. Was it the first time she had seen his crooked smile, the day they had met? He had been carried into the Fanton townhouse by two of the footmen, the leg injury he had sustained at Waterloo still healing. Having made the long and tiring journey from France, he had then faced the entire Fanton family who were waiting to greet him, including the Earl of Shalford, Olivia's eldest brother—an ordeal for any stranger. But how much harder must it have been for him? Olivia reflected. Unable to walk, exhausted and clearly feeling uncomfortable about the number of people waiting to receive him, he had nevertheless behaved impeccably. He had thanked his commanding officer, Olivia's other brother Harry, for the invitation, but insisted he would remove to a hotel on the morrow.

Harry, of course, was having none of it. 'Having resigned from the Army, I am your Captain no longer,' he had said, 'and so I cannot command you. But I do hope you will stay with us until you are recovered.' They had agreed to discuss the matter later, but even then—having known him for all of two minutes—Olivia had been conscious of a strong wish within herself for him to stay.

She had looked at him closely, noting the dust of travel on his clothes and the lines of pain and tiredness etched on his face, yet her thought had been, 'My! How handsome he is!' Surely the beginnings of love had sprung into life in that moment? Like a trickle of water on a hillside in spring, it had begun almost silently. But, during the months of his convalescence, as she had spent more and more time with him, the trickle had grown slowly and steadily, until now a flood of love for him consumed her. He was her first thought in the morning and her last at night. She lived for the times they spent together, especially the precious moments when they were occasionally alone.

He had been ever the gentleman, but she hoped he might love her the way she loved him. She had sometimes sensed something from the expression in his eyes. There was also, she reminded herself, the fact that he sought her out and seemed genuinely interested in all of her thoughts and feelings. There was hope!

And now, he wished to speak to her. Alone.

Heart pounding, she made her way downstairs, through the townhouse and out to the garden beyond. And there he was! Seated on the usual bench, waiting for her. No stick today, she noticed automatically. It had been over a week since he had used the stick to aid with his walking. His crutches had been dispensed with over three weeks ago and it was wonderful to see him healed further.

She smiled instinctively, gladness sweeping through her just on *seeing* him. Her eyes swept over him, noting the polished boots, the well-tailored breeches clinging to his muscular thighs, the smart military coat that suited him so well. How handsome he looked in his uniform! This was only the second time she had seen him fully attired in his dashing regimentals. She strongly approved.

Her eyes scanned upwards to his beloved face. No smile. He looked serious, grave, solemn. Of course he did! This was an important moment.

They exchanged greetings and he invited her to sit next to him. She did so, all the while her mind racing in anticipation of what he would do and say next.

'Lady Olivia,' he began, his deep blue eyes trapping hers. 'I wanted to see you as there is something important I must say to you.'

She nodded. She was not normally tongue-tied, but the enormity of the moment had taken from her the power of speech.

'I am lately returned from Horse Guards Parade. As you know, I was also there two days ago, to report my leg is now fully healed.' Olivia frowned—this was unexpected. 'I returned today, to some surprising news.' He paused, seemed to gather himself, then resumed. 'I am to be posted to Australia.'

'Australia?' What on earth was he talking about? He couldn't possibly be going to *Australia*! 'For how long?'

'For at least two years.' He looked pale, she noticed absently, even as she felt the blood draining from her own face.

'Two years?' She echoed him mechanically, barely able to take it in.

'At least. In reality I am likely to be gone for longer. I am transferring to the Forty-Eighth and am promoted to Lieutenant.'

'Lieutenant?' She swallowed. 'But that is wonderful news! And well deserved. But—must it be Australia?'

He nodded grimly. 'You know my situation. Although there is no shame in my lineage, my father died penniless. Thankfully he had paid for my army commission before his gambling debts overwhelmed him, and my sister Lizzie has a small income from our mother's family. But—' his eyes blazed into hers '—I have no choice. This is a chance to make something of myself.

Today, I am nothing. I am no one. A young ensign, half-crippled, with no fortune, no position in society, nothing. I am truly grateful to your family for offering me a home here these past months, but it has only served to underline my determination to improve my station.'

'But, no!' she protested. 'That does not matter! Money and station are not what is truly important!' Her eyes were filling with tears as shock turned to a dawning realisation. *He was leaving her.* 'You cannot leave—us!' Almost, she had said 'me'. They both knew it.

He stood. 'I am truly sorry. I have allowed a…friendship to develop between us, even though I knew this parting must come. I had no intention of causing you hurt, Lady Olivia.'

She could not speak. Her heart was breaking. She looked up at him in mute appeal. His jaw hardened. He bowed, wished her farewell and was gone.

Chapter One

Surrey—May 1819

'Why must Adam be always telling me what to do? Life is so *dreary* here at Chadcombe!' Olivia sat down heavily on an ornate French chair, uncaring that the mud along the hem of her petticoat was transferring itself to a gilded wooden leg. 'Everyone thinks I am still ten years old!'

Great-Aunt Clara set down her knitting. 'Oh, dear, Olivia—I did not know you were so unhappy here with us!' Her lined face was filled with distress. 'But, yes, how tedious you must find us all!'

With a startled expression, Olivia jumped up and moved to sit beside the elderly lady. 'Oh, no! Darling Great-Aunt Clara, I did not mean *you* are dreary!' She took her great-aunt's hand. 'You know I love you dearly, and I love Adam and Charlotte, but I have spent most of my life here at Chadcombe and sometimes I just feel— oh, I don't know! You will think me foolish!'

'Who is being foolish?' Charlotte, Olivia's sister-in-law, entered the morning room. 'Olivia? But you could never be foolish!' Charlotte leaned over and kissed Olivia's cheek. 'Good morning!' she added cheerily.

Charlotte's elegant morning gown, Olivia noted, had no trace of mud anywhere on its green-silk folds. Its gently draped skirts revealed that Charlotte was expecting a child. She had suffered in the early months with tiredness and the indignity of being frequently sick. Yesterday she had declared she was much better. Olivia was not convinced.

'Charlotte! You are up already—how did you sleep?'

'Perfectly well, thank you!' Charlotte brushed off Olivia's concerns with a wave of her hand. 'Now, what is this about you being foolish?'

Olivia struggled to answer. Suddenly her frustrations seemed churlish. She knew she had what others would view as a perfect life, in a beautiful house, with a loving family. It was just—she felt as though she needed to escape. She needed adventure!

'Our poor Olivia finds it dull to be always at Chadcombe,' offered Great-Aunt Clara tentatively.

Charlotte eyed her keenly. 'Are you moped, love? Remember, Miss Ford and her brother will arrive tomorrow for their visit. You have been looking forward to that, have you not?'

Olivia sighed in frustration. 'I am always happy to see Lizzie, and it will be good to meet—' she choked a little on his name '—Jem again. I cannot say why I am feeling so unsettled. It's just—I feel as though everyone still believes me to be a child!'

'Poor, dear Olivia!' Great-Aunt Clara's knitting slipped to the floor. Olivia retrieved it for her and the old lady patted her hand kindly. 'I can quite understand how it must be frustrating. After all, you must be nearly twenty now.'

'I had my twenty-second birthday last December, Great Aunt-Clara. Don't you remember?'

'*Twenty-two?* Really?' Great-Aunt Clara looked astonished. 'Well, bless me! I do think of you as properly
belonging in the schoolroom! I am so sorry! But, yes, I
remember you had your Season in London last year, or
was it the year before?'

Olivia exchanged a brief glance with Charlotte. 'I
made my debut *four* years ago, if you remember.' She
spoke gently, hoping her elderly relative would recollect. 'After Charlotte and Adam were married? It was the
time Juliana came to stay with us—and she and Harry
got married soon afterwards.'

'Of course! Was that really four years ago? Yes, I
suppose it must be—because we got the new oven and
Charlotte was such a help… And then that dreadful Napoleon and the battle… I was never so relieved as to see
Harry home safe after Waterloo, and married, and now
he and dear Juliana live so close by with their dear little
son—it all worked out so well…' Great-Aunt Clara almost lost herself in a tangle of recollections. 'So, yes,'
she concluded firmly, 'it was three years ago. Or possibly four. So how old are you again, Olivia?'

'I am two-and-twenty,' said Olivia patiently.

'Twenty-two? Twenty-two already!' Great-Aunt Clara
became animated. 'Lord, I remember you when you were
so little and your dear mama would sit here, in this very
room, cuddling you…'

If Clara had wanted to divert Olivia, she was success-
ful, at least temporarily. Olivia could never resist hearing tales of Mama, who had died giving birth to Olivia's
baby sister when Olivia was a child. No one would tell
her what had happened that day and bewildered eight-
year-old Olivia had just wished to know when Mama
would be returning. Now that she was old enough to ask
for the truth, she had never found the courage. To this

day, Olivia felt the aching hole in her life caused by her mother's death and had never fully come to terms with the sense of abandonment she had experienced.

And then, when she was eighteen, she had been abandoned again by someone else she had loved.

Quickly, she diverted her thoughts from *that* old wound. The past was done, finished, gone. She was a different person now—older, wiser, less naive.

After Mama's death, she had been raised by her grieving father alongside Olivia's two big brothers and Great-Aunt Clara, but it was never the same. So now, she plied Clara with prompts and questions, and her great-aunt dutifully obliged, retelling stories Olivia had heard a hundred times before. Olivia had many clear memories of Papa, who had died only a few years ago, but she tried hard to keep alive her hazy memories of her mother.

Today, though, after a time, the old stories did not satisfy Olivia. She could not settle to any task, and eventually Charlotte sent her away. 'Olivia, do please go for a walk, or take Dahlia out and ride! I declare your fidgeting is making me nervous. I have restarted this list for Cook three times!' Charlotte was smiling, but she looked a little concerned.

'I have already walked this morning.' Olivia indicated her mud-stained hemline. 'I shall go for a ride. At least yesterday's rain has stopped—it is a relief to have some sunshine.' She rang the bell and within minutes a housemaid arrived. 'Please, can you send a message to the stables to have Dahlia saddled and ask Susie to come to my room?' The housemaid bobbed in assent and Olivia left the morning room, murmuring her goodbyes.

Charlotte's head was bent to her housekeeping before Olivia had even left the room. She seemed calm, but

Olivia knew how much her sister-in-law missed being able to ride since she realised she was expecting again. Riding was one of the ways in which Olivia and Charlotte had forged a friendship—both were excellent horsewomen and liked nothing more than to gallop neck-or-nothing through the fields and lanes—much to the disapproval of Adam and Harry.

There was, of course, no question of a pregnant lady riding and Charlotte, after two miscarriages, a still-birth, and yet no living child, was being extra-cautious this time. Thankfully, all seemed well so far, but Olivia shared the concern felt by the whole family about Charlotte's plight.

Olivia's bedchamber was a beautiful room, over-looking the deer park in front of the house. It was decorated with delicate wall hangings and curtains in shades of lilac. Right now, Olivia could not appreciate the comfort or beauty of her surroundings. This restlessness within her had been building for an age, but it was particularly strong today.

She was quiet as Susie, her personal maid, helped her don a fashionable blue riding habit complete with military-style silver buttons, a white muslin shirt and riding pelisse.

Olivia stared at her own reflection. Stormy grey eyes, dark curls, fashionable habit. *What is the point of wearing fine things*, she was thinking, *when no one ever sees me but my own family? I could wear my oldest muslin and nobody would care.*

Rejecting the matching hat, she stated firmly that she would ride today with her head uncovered. *Someone will see you tomorrow*, an inner voice murmured. *Jem will be here. After four years, you will see him again.*

Ignoring the thought, she focused instead on her current frustration. This year they were not in London for the Season, because of Charlotte's condition. Oh, but it was hard to be two-and-twenty and stuck in the country! At least in London there were balls and routs, and trips to the theatre, and people who realised you were a grown-up young lady. Not a child. And there were ways to avoid seeing certain people, if you did not wish to spend time with them. A house guest in the country could not be avoided.

Olivia absent-mindedly thanked Susie and made her way to the stables, enjoying the feel of the May sunshine on her shoulders. As always, she felt a rush of love when she saw her fine looking mare, Dahlia.

'Hello, my beauty!' She nuzzled the horse's delicate cheek and slipped her a treat. Dahlia pranced impatiently and had to be told to hold still while the groom handed Olivia up and into the side-saddle.

'I shan't need you, Joseph!' Olivia waved away the head groom, who was just about to offer to accompany her. 'I won't leave our lands, I promise!' He looked disapproving, but refrained from chastising her.

'Where do you plan to go, miss?' He was always concerned when she rode alone, though why he should be, Olivia could not fathom. Nothing *ever* happened here. Well, she recalled, apart from that one time when poachers had entered the Home Wood. But that was almost five years ago.

Still, maybe she wouldn't go to the Home Wood.

'I'll go to the river,' she said decidedly, 'and the Bluebell Woods.'

She could *feel* the groom watching her as she trotted out of the stable yard. She really felt it today—how much she was watched and protected, and *imprisoned*. It was an itch between her shoulder blades and it seemed as though it had been there her whole life. Her brothers. The servants. Great-Aunt Clara. Her sisters-in-law. Why could they not see she was no longer a child? And how was she supposed to appear different to—to other people—if her own family treated her as though she was still a debutante?

Stop it! she told herself sternly. *This is no prison and they all care about you. That is why they do it—they are just trying to protect you.*

The words failed to quell the burning inside her and so she did the only thing she could—she let Dahlia build from a trot to a canter, then to a full gallop through the deer park. She steered Dahlia eastwards through the fields and lanes of the estate farms, until at last she reached the Bluebell Woods. At this time of year, bluebells were everywhere—along the hedgerows, around the estate workers' cottages and there was a good sprinkling of them in the Home Wood. But here, at the most easterly edge of the Chadcombe estate, here was where they grew in abundance.

Olivia directed Dahlia into the woods. Slowing to a walk, she savoured the coolness of the air, the smells of luxuriant foliage and fertile soil, and the magical colours of the woodland. Sturdy browns and greys mingled with lush green, and everywhere the indigo-purple beauty of the nodding bluebells. The canopy of ash and elm, oak and maple filtered verdant sunlight to warm the ferns and flowers on the forest floor. To her left, a startled squirrel raced up a tree, its tail a flash of rich bronze. Birds chirruped and called, and small creatures rustled in the undergrowth.

Olivia felt the tension leave her shoulders. This place never failed to calm her.

She made her way to the river and allowed Dahlia to drink. She dismounted, leaving her overskirts tied up, and tethered the mare to a nearby sapling in the cool shade. The horse promptly tilted one hind hoof and rested, her tail twitching at flies.

The next half-hour was delightful. Olivia wandered through her favourite part of the woods, up and down along the riverside, gathering bluebells as she went. Clara would love them. The day was warm, so, greatly daring, she removed her half-boots and silk stockings and sat down, dabbling her feet in the coolness of the sparkling river. She allowed the idyllic peace of her surroundings to soothe her, and—briefly—put tomorrow's worries to one side. The sun gently warmed her shoulders, the river babbled to itself, and the woodland whispered and swayed, oblivious to its own beauty.

All it needs, she thought, a little wistfully, *is for a romantic hero to appear.* That was what would happen in the novels she and Lizzie delighted in reading.

The river was shallow and perfectly clear. Olivia and Adam and Harry had paddled here often as children— once she was old enough to be allowed to accompany them. Her adored big brothers had played games of dragons, and giants, and knights—much more exciting than the Greek and mathematics that her governess insisted on. At first Olivia had been content to be the damsel in need of rescue, but eventually she had insisted on being a knight, like them. When her brothers laughed, she had tried to box them. In the end, they had allowed her to be a squire.

Olivia had allowed herself to be persuaded, until she discovered her role was limited to carrying wooden swords and crudely made arrows, and fetching the arrows after they had been inexpertly shot at targets on trees.

And now, they were all three grown up and Adam and

Harry were married. Olivia loved their wives—Charlotte and Juliana truly were like sisters to her—but she could not shake the feeling that everyone else—everyone but her—had their lives in place.

She felt stuck in a place between girl and woman— too old to be a girl, yet not permitted to be a woman. At twenty-two, yet still unmarried, she had no place. She had no responsibilities, no cares—but nothing to challenge her either.

Chadcombe was run efficiently by Charlotte, ably assisted by the household staff, while Adam managed the estate. Great-Aunt Clara, who had struggled for many years keeping house for Adam, had settled into retirement with obvious relief. Juliana was mistress of Glenbrook, wife to Harry and mother to darling little Jack.

Of all of them only Olivia had no role, no task, no purpose. *I am a shadow person*, she thought. *I am aunt, sister, great-niece. But I wish to be Olivia!*

The small river marked the edge of Chadcombe's lands, forming the boundary with their neighbours at Monkton Park. As children, Olivia and her brothers had been wary of Monkton Park's grumpy old gamekeeper, who did not, apparently, approve of children. When they had dared each other to venture across the stepping stones to pick blackberries or find conkers on the far side of the river, they had done it in fear he would catch them, and give chase, and shout in a purplish fury that was half-comical, half-scary. He had died a few years ago, but Olivia still carried the fear that, somehow, he would return from the grave to glower and glump at her.From here, Olivia could see a mass of white flowers on the far riverbank. On impulse, she stood and gathered her skirts. Leaving her stockings and boots with the small pile of bluebells, she ventured across the stepping stones barefoot, lifting her petticoats to make sure she was putting her feet in the right places. Reaching the far side safely, she began plucking handfuls of sweet-scented lily-of-the-valley—they would be the perfect foil for the bluebells.

Monkton Park's owners, Mr and Mrs Foxley, were Olivia's friends. Indeed, Mrs Foxley—Faith—was Charlotte's cousin. Olivia had nothing to fear from being on the wrong side of the river. Or so she thought. Old fears run deep, so when a man's voice suddenly spoke nearby, Olivia's heart leapt in alarm.

'"The summer's flow'r is to the summer sweet,"' the voice intoned.

Olivia whirled around to face the speaker.

'Ah,' he said, 'a rose indeed!'

His cultured accent—and his knowledge of poetry—proclaimed him to be a man of information and learning. She took in his appearance at a glance. *My*, she thought, *he is handsome!*

He looked to be a few years older than her—possibly around Harry's age. He had expressive brown eyes, thick, dark hair, and an unfashionably swarthy complexion—as if he had been in a warmer climate than England. His clothing proclaimed him the gentleman—a crisp white shirt open at the neck in a way which Adam would have abhorred, well-fitting unmentionables, boots that gleamed with a polished shine, and a well-cut Weston coat. He was, in every detail, the embodiment of a romantic hero.

Olivia's jaw dropped. Just moments ago, she had been wishing for just such a man to appear. She felt the hairs on the back of her neck spring to attention. Fate had never yet noticed her, or interfered in her life. Was this

to be a turning point? Was this, in fact, the beginning
of a story that would be truly hers?

'George Manning, at your service, ma'am—or miss?'
He bowed gracefully, all the while keeping his eyes fixed
on hers.

She bobbed a curtsy as gracefully as she could, given
her bare feet and the inconvenient way in which her
heart seemed to be racing. 'I am Lady Olivia Fanton.'
Her voice sounded breathless—she hoped he would assume it was because he had startled her.

'Ah! You are the Earl's younger sister, then!'

She inclined her head. 'I am.'

'I am a guest at Monkton Park and my hosts have
naturally informed me of the various neighbours I am
likely to meet. I admit I have had some difficulty in recalling who is who, so at least now there is one person
whose name and face has already seared itself indelibly
into my memory.' His gaze held hers, causing a slow
blush to warm her cheeks.

'I have been gathering wildflowers for my great-aunt.
She adores bluebells.' Her words came out in what she
felt must be a jumbled rush.

'England's bluebells are delightful at this time of
year,' he agreed. 'Er…how far are you from home? I
understand the estate is large.'

She shrugged nonchalantly. 'It is, I suppose. I have not
pondered it overmuch. My horse is nearby.' He looked
at her levelly and her nervousness increased. 'I must
go back—they will be wondering why I am not yet returned.'

He inclined his head, but there was a knowing look
in his eye. 'May I accompany you back to your horse?'

She paused for a second. This was all highly irregular! But she could think of no reason to turn him down. 'Very well.'

He offered his arm and turned towards the stepping stones. Ignoring it, she skipped ahead of him as far as the water's edge. Now she was faced with a new problem. It would be entirely inappropriate to lift her petticoats to cross the stepping stones—for then he would see she was barefoot and might even see her bare ankles! She blushed at the thought. Heaven knows what he might think of her!

Turning to face him, she tilted her head on one side. 'Please would you mind going first? That way I can perhaps take my balance from you.'

His eyes narrowed, but he murmured politely, 'Of course.' He stepped on to the first stone, then the second. She followed, lifting her skirts carefully, trusting he would not turn. They moved carefully across the river, she always a step or two behind him.

So intent was she on keeping her skirts as low as possible, that she nearly missed a step when they were almost there. 'Oh!' she exclaimed, putting a hand out towards him to steady herself. Her hand touched the warmth of his coat. He paused immediately and made as if to turn, Then he half-twisted, his eyes meeting hers. She removed her hand from his back.

'Do please continue,' she implored breathlessly. 'I have my balance again.'

He turned fully and eyed her seriously. Her heart was fluttering like a trapped bird, and her hand wished nothing more than to touch again the warm solidity of his firm frame.

'I am perfectly steady now,' she insisted. 'Please continue.'

He didn't move and she was conscious of the still-frenzied beat of her heart. He could probably hear it, the throbbing was so loud in her chest. His gaze dropped to her mouth, then slowly, allowing her to draw back if she wished, he bent his head and pressed his lips to hers.

Chapter Two

His lips were surprisingly cool and the kiss was gentle, questioning. Before she even had the chance to understand what she was feeling, he was gone again, mild amusement in his expression—perhaps at her lack of response.

'Apologies! I do not know what came over me.' She raised a sceptical eyebrow. 'Well, perhaps I do. I am overwhelmed by your alluring beauty.'

'Or maybe you are simply an opportunist and an adventurer!'

'Ow!' He clutched his chest dramatically. 'She wounds me with cruel words!'

She snorted. 'You are fortunate I did not push you into the water.'

'But a lady like you would not do such a thing, surely?'

'Oh, wouldn't I? I'll have you know I often gave my brothers a ducking on these very stones.'

'Touché,' he said lightly. 'I shall make a tactical retreat on this occasion.' He turned away, then twisted back immediately, as if a sudden thought had struck him. 'Will you promise not to push me from behind?' His eyes were dancing with laughter.

'Will you promise not to kiss me again?'

'Ah! Anything but that!' He became serious. 'No. I will not.'

'Mr Manning, I grew up with two older brothers and I am aware of the ways in which words can be twisted. Now, explain. Are you saying you will not kiss me again, or that you will not make the promise?'

He only laughed and skipped ahead quickly. Reaching the safety of the river bank, he turned to smile a challenge, displaying white, even teeth. 'That is for you to work out, Lady Olivia.'

Olivia tossed and turned, desperately trying to quiet her mind enough to fall asleep. Mr George Manning had disturbed her equilibrium and, really, she could not say why. Of course it was not fate that had brought him to the river at the same time as her! It was merely coincidence. Gothic novels were simply the product of someone's imagination and, much as she and Lizzie enjoyed reading them, she must not be as foolish as to allow such notions to influence her in matters of importance.

Despite this, her mind insisted on playing out every detail of her encounter with Mr Manning—his handsome form and features, the expression on his face as he had taunted her, that kiss... *Perhaps*, she thought, *I should marry. It would take me away from Chadcombe and would certainly be an adventure. A handsome, interesting husband and being mistress of my own home...*

Do not allow foolishness to overcome you! she told herself. *Others might sometimes forget it, but you are no longer a schoolroom miss. You are a grown woman of two-and-twenty and should know better than to be thrown off balance by a handsome face and a few clever* words. *You have been taken in before. It must not happen again.*

She smiled into the darkness of her room. Perhaps she *should* have knocked George into the river! For a few moments she enjoyed the thought of him, dripping and astounded, sitting in the river, his beautifully polished boots ruined...

That was better! Now she felt more certain, less confused, less...powerless.

Anyway—there should be no doubt in her mind. Any man who would surprise a kiss on a maiden he had just met had to be of dubious character. He had taken advantage of her, knowing her to be alone and unprotected. She was right to be wary of him.

Yet, she recalled, he had given her time to turn away from his kiss. And afterwards he had behaved perfectly civilly as he walked her back to the shady area where Dahlia waited. He had even turned his back while she donned her stockings and boots.

At least, she thought, *George Manning is a distraction from the fact that* he *will be here tomorrow.*

Jem.

Jem, who had disappeared from her life suddenly and completely.

Jem of the handsome face and the crooked smile. Memories flooded into her mind and her heart turned over.

Stop! she thought. *Remember what he did. He allowed you to hope, to expect a proposal, when all the time he had no serious intent.*

At the thought, her old anger began to resurface. How dared he behave so callously towards her? He had rejected her, then walked away without a backward glance, uncaring of the devastation he had caused.

She squeezed her eyes tightly closed and turned over. This was all her own fault. She had wished for something different, something out of the ordinary, and Fate had sent her George Manning *and* Jem Ford. At the same time. She was not sure she approved.

Olivia's two brothers had settled perfectly well into married life. Olivia enjoyed the fact that, with the acquisition of two sisters-in-law, there were many more females in her life than before. Great-Aunt Clara was a darling, of course, but Olivia felt she could not talk to her in the way she could talk to Charlotte and Juliana.

So why, when she returned from her ride yesterday, had she not mentioned her encounter with Mr Manning? She could not account for it, since she had always been open with Charlotte and Juliana about her admirers.

She pondered. Perhaps that was it. She was not sure if Mr Manning admired her, or not. Mr Manning—despite his flirtatious words—had not, she felt, revealed his true self. Instead he had unbalanced her with cryptic words and inscrutable expressions. She looked forward to meeting him again, if only to better understand her reaction to him.

Today Juliana and Harry, with their young son, had travelled the short distance from their home at Glenbrook to await the arrival of Lizzie Ford and her brother Jem to Chadcombe. Juliana and Charlotte had both offered to take Lizzie under their wing during Jem's long posting to Australia and had been true to their word. Lizzie, though under the care of her mother's elderly cousin, had been a frequent visitor and she and Olivia had become firm friends in the four years they had known each other.

Lizzie, of course, had no notion that Olivia and Jem

had enjoyed a *particular* friendship during his convalescence and Olivia had become accustomed to commenting politely on those occasions when Lizzie would talk of her brother and his trials and achievements in Australia. He had made Captain a year ago and Olivia had found it in her heart to be pleased for him. It was a sign, she thought, that her heart had healed from the blow he had dealt it.

'I cannot wait to see Lizzie again,' Juliana said with enthusiasm, as the ladies sipped tea in the morning room. 'I confess I have missed her. We have not seen her since last autumn, remember?' She did not mention Jem, which was something of a relief. Olivia did not wish to even *think* about Jem—especially that last day she had seen him, four years ago. Yet his arrival was imminent. Olivia's palms were suddenly damp with fear, anticipation and anxiety.

'Would you not have preferred for Jem and Lizzie to stay with you at Glenbrook, Juliana?' asked Charlotte.

'Oh, no, for I would not subject you to the journey to Glenbrook every time you wished to see them,' countered Juliana. 'Not while you are in the family way. Besides, you have more space here at Chadcombe.'

They all laughed at the old witticism. Everyone regularly teased Adam and Charlotte for having the largest house in three counties. Harry and Juliana's home was perfectly adequate, but Chadcombe was easily four times larger. Despite her laughter, Charlotte clearly remained unconvinced. 'I confess it troubles me a little, Juliana, that they are not staying with you. While Lizzie and Olivia are firm friends, we all know Jem and Harry fought together at Waterloo—there is a special bond between them. I know they have seen each other in London recently, but this is the first time Jem has come to Surrey to visit the family. I am sure they will wish to spend plenty of time together.'

'That is true,' agreed Juliana, 'but we *all* wish to re-kindle our friendship with Jem. Besides, Harry and Jem will see plenty of each other here at Chadcombe. Harry and I shall stay here at least this week and very likely longer. You will be wishing us gone before long—especially if Jack becomes tiresome!'

'Of course I shall not!' retorted Charlotte, smiling. 'You are always welcome. Why, this is Harry's family home!'

Juliana tilted her head to one side, considering. 'There is, I think, a special bond between all of us. I will never forget how Jem arrived from Brussels with his crutches, just a couple of weeks after Harry and I were married. He looked fragile, but was so brave. Do you remember how much pain he was in and the courage and determination he showed in trying to walk again?'

Charlotte nodded. 'Yes, and how you tormented him and wheedled him, Olivia, so that the poor man did not know whether to thank you or berate you!'

'As I recall,' added Juliana, 'he did both!'

Charlotte agreed. 'You were an excellent nursemaid, Olivia. You seemed to know exactly when to be patient and supportive, and when to be challenging. I confess I could not have done it.'

'Fiddlesticks!' said Olivia, blushing a little. 'Anyone could have done it.'

'No,' Juliana insisted, 'they really couldn't.'

Olivia lowered her head. She had indeed cajoled and challenged Jem, who had been entirely frustrated at his lack of mobility, and frequently short-tempered with pain. Somehow, they had sparked off each other in ways that had motivated him to keep practising his walking—

if only to prove to Olivia that he could. She had helped him heal and then he had left.

No one had suspected at the time how deeply attached to Jem she had become and she had explained away her lowered spirits afterwards with excuses about head colds and stomach upsets. Concerned, they had brought a doctor to investigate. He had concluded that she was suffering no serious ailment, but had prescribed a disgusting tonic, and cupped her.

No serious ailment. Not of the body, anyway. It was her heart, her mind, and her spirit which had been suffering. It had been so hard at first. She had cried herself to sleep for many months and everything in her life had somehow reminded her of Jem and the loss of him. Never again would she allow someone that sort of power over her.

Gradually, over the course of four long years, she had learned to push thoughts of him away, to build a wall of numbness around that part of herself. Until now. Finally, today, she was to face him. She prayed the wall would hold.

And what of Mr George Manning? Was he also destined to cut up her peace? She squared her shoulders. At least, if she felt those same early flutterings for another handsome stranger, she would know better than to listen to them. She did not wish to risk her heart being broken again—by Jem or by George Manning. A light flirtation with Mr Manning was acceptable, but she was determined to protect her heart from both men. It would be best to be wary.

'And here is the Chadcombe gatehouse!' Lizzie's voice almost squeaked in excitement as the carriage entered the gates of the Chadcombe estate.

Jem steeled himself to remain impassive. He was not now a wounded young ensign, grateful for the patronage of a noble family. As a man of substance in his own right, he could no longer be prey to the worries of his youth. He was genuinely grateful for everything the Fantons had done for him, and for Lizzie, and counted himself fortunate to be aligned to such a generous family. But he was visiting them now not as a casualty of war, to be protected and supported during his recovery, but as an independent gentleman of means and status.

Making Captain had been a proud moment, but the discovery that he had inherited a neat estate and a respectable fortune from a third cousin had been shocking. He had been, just a few years ago, fourth in line, with no thought of such good fortune ever coming his way. But a combination of circumstances—two younger sons killed at Waterloo and the eldest then losing his life in a carriage accident—meant the lawyers had confirmed Jem as the new heir.

It had seemed not quite real, reading the letter in Australia. Having risen through the ranks on his own merits he was now forced to abandon the army career that he had assumed would be his fate for life.

On his return from Australia, he had been pleased to meet Harry again and they had picked up the threads of their old relationship without much difficulty. Jem genuinely liked his former Captain and was pleased to find the old friendly warmth still present in their recent encounters.

He could not, he knew, expect the same warmth from everyone in the family.

He both dreaded and anticipated seeing Olivia again. During his years overseas, hers had been the face in his mind when he'd reminisced of home. She had been but eighteen when he had known her before and she had likely forgotten their former friendship, long ago. This visit—and particularly seeing her again—would help his transition from the romantic foolishness that had comforted him through the long loneliness of his posting. He was old enough now to be past such things. He was certain of it.

'They have arrived!' Juliana jumped up and moved to the window, her sharp ears detecting the approaching carriage.

They all rose and went outside to greet their guests, Olivia's brothers joining them. Adam and Charlotte stood forward, as protocol demanded, with Great-Aunt Clara, Harry, Juliana and Olivia behind them. The footman let down the step and opened the carriage door for the passengers to alight.

Olivia had only a moment to notice Lizzie's stylish pelisse and her bonnet (topped with three dashing feathers) when her attention was taken up by Jem. His eyes sought hers immediately, it seemed, then moved on to the others.

He was smiling—that familiar lopsided grin—and her heart turned over. *Jem.* How wonderfully terrifying it was to see him again. She schooled her features into warm politeness. *You are no longer a lovesick eighteen-year-old*, she reminded herself. *Be calm. Be gracious. Be twenty-two.*

Lizzie enveloped Olivia in a warm hug. 'Olivia!' It is such a joy to see you again!'

'I am so happy to see you, too! And you, Jem,' said Olivia, as Jem finally reached her.

He took her hand and held on to it, saying warmly, 'We were urging the horses on these past five miles, for the nearer we got to Chadcombe, the more impatient we became!'

Olivia's heart was beating rapidly. Seeing him again was odd—his features so familiar and yet so strange. Thank goodness she was now a confident young lady, and one who had learned to hide her feelings.

Charlotte spoke to Lizzie again and Jem let go of Olivia's hand. She was conscious of a feeling of loss. *No!* she told herself. *It is but a memory—it is not real. Remember how he hurt you.*

She looked closely at him. He looked older—more assured, somehow. It was strange, she thought, how he could look so familiar, yet at the same time so different. Her eyes swept over him. The same wiry frame, but his shoulders were much broader than before. He looked bigger, more self-possessed. Gone was the thinness of the convalescent. He was all man now.

Her eyes moved again to his face. Still handsome, but his features were somehow stronger now. She could find in his face very little of the young man she had known. There was a slight crease in his brow and he looked tired, she noticed. Had the journey been too much for him? Lizzie had told her the doctors had no major concerns about his old injury, but that it did still trouble Jem occasionally.

Olivia had heard this with mixed feelings. She was determined to keep him at a distance and had not forgotten or forgiven him for hurting her. At the same time, her instinctive compassion meant she did not wish to see him—or anyone—in pain.

In the old days, he would never admit it when his leg ached—his pride would never allow it—but Olivia had always known. There would be a tightness along his jaw or in his shoulders, a slight pallor, or occasionally beads of sweat on his forehead.

Today, she had taken the precaution of arranging for a bathtub to be brought to his room and now she nodded significantly at the second footman, who bowed and disappeared towards the kitchens to procure the pails of hot water needed for Mr Ford's bath. Olivia hoped the footman would remember to add the oil of lavender and marjoram she had pressed this morning—Jem had hated taking laudanum for the pain, so she had found other ways of helping him through the days when he had overreached in his attempt to recover.

Perhaps he would not need the bath, but she had thought it best to be cautious. She had agonised over how it might seem to him—she wanted to give him no opportunity to assume she still felt a *tendre* for him, but in the end, had decided that to arrange a bath for an honoured guest was not *too* particular.

Twenty minutes later, the second footman entered the parlour where they were all enjoying tea and conversation, and reported that Mr and Miss Ford's belongings had now been unpacked and their rooms were ready. The footman smelt strongly of lavender and Jem, sensing it, threw Olivia a quizzical look. She raised her eyebrows in innocent enquiry, determined not to understand him. He then glanced at Charlotte who, as hostess, would be the obvious source of such a luxury. Charlotte, however, was busy with Great-Aunt Clara, who had requested more tea.

Olivia was conscious of a strong feeling of danger. She should not have ordered the bath. He must not assume she was still lovesick for him! It was vital that he understood she was not the person she had been. Ignoring the knot of anxiety resting just below her ribcage, she continued to chat with Lizzie, though she struggled to take in what her friend was actually saying. She must get through this with a calm demeanour. It was imperative.

Chapter Three

Jem relaxed in the now-cooling bath, the scent of lavender and marjoram filling his senses and easing the throbbing in his old wound. He had dismissed the footman,
needing solitude to relax and think. His leg rarely pained
him now, but being stuck in a jolting, leather-slung carriage for most of the day had brought back the old ache.

Other old aches had been reawakened this day, and
with unexpected force. Olivia—Lady Olivia—had
blossomed into a stunning woman. He closed his eyes.
There she was, in his mind's eye, serene and elegant.
Her beautiful face, glossy dark curls and intelligent grey
eyes were just as he'd remembered, but there was a new
quality about her that he assumed could only be self-
assurance gained in the years since he had last seen her.

He had not expected to react so strongly to her but, he
reasoned, it was perfectly logical, given the way he had
made her the focus of his dreams these past four years.
Those dreams were not and had never been real—they
were fantastical only, designed to help him cope with
the loneliness of his overseas posting.

He had spent most of his time in Australia with soldiers and outlaws and, surprisingly, he had not taken

long to adapt to the basic—and hard—life in one of the remotest parts of the world. Their fort, which included a prison for outlaws along with the village that had sprung up nearby, was surrounded by fifty miles of emptiness in all directions. Living conditions were basic, diversions were few, and they had all been relieved when occasionally called to one of the settlements further down the coast to take their turn at ensuring public order and supporting the local government officials.

Jem had gradually been offered more and more responsibility, as his commanders had come to appreciate his qualities as a leader. They had genuinely been regretful at his decision to sell out of the army, following the news of his inheritance. They had, of course, understood and wished him well, but he had been pleased to discover that, had he stayed, they had seen in him the potential for high office in the future.

He stood, allowing the cool, herb-scented water to run off him for a moment, before stepping out of the bath and reaching for the soft towels provided by Chadcombe's staff.

Did Olivia arrange this bath for me? he wondered, as he towelled himself dry. *Or was it Lady Shalford?*

He was still getting used to the blessings of civilian life, but being able to bathe in warm water, and with privacy, was a profound luxury.

Or perhaps they do this for all their guests?

Chadcombe was a huge mansion—more like a ducal seat or a royal palace than an earl's establishment—and Jem was struck anew by the gap in station between him and Lizzie, and the Fanton family. Yes, he himself was a gentleman, like Harry, and, yes, he had come into a sizeable inheritance. But there the comparisons ended. He was not sure any gentleman's residence could compare to Chadcombe, and his lack of title was also a crucial point of difference.

Although Harry and the Earl had both married heiresses, their fortunes had apparently not been known about at the time. He was sure the Earl would encourage Lady Olivia to make an advantageous marriage—that she was twenty-two and yet still unwed was telling. During those long four years, each time a letter had arrived from Lizzie, he had unconsciously expected it to detail Lady Olivia's betrothal, or her marriage. Most young ladies were betrothed by the end of their second Season, so when Olivia remained unwed after four years, he had gradually hit on the most likely explanation. Quite simply, he reasoned, no one was good enough for her.

The young girl he had known had not been prideful or self-important but, equally, she had been blithely unaware of the privileges she enjoyed. No door was closed to her. She made friends everywhere she went. At eighteen, she had enjoyed all the advantages of wealth, position and connections.

For her to accept a betrothal, no doubt her suitor would have to pass a number of tests set by the Earl and unconsciously endorsed by Olivia herself. For how could she be expected to consider someone who had neither title nor fortune? Such was, he knew, the way of the world. He understood this without rancour or bitterness. Although his situation had improved a hundredfold in four years, yet still he was beneath her touch. He must not forget it.

Not that he had any particular designs on the lady. He had enjoyed her company during his convalescence and had—not unnaturally—developed some warm feelings towards her. They had, after all, been thrown into each other's company on a daily basis. He laughed a little as he recalled actually believing he had been in love with her. He had been so young back then!

His task now was simply to find ways to be unperturbed in her company, without the undercurrents of old memories or the fantasies of a soldier starved of female company. He would be polite and warm, and at ease.

'Would you do me the honour, Lady Olivia, of showing me some of these beautiful gardens?' Jem waved a hand towards the window, where indeed the prospect was delightful. 'If you are not otherwise engaged, that is?'

They had just breakfasted and Adam had left them to begin his work for the day. Most of the household were still abed—both Jem and Olivia were renowned early risers. Even as Olivia politely agreed to Jem's request, part of her was, with some sadness, remembering their habit of walking together in the garden in London immediately after breakfast.

Olivia had come to love those walks together during his convalescence—he struggling but determined to master his mobility, she cajoling and challenging him, bearing his frustration and elation with equanimity. As the time went on and his walking became easier, they had talked of many things—his childhood in the north of England, his sister Lizzie, who was to visit him in London, some of his experiences in the army, his hopes for advancement once his injury had healed.

He had not discussed Waterloo, the horrific leg injury he had suffered during the battle, nor how it had come about. Harry must know, but he never talked of it either. Adam had hinted her away from questioning them and, ever sensitive, Olivia knew better than to push either of them into reliving experiences they were trying to forget.

During those weeks, Olivia felt she had come to re-

ally *know* Jem and to feel comfortable in his company.
Well, she recalled ruefully, as comfortable as one could
feel with someone for whom one had developed such
strong feelings.

But had she ever truly known him? She had not for a
moment anticipated he would reject her so comprehen-
sively, or that he would disappear so completely, uncaring of the devastation he was leaving behind.

He had been ever the gentleman, she acknowledged.
Never had he spoken of love, or tried to kiss her. But his
eyes had warmed when he looked at her and she foolishly had believed he had cared for her. How wrong she
had been!Afterwards, she wondered if he had seen her
as a child, which had of course offended her eighteen-
year-old dignity. *But I* was *a child*, she reflected now.

Again her mind returned to that last day. Through a
haze of tears she had watched him walk away, unable to
fully comprehend that he was really leaving. Little did
she know then that would be the last she would see of
him for four long years.

It was for the best, she reminded herself fiercely, *because now I am free of my old feelings and can be easy
in his company. Perhaps—maybe—I could even be his
friend. After all, he is Lizzie's brother and I shall no
doubt be forced to see him from time to time. Yes, I can
be friendly*, she decided. *I must put aside my girlish foolishness and the anger that came from hurt pride.*

Chadcombe had extensive gardens, from formal
squares and ponds laid out in the French style to con-
trived wildernesses and a well-developed rose garden
behind the ballroom terrace. She and Jem wandered
through the archways and walks of the garden, the early
flowers budding and unfurling in a promise of the glo-
ries of colour yet to come. Olivia had taken particular

care with her dress today, opting for one of her favourite embroidered muslins, this one with a pretty yellow taffeta ribbon. She told herself she had done so because of Lizzie's visit. There was no other reason.

'I see Lizzie is just as much a night owl as ever!' offered Olivia politely.

'What? Oh, yes, yes, quite!' said Jem. Olivia frowned. What was wrong with him? Unable to account for his distractedness, Olivia lapsed into silence, unsure of what to say.

This was unexpected. Having successfully passed the test of seeing him again, of spending an evening in his company and enduring an entirely restless night—or so she believed—she had emerged this morning with a determination to maintain a distant, friendly air with him. It was vital that he understood she was no longer an infatuated girl. But she had not thought properly about the fact that, as much as she had changed in four years, so also would he. Gone was the open, friendly youth who had so enjoyed her company four years ago. In his place was a stranger and one whom she could not read. At all.

They walked on a few yards more and found themselves at the Fountain of Eros in the centre of the garden. The air was still and the sky cloudy and dull. A wren called sweetly from a nearby branch. Jem stopped walking and turned to face Olivia directly.

His expression was grave, worried. Olivia's heart sank. It reminded her of his appearance in the London garden, when he had said the words that had broken her heart.

Jem was in a quandary. His plan to be calm and easy in Olivia's company had fallen completely flat. Last evening, and earlier at breakfast, he had been intensely aware of her, compelled to keep looking at her, and frustrated by his own lack of self-control. This old passion was proving difficult to conquer!

Give yourself time! he had told himself, even as he'd invited her to walk with him. *Familiarity will help you see her differently.*

As they walked, he was conscious of memories of those *other* days, in that *other* garden. The feelings from back then were once again flooding through him, like a Pandora's box of unwanted emotion. His mind, too, was awhirl. In particular, he was wrestling with a topic that had occupied his mind obsessively during his long voyage to the Antipodes and for quite some months afterwards. *What if I was wrong about her?*

Soon after his arrival in the Fanton townhouse, Jem had heard Harry tease Olivia about a *tendre* she had had for a poet a few weeks earlier—just before Harry had left for Waterloo. The poet, it seemed, had professed his undying love for Lady Olivia, expressing his passion via some excruciating verse, and Olivia had, it seemed, quickly outgrown her infatuation. Harry—then a master in the game of flirtation—had advised Olivia on how she could gently discourage the young poet while avoiding unnecessary drama.

Blushing a little at Harry's teasing, Olivia had confirmed that her feelings for the dashing Mr Nightingale were not what she thought they had been and that, yes, he had gradually responded to her gentle hints by transferring his attentions to another young lady. This lucky damsel had that week received a sonnet to her Glorious Shoulders.

They had all laughed, not unkindly, but Jem had been left with the impression that Olivia was extremely young and untried, and that it would be a long time before her heart would engage in anything deeper than a passing notion.

She will fancy herself in love a dozen times, he had thought.

So when she had, soon afterwards, occasionally looked at him with admiration in those beautiful grey eyes, he had known not to refine too much upon it. Especially when he himself had been struggling to resist an unlooked-for and inconvenient attraction to her.

But what if he had been wrong? What if she had actually developed a deeper attachment to him at the time? His heart leapt in the old way at the thought.

Be sensible! he told himself. These were the same agonies that had haunted him throughout his stay at the Fanton townhouse. *Knowing* she was not for him, yet helplessly obsessing about her, while continually reminding himself that she would forget him as quickly as she had forgotten the poet. Around in circles he had gone, day after day, night after night.

He shook himself. Even if her *tendre* had, in fact, been deeper at the time than her feelings for the unfortunate poet, after four years he would have been long forgotten.

His dilemma, however, was this: Should he apologise to her? He had done nothing to discourage her girlish regard at the time. He had continued to enjoy her company—in truth, he was unsure how well he would have managed his recovery without her encouragement and challenge. He had selfishly taken advantage of her healing company and had failed to discourage her attentions. He was only slightly older in years, but even then, he had been much more worldly-wise than she. And then he had vanished with sudden finality.

If his actions four years ago had caused her any hurt, then to apologise would be the gentlemanly thing to do.

On the other hand, if he was wrong, it might cause awkwardness or confusion. And—did he really wish to know the truth? Had she forgotten him instantly, moving on to the next handsome suitor that caught her girlish fancy? How much of her warmth at the time had been fuelled by pity, or foolish romantic notions of a wounded soldier?

Or had she, like he himself, remembered their time together afterwards with rather more intensity than expected? She was, of course, unaware of the foolish devotion that had stayed with him all the way to Australia and had lingered for a long time afterwards. Raising the topic of their old friendship—and his abrupt departure—might give him an inkling of whether she had ever thought of him afterwards.

Yes, he thought. *I do want to know the truth.*

Mental excuses about apologising or being gentlemanlike were simply that—excuses. He felt compelled to know how she would react if he mentioned their former friendship. He refused to consider why that might be.

Without further deliberation, he decided to throw caution to the four winds. 'Olivia!' he said. 'There is something I wish to say to you.'

Olivia studied his face carefully. He looked unhappy—slightly cross, even. She could not recall ever seeing him like this. How he had changed! She swallowed. What was he about to say? Was it something to do with Lizzie?

Whatever it was, she would remain polite, friendly and serene.

She sat on the edge of the small pool at the base of the fountain, folded her hands in her lap and waited. He looked at her, his jaw set, then looked away. Having paced up and down for a moment, he seemed to gather himself, then turned to her again. His blue eyes seared into hers.

'I debated whether to speak to you at all. To be a gentleman is difficult at times—knowing the right thing to do or say may not be obvious.'

Olivia was lost. *What on earth is he talking about?* 'Whatever it is, Jem, you need not fear me. Although we have not seen one another for many years, I feel as though we have been friends through Lizzie for a long time.'

He stilled, then ran a finger around the inside of his neckcloth, as if he found it too tight. 'Friends. Yes.' He frowned. 'Friends. And therein lies my difficulty. For how could I—?' He broke off and completed another bout of pacing. 'Olivia, do you remember when I first came to live with you all in London, after Waterloo?'

She swallowed, but managed a bright smile. 'Of course! Harry did right to insist that you convalesce with us. And frankly, I am glad of it, for otherwise we should not have met and I would never have known Lizzie, who is now my greatest friend. And I hope we can also be friends.'

'Again, friends!' Sitting beside her, he picked up her hand. Olivia felt a familiar thrill go through her at his touch—a thrill that only he had ever caused. *Stop it!* she told herself. *Jem is trying to tell you something important to him. Now is not the time to be distracted by an old attraction that cannot be.* 'When we met,' he said earnestly, 'you were but eighteen and the sister of my commanding officer. I was a wounded junior officer with no real prospects and little money. Harry had done me the honour of offering me hospitality at a time when I was in desperate need of it. Without him and Juliana, I might have been billeted in a tent or hotel in Brussels for months after the battle.'

'I remember.' Olivia shuddered. 'That would have been terrible, for you might not have recovered so well.'

'I am sure of it,' confirmed Jem. 'Although the journey to London was difficult, I am glad Harry insisted on it. You and the rest of the family were so welcoming, taking a stranger in and treating me with such kindness.'

'You became part of our family, Jem.' Olivia was trying to sound reassuring. Was he, four years later, still feeling guilty about their hospitality towards him? She tried to think of how best to comfort him, without reminding him of her old infatuation. 'Why, for all that we have not seen each other, you are like a brother to me, and Lizzie a dear sister!' The warmth of his hand was making her nerve-ends tingle and causing all manner of distracting feelings in her stomach, so Olivia gently extracted her hand, under cover of patting his arm reassuringly, in a sister-like manner.

He looked down at her hand on his arm. When his eyes returned to meet hers, the expression in his was guarded.

Olivia was overcome by confusion. Why was he talking about four years ago? Did he—did he *know* he had broken her heart? Lord, she hoped not! She summoned the old anger, that sense of betrayal she had felt at the time. But, now that he was beside her, a full six feet of gorgeousness, it was hard to be angry. Instead she knew only confusion and uncertainty, and the compulsion of his blue, blue eyes.

She gathered all her strength. 'I am listening, Jem. Whatever it is, you can tell me.'

He stood, raking his hand through his thick, dark hair. 'I think that is debatable.'

Olivia waited, all her attention focused on him. *How fine he looks!* she could not help thinking.

His strong, muscular frame gave no hint of the serious injury he had sustained, which could have resulted in him being permanently crippled. Now he moved fluidly, pacing again before her. Through her eyelashes, and trying not to be obvious about it, she studied his striking form—slim, muscular legs encased in fine pale breeches and gleaming Hessians, a lithe, wiry torso hinted at beneath an elegant waistcoat and a form-fitting blue jacket. Oh, but he was a joy to behold!

He stopped now and looked at her again. Disconcerted, she blushed slightly, hoping there was no way he could read her thoughts. She looked up at him in mute question. He sighed and shook his head. 'I apologise, Olivia. I am wool-gathering today and it seems I have nothing to say to you after all.'

She looked at him doubtfully. 'Are you certain? You seemed agitated before—I would hate to think you were distressed, when I could help…'

He smiled broadly. 'Not at all!' His tone was jovial. 'Never felt better! Perhaps I need to simply stop thinking about things overmuch. Clearly long carriage rides can make me maudlin. Now, shall we walk back to the house?'

She smiled back, relieved to hear a more typical tone in his voice. 'Of course!' He offered his arm and she slipped her hand into it, relieved that near disaster had been averted and normality had reasserted itself.

Chapter Four

'Do not *speak* to me!' declared Lizzie, with fervour. 'It is not yet noon and I am forced into polite company.' She smiled to soften the words. 'Why, I shall not be fit for conversation for at least another hour!' Lizzie had just joined Olivia, Jem, Clara and Charlotte in the morning room. She had brought her sketchbook—Lizzie was a talented artist and often worked on her drawings and paintings during the afternoon.

'Have you eaten?' asked Charlotte solicitously.

'I have, thank you.' Lizzie leaned forward conspiratorially. 'I confess one of your wonderful housemaids brought rolls and chocolate to my bedroom. I truly appreciate Chadcombe's hospitality—even if you do keep inconveniently early hours!'

Charlotte was just explaining that Adam was with his steward and Juliana and Harry—who also loathed country hours—had not yet emerged from their bedchamber, when the sound of a carriage approaching up the drive alerted them to the fact they were to have visitors. 'Oh, dear,' said Lizzie, patting her hair, 'and I am not long risen!'

'You look charmingly,' said Olivia reassuringly. Lizzie beamed at her. Oh, it was good to have her friend at Chadcombe! Already life seemed less flat. And now, it seemed, they were to have visitors as well. She peeped discreetly through the lace curtains as five people emerged from the coach. 'Two men and three women,' she announced. 'Although they are too far away for me to distinguish who they might be.'

'Do sit down, Olivia,' said Charlotte, 'for they might see you looking through the window!' Olivia complied, sitting beside Jem on a satin-covered couch. She hoped Jem and Lizzie did not think Charlotte was telling her off, as though she were a child. That had not been Charlotte's intention—dear Charlotte would not do such a thing—but, still…

They all rose when the footman announced their guests. 'Mr and Mrs Foxley, Mrs Buxted, Mr Manning, Miss Manning,' he intoned, his final introduction slightly muffled by the scrape of Lizzie's chair as she stood.

Mr Manning! Olivia's heart began to race. She stood, maintaining what she hoped was a neutral look on her face. The ladies dipped into a curtsy, the men bowing politely, then Charlotte stepped forward to greet her guests.

'My dear Faith!' she said warmly, embracing her cousin Mrs Foxley. 'Aunt Buxted!' She embraced Faith's mama next, though with rather less enthusiasm. However, her words were warm and genuine. 'It is so good to see you! And where is little Frederick?'

'We have not brought him, I'm afraid.' Faith spoke in her usual gentle tones. 'We have left him with his nurse.'

Her husband explained. 'We recall the last time he was here, he managed to break not one, but *two* tea cups and we decided that, on this occasion, we should sacrifice his company in the interests of our sanity—and your china!'

They all smiled at this. Master Frederick Foxley was

just past his second birthday and had recently become, as his doting father suggested affectionately, a tyrant.

Olivia could barely follow the conversation. Her attention was fixed on Mr George Manning and her foolish heart was still pounding wildly, and in complete defiance of her wishes. She was wondering if it was obvious to everyone in the room that she and Mr Manning had met before. Oh, how she wished she had mentioned it!

He stood a little to the side, awaiting formal introduction, and Olivia's eyes were compulsively drawn to him. How elegant he looked! His tall figure equalled Jem's—both were handsome, imposing men. Mr Manning had a peculiar stillness that spoke of assurance and composure. His handsome face looked relaxed, though his eyes were busy, observing everyone with keenness and intent.

By his side stood a beautiful woman, with fair hair smoothed into an elegant chignon, pale blue eyes, and the most stylish silk morning dress Olivia had seen outside London. She wore a delicate lace cap, proclaiming her status as a married lady, and, unaccountably, Olivia's heart sank. Had the footman said *Mrs* Manning? Was George Manning, then, *married*?

She was conscious of a strong feeling of disappointment. She and Lizzie had often moaned in private about the fact that so many young men's lives had been lost in the war and that there were usually three young ladies to every eligible gentleman at the balls and routs they attended. And even then, like as not, the most handsome ones were invariably already married. With Jem here, she *needed* the distraction of an eligible man.

She caught Lizzie's eye. Her friend sent her an impertinent look, arching her eyebrows to signal the presence of an *interesting* new acquaintance. Olivia suppressed a smile and stood still, awaiting the introductions.

Mrs Buxted obliged. 'My dear, dear Charlotte! Lord Shalford! Permit me to introduce to you my treasured friend Miss Manning, who is lodging in Albemarle Street, and her brother, Mr George Manning.'

Her brother! Olivia's eyes flew to Mr Manning's face. He was watching her intently and was clearly amused by her reaction. She flushed and looked away. Jem was looking at her, a crease in his brow. Everyone else, she noted, was surreptitiously studying Miss Manning.

Olivia had erred. Seeing Miss Manning's cap, she had assumed the woman was married. Instead, she was clearly wearing it to indicate she was no longer of marriageable age. Now aware that Miss Manning had to be older than she first appeared, Olivia looked for the signs. And there they were—subtle lines at the corners of the eyes, between her delicate brows and at the corners of her mouth. Still, Miss Manning was a remarkably beautiful woman. It was difficult to estimate her age—perhaps she was in her early forties, thought Olivia. At least ten years older than her brother.

'…and this is my sister-in-law, Lady Olivia Fanton.' Charlotte's voice intruded into Olivia's musings, but, thankfully, years of social schooling meant she had reached out automatically to touch Miss Manning's pale, white hand.

The woman's grasp was weak, but she murmured something appropriate with cool politeness. 'I am happy to meet you,' Olivia replied cordially, though, in truth, she scarcely knew what to make of Miss Manning. Briefly, an intent look flashed in those pale blue eyes and Olivia was put in mind of a swan on a lake, sailing serenely by, but with webbed feet pumping furiously beneath the waterline.

'My brother, George,' said Miss Manning, gesturing to him, then pausing to watch as George bent over Olivia's hand to kiss it.

Olivia flushed and pulled her hand away, wishing she could wipe away the feeling of his warm lips on her skin. Her skin tingled pleasantly where he had kissed her hand, but it angered her that she should feel pleasure when she did not choose it.

They all sat, Jem returning to his place by her side. He was still frowning. He turned as if to speak to her, but Olivia's attention was taken up by the new arrivals. By the time she realised he wished to say something, he had already subsided and indicated with a slight shake of his head that whatever he had intended to say was of no matter.

Relieved, Olivia returned her full gaze to George Manning and his sister. Looking at Jem was altogether too confusing. It was easier to avoid it. It was difficult enough being seated beside him and being so conscious of his nearness.

Once again, she reached for that old sense of betrayal. Jem was nothing to her now. An acquaintance. Possibly a friend. No more than that. Having George's admiring gaze on her helped soothe the Jem-related anxiety.

Mrs Buxted was explaining the friendship between them was of recent date, as the Mannings had lived in London for only the past few months. 'We met, would you believe, in Rotten Row, during the evening perambulation,' declared Mrs Buxted. 'We struck up a conversation and Miss Manning was *most* obliging. She was quite willing to listen to me nattering on about my daughters and my dear niece Charlotte, who is now, of course, a countess!'

Olivia squirmed a little at Mrs Buxted's vulgar words. Charlotte, always ready to say exactly the right thing, diverted her by asking about her other daughter.

'Oh, my dear Henrietta is well, though suffering from great tiredness. She has just written to tell me her fifth *petit paquet* will be delivered in the winter!' Since Henrietta's fourth child had been born last November, and her firstborn had just turned five, this news, naturally, caused some exclamations. 'Oh, never worry about Henrietta,' said Mrs Buxted, in a confiding manner, 'she always wanted a large family.'

Faith, Henrietta's sister, looked dubious at this assertion.

'You will be wondering, I am sure,' continued Mrs Buxted serenely, 'why Miss Manning and her brother look so little alike!' Olivia almost gasped. She had met Mrs Buxted many times, yet never failed to be astonished by her impropriety. 'And why should you not, for I wondered exactly the same thing myself!' She patted Miss Manning's arm affectionately. 'You are so fair, my friend, and your brother is so dark in his colouring, so everyone who sees you must wonder at it!'

Miss Manning's expression did not change, apart from a slight hardening of her lips.

Perhaps, thought Olivia, *the friendship with Miss Manning is not so firm as Mrs Buxted says it is.*

She glanced at George Manning. He looked decidedly uncomfortable and as she watched he drummed his fingers on his strong thigh. Olivia sympathised. How uncomfortable the Mannings must be, to have Mrs Buxted talk about them as if they were not present!

'George favours his father,' said Miss Manning coolly, 'while I am like our mother in looks.'

'Are your parents also staying in London?' asked Charlotte politely.

'Our parents died many years ago,' said Miss Manning calmly. 'Smallpox.'

Great-Aunt Clara, who had a morbid fear of the disease, gasped. 'Oh, dear, how unfortunate! I am so sorry you lost your parents, Miss Manning.'

Miss Manning shrugged slightly. 'It was a long time ago.'

Another silence ensued. This time, even Mrs Buxted seemed aware of the tension. She looked from face to face uncertainly.

George Manning spoke. 'We are delighted to have been included in the invitation to stay at Monkton Park. Mr and Ms Foxley are generous hosts, indeed, to have included people they had never met. We are exceedingly grateful.'

Olivia could almost *feel* the tension ease. George's speech struck a perfect note, diverting attention from Mrs Buxted and the topic of the Manning parents' unfortunate demise. Mr and Mrs Foxley both responded enthusiastically, declaring that, of course, they were happy to welcome Mrs Buxted's friends and that visitors enlivened their common routine.

Olivia could not resist sending a thankful glance in the direction of Mr Manning. The look he returned her was half-amusement, half...something darker.

He is interested in you.

He was still looking at her and she, as if turned to stone, was returning his gaze. Becoming aware, she blushed and, breaking her gaze, wriggled slightly in her seat. Beside her, she noticed, Jem's back was ramrod straight. She stole a glance at him. His face was rigid, impassive. Despite George's intervention, Jem was probably still uncomfortable with Mrs Buxted's rudeness. She hoped he would feel at ease soon.

Tea was served and they all supped politely. Charlotte, Faith, George and Clara carried the conversation, while the others remained largely silent—even Mrs Buxted. Charlotte promised to call at Monkton Park tomorrow, which made Olivia sit up straighter. She must go, too!

She was still unsure what her opinion was of Mr George Manning, but one thing was certain—she very much wished to see him again so that she could find out.

Monkton Park was a pretty estate bordering Chadcombe to the east. Since the Foxleys had wed and taken up residence, the friendships between them all had deepened. Olivia had visited many times and had enjoyed seeing how Faith had adapted to her new roles as wife and mistress of Monkton Park. The birth of little Frederick had added to the happiness of the young couple and Olivia always looked forward to seeing how he had changed since she saw him last.

Today though, Olivia's thoughts were not on Frederick, or Faith, or indeed any of Monkton Park's permanent residents. Foolishly, her preoccupation was solely with only two people: Jem and the enigmatic George Manning.

The carriage lumbered on and Olivia let the lull of voices wash over her. Lizzie and Juliana were engaged in some frivolous talk about Juliana's new fan, while Jem and Harry remained silent in the facing seats. The others were travelling in the new carriage, which gave more comfort and safety for Great-Aunt Clara's old bones and Charlotte's delicate condition. This could well be Charlotte's last excursion away from home, as her confinement was only weeks away.

They had completed their courtesy call earlier in the week, staying for less than an hour. Olivia had enjoyed no further conversation with Mr Manning, as he had been seated with Lizzie during their call. However, Faith had invited them all to a dinner party tonight, in honour of her guests. They would all stay the night, as there was to be no moon, which would make it too dangerous to travel the road home.

'Lord, I am hungry!' announced Lizzie. 'I deliberately took no nuncheon, as I knew we were to dine out tonight, but now I wish I had indulged myself. Even some thin gruel would be welcome for my present distress, for I declare I shall faint if no one feeds me soon!' They all chuckled at Lizzie's pronouncement—even Jem, who seemed generally more taciturn than he used to be.

Encouraged by this sign of animation, and under cover of Juliana and Lizzie's speculation about what food might be offered by the Foxleys tonight, Olivia leaned forward and spoke to him.

'It will be good to spend time with the Foxleys together, as we did that summer when you stayed with us in London. Do you remember? We went for a picnic.'

'Of course I remember!' he retorted. 'You wore a yellow dress and I gave you a yellow flower that matched the colour exactly.'

She smiled, surprised he had remembered. She still had that flower, had treasured it. She could still recall the thrill that had gone through her when he had handed her the flower.

Finally, she had thought, *here is a sign he is interested in me!*

How wrong she had been. She had read too much into the situation, had been wilfully blind. He was looking at her expectantly, so, in a rush, she responded.

'As I recall, I told you my dress was a perfect shade of *jonquil*, not yellow. A high-class dressmaker would never make anything in a colour as common as yellow!'

'Yellow,' he repeated and there was a definite twinkle

in his eye. 'It did not suit your complexion. You were decidedly sallow that day.'

She took this in good spirit. 'Sallow? *Sallow?* I did *not* look sallow! Why, did not Charles Turner tell me I looked beautiful that day?' Her eyes danced with merriment.

'"Angelic", I believe, was his epithet.'

'Angelic, then. He certainly did not call me sallow!'

Jem rubbed one long finger thoughtfully along his jawline. 'He may not have said it *aloud*, but—'

'But nothing!' She decided to enlist Lizzie's assistance. 'You remember my jonquil dress? I wore it to the picnic in London when you visited Jem that summer. Now, did I look sallow in it?'

'I cannot remember the particular dress, I'm afraid,' Lizzie admitted, 'but I am certain of one thing. You could never look *sallow*, Olivia!' She glared at her brother, but with a smile lurking in her eyes. 'Jem, you should show some discretion when talking to ladies about their looks. Why, we are sensitive creatures, easily crushed by criticism!'

Olivia glanced at the other ladies. Both Juliana and Lizzie wore similar expressions of mock outrage— mirroring her own. She decided to test the men.

'So then, Jem—and you, Harry!'

Harry flung his hands up. 'This is nothing to do with me and I will not engage with you!'

'Coward!' muttered Jem.

Olivia ignored this. 'What would you say about our appearance tonight?'

The men exchanged glances. 'You expect, I suppose,' drawled Jem, 'a dozen outrageous compliments on your dresses and your hair, and no doubt any further attributes, possessions and qualities.'

'At *least* a dozen!' confirmed Olivia, her eyes brimming with mischief.

'A dozen and no more!' He eyed Olivia from head to toe, then quickly scanned Juliana and Lizzie. 'I can affirm,' he said theatrically, 'that you each have beautiful dresses and hair, and—er—' his eyes scanned them again, a hint of theatrical panic mixed with his amusement '—gloves!' he said triumphantly. 'That is surely a dozen things!'

'It is only three and well you know it!' challenged Juliana.

He shook his head. 'There are three of you and I named four items, so that is twelve!' He nudged Harry in the ribs. 'Wouldn't you say so, Captain?'

His former commanding officer smiled broadly. 'I heard only three for each lady, so that is nine.'

Jem clutched his heart. 'Betrayed by my comrade! But none of you can count!'

'What do you mean?' asked Lizzie.

'I know *exactly* what he means', said Olivia, dimpling. 'He is counting the gloves as two separate items!'

Jem nodded, smiling indulgently. 'You always understood me, Olivia.'

Jem's tone was entirely familiar to Olivia—it was exactly how he always had spoken to her when she was eighteen. She sighed inwardly. How often had she wished he would see her as a woman, not a girl? She frowned, her thoughts returning full circle to the realisation that no-one, including Jem, saw her as an adult, even now.

Yet, as they travelled on to Monkton Park, Olivia recognised with some surprise that she felt the glimmerings of peace. To her right the sky was colouring up for what promised to be a glorious sunset—glowing purple and gold and orange-red. Although the same frustrations dogged her, at least here, in this very carriage, were people with whom she felt at ease.

Jem sat back, enjoying the sensation of simply *looking* at her. She'd blossomed into quite a beauty. While she had been striking at eighteen, at twenty-two she was simply exquisite. As to her character, it was too early to tell, but he suspected her nature was basically unchanged.

Yet some changes were apparent. Gone was the naive girl who had glowed in his company. In her place was someone more reserved, less easy to read. It surprised him just how much he desperately wanted to get to know her all over again.

Who knew what experiences she'd had in the intervening four years? Had she fallen in love? Four years ago, he had foolishly allowed himself to become lost in her company, knowing it was destined to lead nowhere. The Earl, Olivia's brother, had barely been aware of his existence.

And why should he? As a family they regularly hosted guests and the Earl had been busy with Parliament, his duties to the estate and his new marriage to Charlotte. He had spent little time with Jem and, although unfailingly polite, had showed no particular interest in him. Any suggestion of a relationship between Ensign Jem Ford and the sister of the formidable Earl of Shalford had been unthinkable.

Knowing he was a guest in their home and that he was trusted by her brothers to behave appropriately towards Olivia, he had acted the gentleman throughout and never so much as kissed her.

I was a damned fool! he thought now, as the realisation of the lost opportunity washed over him anew. *I should have kissed her while I had the chance—while she might have wanted me to.*

Desire flooded through him at the thought.

Or perhaps not, he thought a few moments later, as his rational mind reasserted itself and he pictured the ramifications. Olivia might have responded with enthusiasm and his heart skipped at the notion of the joy that would have brought to him then, but had the Earl discovered them Jem would undoubtedly have been banished from the Fanton home—and from Olivia's life.

How might it have changed her feelings for him? Could he have secured her deeper affections, if he had breached the boundaries around them? Eighteen-year-olds were not normally renowned for constancy. Even if he'd tried to fix her interest—which would have been madness—it would not have survived four years apart.

Which brought him right back to the present, sitting opposite her in a carriage, desire and yearning confusing his senses. He glanced at her again. She was looking out of the window at the beautiful sunset, calm and serene. Certainly there was no awkwardness in her dealings with him—she was friendly, warm and gracious. Equally, there was no indication of any warmer feelings.

We had our chance, he thought, *and we let it pass us by. The opportunity was lost.*

The realisation hit him like a blow to the stomach.

Chapter Five

'Lady Olivia, your seat is here.' Olivia thanked Faith and moved to the table. The footmen were already bringing dishes into the dining room and the smells were wonderfully appetising. Faith continued to seat the ladies according to her plan and soon the men, too, were moved into position. Olivia had Charles Turner on her right and George Manning was placed on her left. Jem was opposite, between Amy Turner and Mrs Buxted.

During the first course, Olivia chatted easily with Charles, whom she had known all her life. His sister Amy, she noted, was being gently entertained by Jem. As she watched, Jem spoke softly to the girl, who was just seventeen and not long out. Poor Amy tended to still be tongue-tied at formal events.

Knowing how anxious Amy was likely to be tonight, Olivia could not help but be glad she was seated next to Jem. He had sensed—without anyone having to prompt him—that Amy would need kindness and reassurance tonight.

And, she reflected, *perhaps it is best for me to have a break from the confusion Jem causes in my heart.*

Was it inappropriate to feel interested in Jem's actions? After all, she and Jem had not seen each other for years. Why, then, did she feel it was natural and right for her to think of them having some sort of special connection? Looked at from that perspective, she could not justify it. She was making assumptions based on something that existed only in her own imagination. It had not even been real in the past. She looked across the table again, this time focusing on Amy. 'Your sister looks beautiful tonight, Charles!'

Charles snorted in response, glancing across the table. Amy's fair hair was drawn up into a high topknot and her pretty face was framed by elegant side curls, emphasising her delicate features. Her cheeks were slightly flushed and her eyes sparkled.

Her elegant gown, as she had confided to Olivia while they had been assembled in the parlour, awaiting the call to dinner, was new and specially made for tonight. Formal dinners did not come along very often and Squire Turner must have been persuaded by his wife that on this occasion Amy required new finery. The dressmaker had outdone herself. Amy's gown was of rose silk, trimmed with lace, and was perfectly suited to her age and her complexion.

'Hard to believe she is now out,' said Charles. 'I still think of her as no more than twelve and suited to the schoolroom.'

'Oh, Charles, you sound like your papa!' Squire Turner had long bemoaned the fact that his little Amy was making her debut this year and that she scarcely seemed old enough to be out. Olivia was not the only one to suffer from an over-protective family. 'Amy is perfectly ready for company. Why, just look at her, conversing so easily with Mr Ford.'

Her brow creased. When she was eighteen, Jem had

been kind to her in just the same way. And she had blossomed under the warmth of his attention, misinterpreting
his kindness for something deeper. She swallowed as
the realisation sank in. She had spent four years feeling angry with him, alongside her heartbreak. Yet now,
she suddenly wondered if perhaps it was she who had
been at fault, for assuming feelings on his part that had
never existed.

Charles grimaced. 'I see them,' he muttered.

'What? Don't you like Jem?' Olivia was puzzled.
Years ago, Charles and Jem had met in London and always seemed at ease with each other.

'Jem is the best of fellows, I am sure,' said Charles.
'But one does not like to see any man flirt with one's
sister.'

Olivia laughed. 'He is not flirting! He is simply conversing with her to make her feel at ease. Why, you sound
like my brothers when I first came out! Every man who
spoke to me was watched and criticised!'

'It is a brother's fate, I suppose,' he said morosely.
He glanced back at Jem and Amy, who were talking
quietly, their heads close together. 'I know what I see,'
he growled. 'Perhaps I shall become accustomed to it
in time.'

The footmen moved in to clear away the soup and
the fish course was served. At the head of the table, this
was the signal for Faith, as hostess, to turn the conversations. With relief—for the conversation with Charles
was creating unexpected anxiety—Olivia saw Faith turn
away from Adam, who was seated on her right as guest
of honour, and strike up a conversation with Harry, to
her left. With the table now turned, everyone else now
ended their conversations and turned to the person on
the other side. For Olivia, that meant speaking directly

to George Manning for the first time this evening—apart from the formulaic greeting on their arrival. Even then, she had noted how his gaze had swept over her face and her form, before his dark brown eyes had pinned hers in an intense gaze that had made her reach for her fan.

Now, she was conscious of bracing herself for the encounter, but also that she felt *alive* having him beside her. She was grateful to have the distraction of his company. He had Lizzie on his other side—Faith had seated him between them deliberately, Olivia was sure.

'Good evening, once again, Lady Olivia,' he growled. 'May I offer you some salmon? You look stunning by the way.' He tagged on the compliment as if it were an afterthought, leaving Olivia unsure of his sincerity. Such a contrast with Jem and Harry's laughing repartee earlier!

'Er…yes, thank you.' Olivia had not felt so uncertain for a long time. Why, she was as tongue-tied as Amy! She forced herself to speak. 'And some of the potato pudding, please.'

Soon her plate was laden with all her favourite dishes and she and George tucked in. 'Tell me, Lady Olivia,' said George, eyeing her intently, 'do you visit Monkton Park frequently?'

His innocuous question was clearly designed to put her at ease. Although she was half-aware he was using all his social charm on her, Olivia could not resist gradually relaxing as they made small talk. They chatted of Surrey, the families who lived hereabouts and his impressions of the countryside. It reminded him, he said, of parts of northern Spain. He had also previously lived in Salzburg, Venice, Brussels, and, most recently, Paris.

'Have you travelled in Europe, Lady Olivia?'

'Er…no. I have been to London, many times. And I have visited friends in Lincolnshire.'

Lord, had she really just said *Lincolnshire*? It was a perfectly good part of England and she had had an enjoyable time visiting her friends there, but it did not begin to compare with the exotic places he had seen.

He was nodding politely. 'Alas, I have not yet visited Lincolnshire. In fact, there are many places in this, my homeland, that I have not yet had the pleasure of seeing. But, for now, I am content to gaze on the beauty of Surrey.' His eyes blazed into hers and her colour rose. He leaned forward and spoke into her ear. 'I noticed at Chadcombe you did not mention the fact that we had met before.'

Now she was totally flustered. He smiled at her confusion. 'Never fear! It will be a secret between us.'

She frowned. She did not keep secrets from her family! Thankfully, the servants moved in to replace empty dishes with full ones and she was given a brief respite from his focus as she turned back to Charles.

When it was time to turn once more, she felt more ready for him.

'You mentioned you lived in Brussels, Mr Manning.' Her tone was polite, not too interested. *Good.* 'Was this before or after the great battle?'

'Waterloo.' He frowned, then grimaced slightly, as if struggling with his own thoughts. 'I will never forget it as long as I live.'

She caught her breath. 'You were there?'

He nodded grimly. 'I was. I fought that day. Longest day I've ever spent.' His eyes grew distant. 'We lost some good men.'

She swallowed. 'I apologise. I did not wish to distress you.'

He caught her gaze. Helpless, she could not break free. 'I am glad you mentioned it. I feel I could tell you things—things I could not normally say.'

Her eyes widened. 'Oh.'

Do not act so scatter-witted, she told herself. *Say something meaningful!*

'What things?'

He seemed not to notice her tongue-tied stupidity. 'We men are changed by war. The things we saw, the experiences we went through...' He shook his head.

Much moved, she was tempted to reach out and touch his strong hand. She resisted. Instead, she said softly, 'There were good tales told about that day, too. Tales of heroism and bravery.' The conversation was making her feel decidedly uncomfortable. Oh, why had she mentioned the battle?

He looked at her keenly. 'You are right.' He hesitated, then spoke in a lower, quieter voice. 'There is something—a thing I have not told many people. But it makes me feel better about that day.'

'Yes?' She could not resist encouraging him, for now she really wanted to hear his tale. He leaned forward, so close she could feel his breath on her cheek.

'It was during the battle. We were under attack from all sides. We had already lost dozens of men from our section. Beside me, a horse was killed—its throat cut by one of those French monsters.'

Olivia, thoughts of her beloved Dahlia in her mind, immediately recoiled in horror. Raising her hand to her mouth, she gasped.

'Oh, dear! Pardon me, Lady Olivia, for I did not mean to distress you. It is just—that day will stay with me...' He shook his head sorrowfully.

Olivia immediately felt guilty. Here she was, upset at even *hearing* his tale, when he had been forced to experience these awful events first hand. Though Harry and Jem had both been soldiers, they had never spoken to her in depth about the horrors of their soldiering days. Frankly, she preferred not to think of the details. Now, here was a man who had chosen to confide something to her. It was, no doubt, a privilege that he should do so. She must be brave and grown-up about it.

She rested her hand on his arm. 'Please, continue.' Dinner was forgotten. She would focus only on him.

He smiled gratefully. 'Thank you.' His eyes became distant again. 'One of my colleagues became trapped underneath the horse. Despite the fact that we were fighting hand to hand at that point, I knew I had to do something.' He was sitting straighter and his hand gestures had become quite animated. Still, his voice remained low. 'Ignoring the danger to myself, I pulled him out from underneath.'

Olivia was fascinated. He told the tale so simply, but it was compelling. 'Why, Mr Manning, you are a hero!'

He brushed away her words with a gesture. 'Never say so! I only did what anyone could have done.'

This she could not accept. 'I think not! Others did not do it. *You* did. That means something.' Her eyes were shining. Suddenly she saw him in a whole new light.

Of course, she knew there had been acts of heroism at Waterloo. She had read about some of them in the newspapers. But to actually meet a real hero—here in Surrey! Once again, her heart was beating rather fast.

'I hope you got a medal!' She had seen Harry's and Jem's Waterloo medals. Made of silver and with their names etched on the back. Both Jem and Harry had treasured them.

'Alas—my medal was stolen!'

'Oh, my goodness, how shocking! Where did this happen?'

His eyes flicked, briefly, to the side. 'Oh, somewhere

between Brussels and Paris.' He thought for a second. 'I had packed it away for safekeeping at the bottom of my valise. Someone must have found it and taken it—perhaps at one of the inns.'

'But that is terrible! Why, everyone knows how precious those medals are!'

'Indeed, and I have no doubt it was sold on for a great sum. I shall never see it again.' He sighed quietly, then shook himself. 'But we must not speak of such sad events. Not tonight, when there is a fine feast before us, and good wine, and—' he sent her a sidelong look '—excellent company.'

She blushed again—really, one would think she was but a schoolgirl! There was one final thing she wished to say to him. 'Mr Manning.'

'Yes, Lady Olivia?' His eyes were smiling.

'It may be helpful to know that my brother Harry and Jem—Mr Ford—both fought at Waterloo. I believe men often like to talk together about such things.'

The smile faded. He glanced at both men, his gaze sharp, interested. Then he turned back to her. 'Thank you for telling me. I generally prefer not to speak of it. Just now was different—your powers of persuasion got me talking about things I would not normally discuss.' He lifted her hand. 'I do hope you will keep what I told you to yourself?'

'Of—of course.' Olivia felt so sorry for him. He had been through a harrowing experience at Waterloo, but did not wish his heroism to be widely known. Her heart melted as she considered how difficult it must be. At that, Jem happened to turn his head to look at them. His eyes flicked briefly to where her hand still rested on Mr Manning's arm, then he looked away again.

Once again, George turned to talk to Lizzie, but

Charles, on Olivia's right, would only sigh morosely into his blancmange. Eventually, after some gentle questioning, he mumbled something about Jem leading his sister astray. Olivia looked across the table—and what she saw surprised her. Jem and Amy, who were speaking again, seemed to be getting along famously. Amy looked relaxed and comfortable, and was involved in telling Jem a long story, by the looks of things. And Jem! He looked as if he was fascinated by Amy's tale. In fact, he looked as if he was fascinated by Amy. His eyes never left her. He seemed completely absorbed in her. It was most disconcerting.

'I see what you mean, Charles!' Olivia swallowed hard.

'I did tell you so, Olivia. He's hanging on her every word! And years ago I used to think Jem a sensible fellow!' He took a long sup from his wineglass. 'Depend upon it, she will have every fortune hunter in the country following her—and how am I to steer her through it?'

'Well, you surely cannot accuse Jem of being a *fortune hunter*! Of that you must acquit him!'

He eyed her balefully. 'Oh, I know he is well circumstanced—came into quite an inheritance, did he not? But one can never have too much money, y'know!'

This she would not accept. 'No—you do them both a disservice! Jem would never pursue a young lady just because of her dowry and she is—why, she is beautiful and kind, and clever…' Her voice tailed off.

'Is she? I'll take your word for it. Yes, I see your fierce look! Very well, I accept that Amy is pretty. And she is a good sort—' He took another swig. 'Perhaps I don't want her to grow up and leave us!'

'Oh, Charles! All will be well, you'll see!' Even to her own ears, she did not sound convincing. Olivia sighed. She only wished she could believe her own words.

* * *

Jem tried to concentrate on what Amy was saying, but to no avail. Rage had taken him over and he wanted nothing more than to plant a facer squarely on Manning's nose! Olivia had looked as though she were entranced by him. What on earth had Manning been saying to trigger the rapt look on Olivia's face as she listened? Oh, he knew that expression well—she had used to look at him in just such a way.

No longer. Manning was the new flavour in her world. He was sniffing round her—and making headway, if Jem was not mistaken. Not that it was any of his business, he reminded himself. Olivia was her own woman and had probably encountered many such handsome tryers over the past four years. His own reaction was simply because he had made her the focus of his foolish dreams for so long. Perfectly logical that his mind would struggle to separate reality from fantasy. Olivia was not his, had never been his.

Chapter Six

Doves and wood pigeons were all very well, thought Olivia, in paintings. She quite liked them when they were in pies, or roasted in onion sauce. But when at least ten of them had taken up residence in a tree directly outside one's bedroom window, cooing and calling relentlessly, it was the outside of enough!

She could tell it was very early. There were no sounds of activity in Monkton Park, as the family, guests and servants were all still abed. She turned over again. A restless night in a strange bed—though the guest rooms at Monkton Park were comfortable and beautifully furnished—had left her feeling as though she had not slept at all. Fragmented dreams of running from danger, Amy laughing at her and dead horses had troubled her night, and the birds outside her window had now woken her far too early. Sighing, she sat up. There was no point in just lying there.

Fifteen minutes later, having washed, tied her hair up as best she could and donned her riding habit, she left the bedchamber. She had already arranged with Faith to take Faith's mare out for a gallop before breakfast—

though neither of them had anticipated that she would be out this early! She would have to saddle the horse herself, as the stable boy was likely still asleep. Thinking of this, she was pleased she'd managed to dress without needing to ring for a maid. She'd been raised to be as independent as possible and to consider the needs of the servants—they needed their sleep just as much as anyone else. The only bits she'd missed were the silver buttons at her wrists, but she had turned the sleeves up slightly and thought they looked fine.

Tiptoeing along the landing, so as not to awaken the other guests, she got a fright when a door on her left suddenly opened!

'Oh!' the exclamation left her, sounding rather loud in the early-morning hush. She froze, watching helplessly as someone emerged.

It was George Manning. He was wearing a rather extravagant dressing gown and his feet were bare. He was closing the door softly when he heard her exclamation and whirled around to face her, looking just as startled as she felt.

'Oh! Lady Olivia! I—'

He broke off and just looked at her. She also could not think of what to say. Absently, she noticed with interest the dark hair visible through the open V of his dressing gown. Her heart was pounding rather loudly in her ears and her palms were moist with sudden sweat.

Downstairs, a clock struck the hour, its chimes faintly sounding up the elaborate staircase ahead. Four—five—six… Nothing more. Six o'clock. Lord, how early it was!

'Are you going riding at this hour?' His expression was shocked.

She lifted her chin. 'I often go riding before breakfast—Mr and Mrs Foxley know me well, so they would not be surprised. Although…er…six o'clock is early, even for me.' As she spoke, all the time she was wondering what on earth he was also doing awake and where he was going in his dressing gown!

His eyes darted away, then back again. 'Most un-usual. I…er… I am going to the terrace to smoke a cigar. Disgusting habit, I know, but sometimes when I can-not sleep…' His voice tailed away. 'You may wonder,' he resumed, 'why I do not simply blow a cloud in my chamber. Well, I confess…' he smiled broadly at her '… I have run out of cigars, and was intending to purloin one of Foxley's from the dining room.'

'I see.' She didn't, not really, but she supposed it made sense to him. 'Shall we go downstairs, then?'

He assented and fell in beside her.

This whole situation is peculiar, she was thinking. *Here I am, at six in the morning, descending a staircase in Monkton Park, accompanied by a gentleman wear-ing a dressing gown and*, she speculated, *very little else*.

Beside her, he retied the belt of his gown more tightly and Olivia stifled a nervous giggle. His height and breadth was imposing and she could occasionally catch the scent of him as they moved down the stairs in unison.

In the hallway, she wished him a polite adieu, find-ing she could not quite look him in the eye. He bowed gallantly, though the effect was made somewhat strange by the bare feet and by his attire. She had never seen any man apart from her papa and her brothers dressed for bed before.

There was something exquisitely *dangerous* about the whole situation that had Olivia's heart pounding. Once again this handsome stranger was disconcerting her. Ex-pressing a wish to see him at breakfast, she made for the front door. Thankfully, the bolts slid back easily, and she emerged, relieved, into the early morning sunlight.

'May I offer you some beef, Lady Olivia?' George Manning was all attention and had solicitously been offering her a range of breakfast foods since she had taken a seat at the table. Jem and Amy were there, too, as well as Faith and a sleepy-looking Lizzie. The others were presumably still in their chambers.

George Manning was too much, Olivia felt, for breakfast time. Too dashing, too debonair and far too confusing. Attired now in the palest pantaloons, a snowy white shirt, and well-fitting coat, he looked just as attractive—and dangerous to her senses—as he had at six o'clock.

Jem, too, looked handsome in elegant morning dress. With a single glance, Olivia noted the way his fine buckskins clung to his thighs and how his morning coat was moulded to him like a second skin. She could not bear to look at him, yet wanted nothing more than to look at him. To cover her confusion, she sent him a sunny grin.

He responded with a slow smile, then turned to answer a question from Amy. Olivia's own smile faded. She made a careful study of her breakfast.

'Good morning, Emma!' George rose to greet Miss Manning, who had just entered, wearing a handsome and expensive-looking morning gown of blue merino, trimmed with a deep flounce at the hemline.

'Morning, George! Good morning, all!' They all murmured their greetings, then Miss Manning took her place. Olivia watched curiously as George ensured his sister had all she required. It gave her a feeling of reassurance to see George being so solicitous towards his sister. She often felt that observing family relationships provided an insight into character.

Reassurance? She suddenly caught the direction of her own thoughts. Why should she need reassurance? She knew, after what he had told her last night, that George Manning was a hero. She could not imagine how he had managed to be so brave, saving another while putting his own life at risk. That was all the reassurance she needed as to his character.

'What do you think, Olivia?' Jem was speaking to her. Wrenching her gaze away from Mr Manning, and hoping her feelings hadn't been showing on her face, she looked at Jem.

'I'm sorry, Jem, what did you say?'

His expression did not change; he merely looked at her levelly. 'I was wondering if we should all take a turn about the gardens after breakfast.'

Disappointment stabbed at her. Was she not, then, to enjoy a tête-à-tête with Jem alone?

She shook herself. She had no right to any particular attention from Jem. She swallowed her regret without looking at it too carefully. 'Yes! Let us all go! That is, everyone who wishes to.'

'Capital idea!' said George. 'Emma, how about it?'

Miss Manning looked at him and some unspoken message seemed to pass between them. 'Very well.'

Olivia sighed inwardly. She had not yet warmed to Miss Manning. Conversation with her last night after dinner had been stilted and Olivia had been relieved when the men had rejoined them. Miss Manning was a woman of few words, yet she was not, Olivia surmised, lacking in confidence. She seemed serene, self-contained and unconcerned—as if all of them were children at play around her feet, to be ignored. She was perfectly polite and responded to questions when asked, but seemed uninterested in her fellow guests.

George was his sister's opposite, Olivia mused. Not just in looks, but in character. While she was quiet, he was jovial. If Miss Manning was uninterested, George was *extremely* interested. In everyone. Lizzie had confided to Olivia that George had been flirting with her, too, drawing her out, asking her about her likes and opinions in the same way he had talked to Olivia.

The man's a flirt! Olivia thought now, not without a hint of disappointment. When he talked to her, he had given her the impression that he was *particularly* interested in her. Yet Lizzie had felt the same.

'Let us both enjoy his attentions, then!' Lizzie had suggested last night. 'He is prodigiously good-looking, after all!'

Lizzie and Olivia had developed the habit of chatting in animated tones after each ball, picnic and rout, speculating about the young men and enjoying the thrill of the attention they received as young ladies. If she and Lizzie could flirt, then why should she feel uncomfortable with the men who dallied with them in turn? Especially when she now knew that Mr Manning was a man of integrity, beneath the flirtation.

Yet something about last night had rocked her. She felt unsure, as if her peace was threatened. Anxious knots had formed in her belly. Logically, though, she could not identify the threat.

Perhaps it was just that George Manning seemed so much more *dangerous* than the young men that she was accustomed to. He was like a romantic hero from a Gothic novel. She easily could picture him fighting heroically in battle, rescuing damsels in distress and defeating one's enemies.

Ooh, she liked that idea! Were she ever to be in distress, she could think of worse fates than to be rescued by the dashing Mr Manning. She resisted the idea of placing Jem in that role in her imagination. It was altogether too disturbing.

'Olivia?' Everyone was looking at her.

'Sorry, Amy, I was wool-gathering and daydreaming! I did not sleep very well last night. What did you say?'

'Just that we should probably bring shawls for our walk. There is apparently a blustery wind this morning.'

In truth, the day was rather breezy. Olivia nodded. 'I know—I was out riding before breakfast.'

She could *feel* George's eyes on her. Avoiding his gaze, she nevertheless felt a slow blush flood her cheeks. Oh, why had she mentioned that?

Faith was frowning. 'I am so sorry that you did not sleep well, Olivia. I do hope your bed was comfortable. Or was it, perhaps, something you had at dinner? I did wonder about those prawns…'

Olivia was mortified. 'Oh, no, Faith, you mustn't think that! The food was delightful and the room so comfortable. But you know me of old—I often struggle to sleep when away from home—especially on the first night.'

She continued to reassure Faith as the ladies all climbed the stairs in search of shawls. She would hate for her thoughtless words to upset her hostess, who had been so kind. As they continued along the landing, Olivia absent-mindedly noticed Miss Manning enter one of the bedrooms. It was only when she got to her own chamber that she thought about what she had seen. Miss Manning had gone into George's room!

She shook herself. That should not surprise her. Miss Manning's shawl might be in George's bedchamber— she might have left it there at some point. The woman was perfectly free to enter her brother's bedroom if she wished. Olivia shrugged.

She picked up her own shawl—a beautiful, soft Indian wrap in subtle shades of blue—checked her appearance in the mirror, then hurried back downstairs. As she descended, she became aware of male voices below. Jem and George were conversing.

'Delightful! Mr and Mrs Foxley have been most kind.' George's voice.

'They are generous and trusting people, that is for sure.' That was Jem, but there was a puzzling edge to his voice. 'Some might say they are too trusting.'

'And do *you* say so, Mr Ford?' Now it was George who sounded strange. His tone was silkily polite, but there was a barb in it. Olivia's pace slowed. What on earth was happening?

'Time will tell, no doubt, Mr Manning. We all of us must navigate our way through life as best we can, balancing generosity with self-interest.'

'Indeed.' George's tone was curt. Olivia was now at the bottom of the staircase and George's eyes flicked briefly towards her. 'I am one of those who will always put others first.' His voice was a little louder. 'Self-interest is unknown to me.' Now he turned towards her 'Ah, Lady Olivia!' He swept forward, making an elegant bow. 'So happy to see you again—and what a fetching shawl!'

Olivia could feel herself blushing. His gallantry was pleasant—but she must not let him see that. She kept her tone even. 'I have only left you for five minutes.'

'When you are gone, Lady Olivia, five minutes is like five hours!' He smouldered at her, humour glinting in his eyes, and she could not prevent a giggle. Really, the man was outrageous!

She turned towards Jem. 'What do you think of my shawl, Jem?' She lifted the ends up to show him the beautiful fabric.

'Very nice,' he retorted bluntly.

One side of the shawl slipped from her grasp briefly and Jem grabbed it, his hand brushing her arm as he replaced it. A familiar thrill went through her, making her quiver. She was relieved when her thanks came out in a normal-sounding voice.

The others arrived then, in a bustle of muslin, walking boots, and conversation. Lizzie, speaking in Olivia's ear, confessed that she was looking forward to the walk, even though it was at such an ungodly early hour. Faith, all smiles, had brought little Frederick and the women were invited to exclaim over him. Overwhelmed, he sought comfort in his mama's skirts, until she picked him up. He then promptly tucked his face into her neck and pretended not to hear the ladies call his name.

'He will not be so bashful after a few minutes—just wait and see!' said his doting mother.

And so it proved. Frederick's shyness lasted only until they had reached the end of the first path, barely a hundred yards from the front door. Soon he was running and yelling, and fighting imaginary enemies with a stick he found under an elm tree.

'He is determined to be a hero, for his papa has filled his head full of stories,' said Faith indulgently. 'He has told me that if a "Bad Man" comes, he will fight him.'

'Well, good for you, Frederick!' said Lizzie, 'for we have need of heroes in this world.' She linked her arm with Olivia's. 'Is that not true, Olivia?'

Olivia laughed, glad that Lizzie had distracted her from another rather stilted conversation with Miss Manning, who was on her left. 'Strangely, I was just thinking earlier how exciting it must be for the heroines in those Gothic novels who are rescued from danger by a dashing hero!'

Miss Manning, looking thoughtful, said, 'I have never wished to be rescued. I would much prefer to rely on my own resources.' She indicated George, who was walking ahead, engaging in animated conversation with Amy and Charles. 'My brother is a strong, talented person, but even he would know better than to suggest that I might ever be in need of rescue.'

Olivia and Lizzie exchanged glances. 'Such a pity, Miss Manning—for I am sure that George would love the opportunity to rescue someone.' Lizzie's tone was playful.

Miss Manning snorted. 'Undoubtedly. It is in his nature to be dashing, and flamboyant. I have known him too long to see it clearly now.' She pursed her lips. 'But he is a man of many talents. His wife will be a lucky woman.'

Olivia's eyes widened. Lizzie's grip tightened on her arm. 'Is Mr Manning, then, considering entering the married state?'

'I believe he is now of an age where he is beginning to consider settling,' said Miss Manning. 'It would take a special woman to win him, I believe.'

Well! George Manning, handsome, debonair, heroic—and in want of a wife! Olivia squeezed Lizzie's arm and got an answering nod from her friend. They had much to talk about.

Within a very few moments, they managed to separate themselves from the rest of the party, by the simple expedient of Lizzie pausing to study a random hedgerow, speculating whether it was hawthorn or a blackthorn.

'Blackthorn,' said Olivia. 'See the shape of the leaves?'

Lizzie pretended to inspect them, waiting until the others were out of earshot. Then she straightened, saying excitedly, 'Well! Miss Manning could not have said it more plainly!'

'I know! He is in search for a wife!'

They clasped their hands together excitedly. 'Imagine walking into a ballroom in London as Mrs George Manning!' said Lizzie dreamily.

'*And* he is a war hero!' announced Olivia.

'What!' shrieked Lizzie. 'Tell me what you know!'

Olivia told her, swearing her to secrecy. Lizzie's eyes opened wide. 'Poor Mr Manning! What a terrible situation to be in!' She reflected. 'I had not thought much about the fact that there are all those horses on the battlefield. But I know that Jem's injury happened when a horse fell on him.'

'Really? I had not remembered that—but then, he has never spoken of it to me directly. And I never heard anything about Jem's life being in danger at the time.' Olivia frowned.

'Anyway—Mr Manning! What a catch he would be!'

'I wonder if either of us will receive a proposal from him?' mused Olivia.

'If he proposes to you, I shall sacrifice myself and stand aside!' said Lizzie, the back of her hand on her brow, in a fair imitation of an actress in a tragedy.

'As will I!' confirmed Olivia. 'Though it won't come to that. Why would someone like him offer marriage to a provincial miss like you or I?'

'We are attractive, well dowried and of good family. Why, you are daughter and sister to an earl!' Lizzie retorted.

'I suppose,' said Olivia doubtfully. 'But he is so well travelled and so sophisticated. We must seem like bumpkins to him.' She was thinking of his dressing gown. If Adam or Harry dared wear something so unusual, they would be secretly laughed at by every servant who saw it—never mind having to survive the reactions of their wives and siblings. It had looked strange to Olivia's country eye—but then, she and her family did not mingle with the fashionable set.

'Bumpkins or not, I know when a man finds me attractive. As do you. We shall flirt and encourage him, and see what happens. It will be amusing!' Lizzie's glee was infectious. Olivia could not help smiling.

'Very well.'

'Ladies!' It was George, approaching with a dazzling smile. 'I feared the others would leave you behind, so I came back to accompany you. We are to walk in the direction of the river.' He gave Olivia a speaking look. 'I have been there already—a delightful spot. There are even stepping stones.'

Now Olivia's blush was intense. He was remembering that kiss! Thankful that Lizzie was looking at George, rather than her, she took his arm, Lizzie took the other and they dawdled towards the river in companionable conversation.

Despite the breeze, the day was warm when the sun came out and so the ladies spread their shawls on the grass and sat on them. Master Frederick and Jem were amusing themselves by throwing stones into the river, the child completely relaxed in Jem's company. The other gentlemen stood around chatting, apart from George Manning, who produced a book of poetry, and shared his favourite verses with them. It was exactly like a scene that Olivia and Lizzie had read in their latest novel—so romantic! Olivia could not help but stare at George—he had sat near her and Lizzie on the grass and his warm voice knew just how to give expression to the poetry. She had never met anyone before who looked and behaved just like one of the Gothic heroes.

She glanced briefly at Jem, who was clearly enjoying little Frederick's company and completely ignoring the ladies. Well! At least Mr Manning knew how to behave as he ought!

George's romantic poetry reading reminded her of Mr Nightingale, a young poet she had known who had, he said, adored her. That had been during her come-out—only a short time before she had met Jem. The poet, then Jem, now George—in truth, these were the only men she had felt more than a passing interest for. And two of them were here at once!

Faith, after an exchange of nods with her husband, called their attention.

'Dear friends,' she said, 'we are so enjoying everyone's company. This is the largest party we have ever hosted at Monkton Park and it has made us greatly daring. We have decided—' she took a breath '—to host a ball!'

Their reaction was all that Faith must have wished. Everyone exclaimed and wondered, and expressed their joy at the news. Amy checked with Charles that she would be permitted to attend and, when he said he expected the Squire would agree to it, she clapped her hands in delight.

Jem returned from the riverbank to join in the clamour and Olivia was struck by the realisation that she might now, after four years, finally dance with him. His injury had prevented him from even attending balls and routs four years ago.

Is he a good dancer? she wondered, then was suddenly assailed by the thought of dancing with him.

Quickly she turned her thoughts to George Manning. She expected he was an excellent dancer. Oh! She might dance with *both* of them at Faith's ball!

The thought created mixed feelings—dancing with

George in a crowded ballroom would be a real thrill. Such a handsome partner! Dancing with Jem would be challenging in a different way—she must keep her heart from him. She would not risk being hurt a second time.

'Jem, you will not like what I have to say.' It was Lizzie, looking at her brother with mischief in her eyes.

He sighed. 'Do your worst!'

She laughed. 'You have guessed it, I see. Yes, I shall need a new ballgown. I know that you will want your only sister to be properly attired for such an important event! And I do know that we brought evening wear, but that was before I knew we would be attending so prestigious an event as the very first Monkton Park ball!'

He agreed resignedly and before long a trip to Farnham had been agreed, to visit the dressmaker's. Lizzie, Amy and Olivia were going and Jem, Charles and George gallantly offered to accompany them.

'You do know what this means?' Charles asked the others. 'We shall be required to carry *dozens* of parcels and will all end with sore feet and sore arms, and sore ears from the chatter!'

'Oh, no!' the ladies all clamoured to reassure him. 'It won't be like that at all!'

Chapter Seven

'I told you! I knew this is *exactly* how it would be!'
Charles, with an air of Cassandra in Troy, reminded Jem
and George of his prophetic words, as Lizzie handed another parcel to George with a smile and a word of thanks.

'It is a pleasure and a privilege to accompany the ladies!' declared George, fixing Lizzie with a warm smile.
Charles muttered a profanity under his breath.

They had been in Farnham for two hours. Olivia, Lizzie
and Amy had all been measured for new ballgowns—the
men retiring to the Jolly Farmer for cool beers while the
ladies deliberated over French lace, blue silk and frothy
gauze. They were to return on Tuesday for a first fitting.

Afterwards, the ladies had led the gentlemen up and
down the town, in search of bargains. Between them, they
had purchased stockings, gloves, ribbons and fichus—
for, they assured the gentlemen, a fraction of what the
items would cost in London. Despite Charles's jesting
complaint, each gentleman had no more than two small
parcels to carry.

The carriage was stabled at the Jolly Farmer and so,
finally convinced there was no more shopping to be
done, they began retracing their steps up Bear Lane to-

wards South Street and the Long Bridge. Olivia was feeling happy and content. She loved Lizzie and Amy and it had been wonderful spending time with them in the dressmaker's. Charles was a dear and the other two...

No, she could not think too much about Jem right now—mainly because George was making it impossible to think of anything other than him. He complimented the ladies and gave them small gifts. When no one was watching, he sent her smouldering looks that made her pulse race. Even now, he had fallen in beside her—displacing Jem, who dropped back to walk with his sister. Further back, Charles and Amy were contentedly bickering over her parcels. Olivia tried to concentrate. George was telling her a convoluted tale from his time in Rome—involving an elderly lady who was robbed of her reticule. George had managed to catch the assailant and retrieve the reticule, but the old lady had berated him anyway.

'How unfortunate!' said Olivia 'She was probably upset about what had happened and mistrustful of everyone.'

George replied, but Olivia barely heard him. They were passing a rundown-looking tavern and her eye was caught by a young boy sitting on the ground outside. His shoulders were slumped, he had a black eye and he looked rather woebegone. As if sensing her gaze, he looked up and their eyes met.

In an instant, Olivia recognised anguish, such as she had never seen in the eyes of a child. It took her aback, made her catch her breath. She kept walking, but turned her head so as to maintain eye contact with the boy. He was around seven or eight, she guessed, a sturdy boy with fair hair and empty blue eyes. Too young to bear such pain.

Later, as the rumbling of the carriage home lulled them all into silence, all she could think about was the child.

Tuesday dawned cool, dull and grey, with the threat of rain. The prospect of another trip to Farnham, so soon after their last interesting excursion, was daunting. The roads were poor in places and the journey long. Yet the young ladies were determined.

Olivia was, of course, looking forward to trying on her new ballgown. She had opted for deep blue satin, with a gauze overdress and embroidery of silver thread. If the dressmaker had done as good a job as she promised, Olivia's dress was likely to be stunning.

The Foxleys would now be in full preparation for the ball, which was to take place on Tuesday night, exactly three weeks hence, under a full moon. Amy had stayed at Chadcombe last night, ready for their return trip to the dressmaker. She was patently excited about her first ball and she had plagued Olivia and Lizzie with a thousand questions about what would happen.

Although she had had lessons with a dancing master, Amy was nervous about forgetting the figures and begged the ladies if they might practise. On this basis, they had persuaded her to stay tonight as well. Charlotte had promised to play for them and so they would have their own, private practice.

Despite her gaiety, Olivia's thoughts kept returning to the small boy and wondering how he was. He was most likely an orphan, doomed to a childhood of servitude. Officially, the parish authorities talked of apprenticeships, but everyone knew that, in many cases, the orphans were not well treated. There were simply too many of them. The parish authorities, relieved to have placed another waif into a settled situation, just moved on to the next child, the next family.

Today, she was determined to walk by the tavern again, in the hope that she might get a glimpse of the boy and reassure herself that his situation was not as dire as she had made it in her own mind.

Charles, citing their unreasonable behaviour on the last trip, had pleaded pressing engagements and excused himself from today's excursion. And so it was that the three young ladies had only two escorts today—Jem and George.

Seated in the carriage, facing the two gentlemen, Olivia could not help but compare them. Both were similarly attired in the breeches, waistcoat, cravat and well-fitting coat that society dictated was *de rigueur* for young men. Both wore dark boots, polished to a gloss. In the carriage, they had removed their hats, which rested on their knees. George's was a smart beaver, while Jem had favoured a stylish Parisien. Olivia's gaze wandered—to two pairs of long slim legs, closely encased in tightly fitting inexpressibles that revealed hard muscle beneath.

Exhaling slowly, she allowed her gaze to travel upwards, past stylish waistcoats hugging firm chests, before coming to rest, in turn, on their two faces. Judicious use of her fan allowed her to do so surreptitiously, she hoped. Two handsome men with dark hair, attractive features and strong jawlines. But—and here was the difference—the eyes!

Jem, whose familiar blue eyes still caused her heart to flutter each time she looked into them. George, his dark brown eyes full of secrets and dangerous intent when he looked at her.

Jem, whom she knew and trusted—who offered her friendship, nothing more. George, who had kissed her and flirted with her—a stranger yet, but one who intrigued her. Could he be the one who might rescue her from the well-meaning protection of her family?

If only Jem would look at me in the way George does! she thought fleetingly. *Stop it!* she told herself firmly. *There is no sense in it. No point. Jem hurt you and made it clear that he was not interested. At least George is interested! It is best to focus on a man who might prove to be a perfectly good option as a husband. If I ever marry, that is.*

But what of love? Choosing a husband should not just be a case of availability. Seeing Adam and Harry so content in their marriages—and their wives so adored—made her yearn for the same for herself. Could she love George? Would she want him to love her? She simply did not know.

Chapter Eight

The young ladies emerged from the dressmaker's satisfied with their gowns. They were loosely pinned and needed finishing, but the dressmaker was doing a great job. Both George and Jem had indicated that they had separate matters of business to deal with in the town, so George had suggested they all meet up afterwards at a coffee house on Castle Street.

As they entered, they heard a call. It was George Manning and they waited while he crossed the road to them, dodging a lumbering carriage. He made his bow.

'Well, this has worked out perfectly! Who would have thought that we should all arrive at exactly the same time?'

'All?' asked Olivia. 'Is Mr Ford with you, then?'

'Mr Ford? Oh, no, no. I know not where he might be. But I am sure he does not mean to be rude, or to neglect you. I have learned,' he reflected, a hint of sadness in his tone, 'that not everyone is as considerate as I was raised to be. Now, do let us go in and enjoy some refreshments. I am sure he will be with us shortly.' He stood back and ushered them inside with a sweeping gesture.

* * *

Jem took another sip of beer. He had completed his business within a short time and retired to the Jolly Farmer for another taste of their home brew, which was of excellent quality. The path before him was in no way clear and he continued to question why his thoughts turned to Olivia so frequently. He forced himself to look honestly at his own heart.

Olivia was, of course, beautiful and quick-witted, and her figure was extremely pleasing…but he had known many young ladies and surely some had been as beautiful as Lady Olivia Fanton. Other ladies had attractive figures and good minds…why should he have developed a preoccupation with this woman in particular?

Was it simply a sense of something unfinished from before—that he had wanted to kiss her and never had the opportunity? Or was it the fact that he was unsure whether she was interested in him now or not?

In truth, he could not read her. At times she seemed to welcome his company—she showed all the appearance of enjoyment when they walked together in the mornings, as they had used to. Yet there was nothing coquettish about her. She did not simper, or flirt, or encourage his attentions.

Apart from that incident with her shawl, he remembered. Manning had been paying her outrageous, insincere compliments—a game that Jem refused to join. He had helped restore Olivia's shawl to her and had felt a rush of desire as his hand had brushed her bare arm. For an instant he could have sworn she had felt it, too, but afterwards he had come to doubt it.

Everything was complicated by George Manning's presence. Manning preened and flattered, he complimented the young ladies and drew all eyes to himself.

Jem's right hand formed into a fist. He would dearly love to land a jab right into the centre of that insincere grin! There was something about the man he just could not like. He reviewed his acquaintance with Manning, trying to identify when and how he came to abhor him. Ruefully, he acknowledged that it had begun on their very first meeting, when Olivia had sat up straighter and smiled more brightly when the interloper arrived.

Interloper? How could Manning be an interloper, when he, Jem, had not seen Olivia in four years and when she was only his friend? He had no claim on Olivia's affections, beyond the ties of companionship.

Could his negative view of Manning be as simple as jealousy? He disliked the thought. As a rational man, there was no need to allow unwanted emotion to influence him. As it had four years ago.

His eyes became unfocused as he allowed his mind to drift back to the idyllic days of his convalescence at the Fanton townhouse. He had believed Olivia to be the ideal young lady—beautiful, kind and smart. She had plagued him and tortured him, he recalled with a chuckle, and without her, he was sure his recovery would have taken longer. But he had not tried to fix her interest— how could he?

How young and green he had been—wounded in body, mind and spirit, still reeling from Waterloo and the horrors of the battlefield. No fortune, no prospects, no position in society. Harry had seen him as a boy in need of protection—there was no chance he would have been seen as a suitable suitor for the Earl and the Captain's younger sister.

Jem's mistake had been in assuming he could forget her.

He laughed hollowly, uncaring of the curious glance

of the farmer at the next table. He shook his head, reviewing his clumsy attempt to speak to her in the garden. At the time he had told himself that he wished only to be sure that she had taken no hurt from him. In truth, he now acknowledged, deep down he had been curious to know if any feelings she might have had for him had survived the years apart. His resolution had faltered at her warm but distant friendliness. Looking at her innocent, bewildered face, and hearing her refer to their friendship, had rocked him. Then she had said he was like a *brother* to her.

It had pained him, but self-preservation had taken over and he had managed to smooth over any awkwardness. In truth, he had not been aware of the true depth of his own interest in her. And, later that day, he was relieved to have not disgraced himself when he saw that she was interested in George Manning.

The wave of rage and jealousy that had threatened to overcome him had been unanticipated. He had had to use every vestige of self-control to hide it from her. If Olivia knew his thoughts, she would rightly be bewildered. He must let go of this disobliging and unhelpful fixation.

The clock on the mantel chimed the hour. He was late! Lost in thought, he had also lost track of time. He drained his mug, threw a coin on the table and stalked outside.

'So glad you have decided to join us, Mr Ford.' Manning's tone was smooth, but Jem detected a barb in it. He took his seat at the coffee-house table, between Amy and Lizzie. Manning, of course, was beside Olivia, with Lizzie on his other side.

'I have no doubt you have been ably entertaining the ladies in my absence,' Jem returned snappily.

Damn it—Manning had got under his skin!

'Indeed he has, Jem,' said Lizzie mildly. Jem was not fooled. His sister was not impressed by his tone. And Olivia had the faintest of frowns as she looked at him. Manning's smile widened and the look he threw Jem was one of triumph. Under the table, Jem's hand tightened into a fist once more.

'Excuse me,' said Olivia, rising. The gentlemen rose as she left the table, heading towards the back of the building, where a staff member directed her towards, presumably, the privy. Jem sighed inwardly. He had allowed his antipathy towards Manning to show and had let himself down in the process. Olivia had looked confused and a little upset as she had left. And with reason. Society's rules were unalterable—rudeness in mixed company was inexcusable.

He quickly apologised to the others—making no excuses. When Olivia returned he would apologise to her, too. But for now, Manning's air of triumph was grating on him. Fearing he might say something worse if he looked at the man's smug visage an instant longer, he made his excuses and went outside into the street for a moment to clear his head.

The rain which had been threatening all day looked imminent. Dark clouds were visible overhead and a stiff breeze had sprung up. Jem walked up the street a little way, trying to shake off the rage that had gripped him. What on earth was wrong with him? He had endured much greater challenges in his military career without losing self-control. It was becoming increasingly difficult to smile and be civilised when he saw Manning with Olivia. For the sake of keeping both his pride and his friendship with her intact, he must endure, at least until this inconvenient fixation went away.

Now the rain was falling, silently and steadily, and the few people who were around raised their hoods and donned hats. As he turned back towards the coffee house, lost in thought, he almost collided with a large man hefting a heavy sack. Apologising automatically, he stepped to the side, not really seeing anything, as the man, his face obscured by his serviceable hood, deposited the sack into the back of a farm cart. The man's horse—a sorry-looking skewbald with brown markings on its face—was already soaked. If a horse was capable of looking miserable, this one did.

'I know just how you feel,' Jem muttered to it, under his breath. Pasting a polite expression on to his face, he ran lightly up the three stone steps and back into the coffee house.

Olivia crossed the yard, her thoughts full of the strange incident she had just witnessed. There was definite animosity between Jem and Mr Manning. She had never known Jem to be rude and she could not account for his antipathy towards George Manning. Why, Mr Manning was all charm! She was confused and more than a little disappointed by Jem's tone towards Mr Manning. It had felt like an unprovoked attack and not something that fitted with her view of Jem.

Distracted by her own thoughts, she did not notice a shadowy figure emerge from the stable. Quick footsteps sounded behind her, but before she had the chance even to turn, she felt a painful blow to the head and the world went black.

Stepping back inside the coffee parlour, Jem threaded his way carefully towards their table, and took his seat. Amy, who had been midway through a tale, broke off to greet him, as did George and Lizzie. No one commented on his absence.

Of Olivia, there was no sign, which was surprising. She had left before him—surely she could not still be at the privy? Perhaps there had been a queue? It would be impolite to ask, so they all sat on, Jem gratefully moulding his cold hands around the hot cup of coffee he was given. How quickly the weather could change to autumn—even in May!

Manning responded to Amy's tale with one of his own. Jem, determined not to allow Manning to rile him again, was not really listening. It was yet another of the man's stories where he pretended to be humble yet managed to come across as the central figure in the tale. Glancing at Lizzie's and Amy's rapt faces, he wondered again why George Manning had such a different effect on him.

Because you're a man. The answer came unbidden into Jem's mind. He reflected. Yes, Manning did not much bother with men. His attention was all for females.

Which was strange, Jem mused, as Lizzie had mentioned that Manning had served in the army, even fighting at Waterloo. Most ex-soldiers had a certain affinity for male company, yet Manning mostly ignored men, focusing instead on any females present. He knew he should ask Manning about his time in the army, that it would be polite to do so, but he did not really wish to know more of George Manning. Nor to give him more opportunities to brag and crow.

'I wonder if all is well with Olivia?' said Amy, a frown creasing her forehead.

'I was just wondering the same thing. I shall go to her,' said Lizzie, rising and walking though the far door, towards the back of the building. George took out his handkerchief and mopped his brow. Jem drummed his fingers on the table.

After a moment, Lizzie appeared, hurrying towards them through the busy room. Looking at her face, Jem felt the hairs on the back of his neck stand up. He rose, knowing something was terribly, terribly wrong.

Chapter Nine

Everything was black. It was rather like awakening from deep sleep, except everything was different. Everything was *wrong*. Her body ached, all over, and she was freezing cold. She could distantly hear the jingle and clop of a horse and the creaking of a carriage or cart. She was moving, travelling somewhere! It was altogether confusing.

Instantly, she became aware that she had a terrible headache, which made her moan with pain as soon as she became aware of it. Her voice sounded strange, muffled. There was something around her mouth! In the same instant, the smells assailed her. Blood—her own blood, she knew instinctively—and something else. Hemp sacking! It was all over her! She was trapped!

Panicking, she began moving violently, trying to kick free with her legs, twisting her head to try to escape the gag that was tied tightly around her mouth. She couldn't breathe! In her panic, her breathing became dangerously rapid and her frantic movements served only to further entangle her in the folds of the sacking. When she turned her head, pain exploded into her brain. The blackness closed in once more.

* * *

'She isn't there!' Lizzie's face was white. 'I do not know where she is!'

'What?' Amy's voice indicated her dismay. 'But she has not got her redingote or her reticule. She would not go outside without them, especially on a day like this.'

'Perhaps she had personal business to attend to,' said George.

'She would have told us—not just disappeared without saying!' Lizzie's voice was high-pitched as anxiety set in.

'And she wouldn't have disappeared in a way which was guaranteed to draw attention to her,' added Jem quietly. He felt a cold sickness in the pit of his stomach. 'Lizzie, show me where she went.'

Lizzie nodded, then led him through the tea room and down a dark corridor. Amy and George followed.

'They have no comfort room inside, just an outside privy,' Lizzie said, opening the back door. It was now raining heavily. The backyard was neat and well swept. A stable was built against the back wall and beside it stood the small hut that must be the privy. Jem crossed the yard and opened the door. Nothing out of the ordinary. Quickly, they searched the area all around. The ladies had entered the stable, George following. They were calling Olivia's name. Jem stepped inside. A lone horse munched contentedly. No loft. No sign of Olivia.

A growing realisation was dawning—though he hoped he was wrong. Abruptly, he turned on his heel and went back outside. Walking around the side of the house towards the street, he emerged in the exact spot where the cart had stood. Where the unknown man had placed that very large sack into the back.

For a second, he almost felt faint. A coldness came

over him, leaving a tight knot in his belly. It brought him back to the battlefields of France and was a feeling he hoped never to experience again. She had been taken. He knew it, knew it as well as he knew his own name.

His mind raced. As if back in the army, he quickly made sense of the hundreds of thoughts crowding into his mind. Running back towards the stable and uncaring of the rain, he began barking instructions. 'Lizzie! Take Amy inside and write a note to be taken to Chadcombe. Ask Adam or Harry to come.'

Lizzie nodded. 'You think she has been kidnapped.' She was pale, but calm.

'I do. And I am going to try to recover her.'

'Recover her? But how?' George had finally found his voice. 'You can have no idea where she is!'

Jem looked him in the eye. 'That will not stop me from searching for her.'

'Of course, of course!' George remained standing in the stable doorway. 'But—are you certain she has not gone somewhere of her own will?'

'Of course nothing is certain! But I *know* Olivia—we all do—' he indicated Lizzie and Amy, who were already dashing across the yard to the house '—and we know she would not leave her friends without an explanation!'

'No need to take that tone with me, old chap! My acquaintance with Lady Olivia may be of recent standing, but I am just as eager as you are to see her safe!'

Jem bit back the retort on his lips, managing to say, through gritted teeth 'Then do something about it! Go and ask the staff if they have seen anything!' Without waiting for a reply, he spun on his heel and left him, returning to the street.

Reaching the front of the house, he looked left and right. Not twenty minutes ago, in this very spot, she had been taken. The cart had been facing towards the Castle, and the road to Upper Hale and Fleet. It was as good a place as any to start.

Quickly, he went back into the coffee house. Although Lizzie and Amy had managed to be discreet, and there was no general to-do, the staff were now clearly aware of the situation. A red-faced, middle-aged man immediately came forward, anxiety creasing his brow.

'Sir! I am Geoffrey Bayliss, the owner of this establishment. I have only just heard about this terrible, terrible situation. Has the young lady been located?'

'No. I must search for her—immediately. Can you tell me where might I hire a horse?'

'You are welcome to the use of my saddle horse, which is out the back.' The man was wringing his hands together. 'That such a thing could happen in my establishment! I can assure you, sir, nothing like this has ever dared to occur here before!'

Jem's mind was elsewhere. 'Yes, yes. The ladies are writing a note which must be delivered to Lady Olivia's brother, the Earl of Shalford.'

The man's eyes grew round. 'An earl? Oh, Lord, an earl! Why must it be an earl?' Mr Bayliss seemed to take Adam's status as a personal affront.

'He must be apprised of the situation as soon as may be arranged.'

'Indeed he must! Why, I shall ride to him myself…' He faltered. 'But—you are taking the horse…'

With some difficulty, Jem managed to answer him in a calm tone. 'Then find someone else to deliver the note.'

'Yes—Abe from the Goat's Head can do it! He is bacon-brained, but a good fellow for all that.'

'The Earl—and possibly his brother—will no doubt

arrive here later. Can you arrange for suitable rooms for them and me?'

'I shall and will! The Goat's Head is not normally the place for earls, but it is clean and Mrs Huddlesford is a fine cook. Her mutton stew is renowned in these parts.'

Mrs Huddlesford's mutton stew was of no interest to Jem. While Mr Bayliss gave instructions to his manservant to saddle the horse, Jem rushed to where Lizzie and Amy sat, Lizzie writing intently. George Manning was hovering nearby, looking worried. Jem ignored him.

'I am borrowing a horse and going to look for her.'

'Oh, Jem!' Lizzie looked up, her eyes heavy with unshed tears. 'Please find her!'

'I will do my damnedest! Tell Adam to put up at the Goat's Head. I shall meet him there after sundown.' She nodded. 'Best for you to return to Chadcombe—nothing you can do here.'

'No! We cannot go home without Olivia!' Amy sounded as though she might cry. 'We can search the street, ask everyone if they have seen her. Oh, this is dreadful!'

'Ladies, please!' Manning had finally decided to intervene. 'We must remain calm. No doubt Olivia will walk through the door at any time! And until she does, I will be at hand to comfort and protect you!'

Jem eyed Manning scornfully. Even now, the man was trying to turn Olivia's disappearance to his own advantage. Rather than help with the search, his priority was to make headway with Lizzie and Amy. Jem's contempt for him increased further.

Catching his gaze, Manning looked uncomfortable for a second, then raised his chin defiantly.

Jem had no time for this. *I must go!* Patience had finally left him.

Bidding them farewell, he retreated to the yard, where the horse, now saddled, was just being led out of the stable. He accepted his hat from the manservant, mounted, then rode out into Castle Street.

The cart would only move slowly, especially now that the rain was softening all the roads. His best hope was that it had set off in the direction of Fleet, and that he could somehow catch up with it before it reached its destination. As he passed the alleyways and side streets of Farnham, he knew that she could be in any building, on any street in the town. The thought of the task ahead was daunting. How on earth could he find one slight girl, abducted for an unknown reason by an unknown person, amid all the buildings, roads and farms of Surrey? Just for a moment, he was overwhelmed by the realisation that this was *Olivia* in danger. Anxiety flooded through him. Knowing better than to fight it, he allowed the feeling to course through him. It would not change anything, nor deter him from his purpose. Her life might depend on it.

He rode through the rain out of the town, as fast as Bayliss's horse could manage, along roads bordered on both sides with hop gardens. There were only a few farmhouses and at each one he made his way up the laneway, located the stable and dismounted to look inside. While there was nothing distinctive about the cart and he had not got a good look at the man's face, he did remember that the miserable-looking horse had unusual markings on its face—two brown patches that looked like strange eyebrows. At the time, he had barely noticed it, but it was the one detail that came to him afterwards. It wasn't much, but at least it gave him a start.

On he went, through every village and hamlet, all the way to Fleet. There was no sign of the cart, the miserable horse, or Olivia. Mr Bayliss's horse was now soaked and shivering. Unless he wanted to kill the poor creature, Jem knew he had to stop. Finding a decent hostelry in Fleet, he gratefully handed the reins to a groom and went inside. While they saw to his horse, he had time for a mug of broth, some hot coffee and a seat by the fire.

There was no way she had been brought this far. He would have easily caught a slow cart on muddy roads. Only stubbornness had brought him all the way to Fleet. Logically she must, therefore, be still in Farnham—or on another road out of it.

Who had taken her and why? Surely that was the key to finding her. What possible motive could lie behind the forced abduction of a lady?

Overwhelmed, he finally allowed images of her to flood his mind. Olivia, laughing. Olivia, pensive. Olivia, confused, that little crease on her brow appearing as she considered something. Oh, he knew all her moods, all the impulses that drifted across her face like clouds scudding across a blue sky.

Olivia! Anguish coursed through him as he imagined the ordeal she might be going through right now.

She was gone. Taken by some evil person. Why? He forced himself to consider the question. For her beauty? For rape and violence? He shuddered. He knew what evil men were capable of. But they usually chose vulnerable women—women who were friendless, or who would not be missed. It would be the height of foolishness to target an aristocratic lady. It simply did not make sense.

The image of the sacking over the man's shoulder came back into his mind. Long and narrow, it had clearly concealed Olivia. The fact that he had not seen any movement meant that she was probably unconscious when the man had casually deposited her in the back of the cart. Unconscious. Or dead.

His heart lurched with fear. *No!* It must not be so! *Oh, God!*

He looked down. His hands were white where they gripped the mug. Lifting it to his lips, he emptied it and rose. It was time to return to Farnham. He must find Olivia!

Chapter Ten

The Goat's Head was a respectable inn located on Castle Street, only a hundred yards from the coffee house. Having relinquished Mr Bayliss's exhausted horse into the care of its owner, Jem walked slowly to the inn. He was stiff and sore from so much riding in one day and he had barely made it back to Farnham before darkness. As he pushed open the door, for one moment he dared to hope that his search had been in vain and that Olivia had been located, safe and well.

It was not to be. As soon as he mentioned his name to the landlord, the man offered him sympathy and told him that his friends were waiting for him in the parlour.

'I have reserved all three bedchambers for your party, sir—one for the two young ladies and the other two rooms for you four gentlemen. Lord Shalford's groom will sleep in my spare servant's room. I am Huddlesford, by the way.'

Not three *young ladies*. Lizzie and Amy must have resisted all attempts to send them home. He thanked the landlord.

Sighing, he opened the parlour door. Five sets of eyes immediately turned to him, revealing various levels of anxiety.

'Jem!' Harry was first to react, rising from his seat to come and shake his hand. 'You are frozen, man. Come and sit by the fire.'

'Any news?' The Earl looked grave.

'None.' Lizzie was helping Jem out of his wet coat. He flashed her a grateful look. 'I went all the way to Fleet. Not a sign of her. I do not believe she went that way.'

Jem unbuttoned his waistcoat and loosened his cravat. Water continued to run down his chest from his sodden cravat; he ignored it.

'What made you search there?' The Earl looked puzzled. 'I mean, what makes you think she was taken to Fleet, rather than anywhere else?'

Jem hesitated. He was reluctant to mention the man with the sack in front of Lizzie and Amy. It was too powerful an image, too distressing.

Harry, always quick off the mark, intervened. 'Stop plaguing him with questions, Adam! Five minutes won't make a difference. Here, Jem, let me help you with your boots.' Harry knelt before him and loosened his boots—a service Jem had performed for Harry many times when they had been quartered together in the army.

Jem gripped his shoulder and gave him a speaking look. Harry nodded subtly, the tiniest of movements. 'Lizzie, Amy, could you procure some towels and hot water from the landlord? This man is frozen!' In truth, Jem was still shivering and could not yet feel the warmth of the fire beside him. 'Have you eaten?'

'Broth and coffee, two hours ago,' confirmed Jem.

'Pfft!' Harry was not impressed. 'You need something more than that!'

'Definitely!' Lizzie shook out Jem's coat and hung it over a chair. 'I shall order food, too. Come, Amy.'

'I shall accompany you ladies,' said Manning. He was

looking rather put out, but Jem's brain was too tired to try to figure out why.

As the door closed behind then, Harry rolled his eyes. 'Thank goodness gorgeous George has gone, even if it is only for a few moments. I have had quite enough of his faux sympathy.'

'Don't you like Manning?' Though wretched with distress, tiredness and near despair, Jem was extremely interested in Harry's opinion of Olivia's suitor.

'No,' said Harry bluntly. 'He is all smiles and empty charm. He has been singularly useless today.'

'Jem,' interjected the Earl, 'tell us what you know.'

Briefly, Jem told them of the cart, the man, the distinctive horse and his fruitless search through the Surrey countryside. 'Perhaps it was nothing to do with Olivia's disappearance, but I had to try.'

The Earl looked at him squarely. 'Thank you, Jem. I really appreciate it. And it might well have been her. How else could someone have taken her out of the back yard of the coffee house?'

'I think we need to work out *why* he took her.' The Earl and Harry exchanged glances. 'What?' It dawned on him. 'You know something!'

Fishing inside his pocket, the Earl withdrew a scrap of paper and wordlessly handed it to Jem. It had been written with a bad pen, on cheap yellowish paper, but the gist of it was clear enough. If they wanted the young lady to be returned alive they must pay handsomely. They must await further instructions and remain at the Goat's Head.

'Ransom!'

'Yes. He, or they—whoever this is—sent this note to me an hour ago.' The Earl looked forbidding. 'By God, when I get a hold of them…' His hand formed a fist.

'And me!' said Jem grimly. 'But, Lord Shalford—'

He scratched his chin thoughtfully. 'How did they know you would be here?'

'You should call me Adam,' said the Earl. 'Yes, we wondered that, too. The note was addressed to "Lord Shalford, the Goat's Head", so either they were told we were here, or perhaps this is the only place in town where an earl was likely to stay.'

'We asked Huddlesford—the landlord—who had delivered it,' added Harry, 'but he never saw the person. The note simply appeared, he said, in the taproom.'

'Curious,' mused Jem. 'When I passed through the taproom just now, there were only a couple of people there. You would think the landlord might have noticed someone come in out of the rain only to deliver a letter.'

'We thought the same and have questioned the locals in the taproom. They are perfectly respectable local farmers, meeting to arrange the sale of some livestock, and both swear they saw no one come in during the time that the letter appeared.'

'So either they are lying, or the letter did not come through the front door.' Jem rubbed his finger thoughtfully across his chin. 'What of the staff?'

Adam nodded. 'There are only the Huddlesfords and two servants—a serving maid who is on her night off and a manservant who came to Chadcombe with Lizzie's note. He seemed rather…er…limited. Not the sort of man who might plan and execute a kidnapping for ransom.'

'That would be Abe,' said Jem. 'I have it on excellent authority that he is bacon-brained.'

Harry gave a short laugh. 'A good description. Yet, he could still be involved. I should like to know who he has had dealings with today.'

'And where he is now,' added Adam. 'We are not long arrived ourselves. My groom, Joseph, is tending to the horses—my carriage is stabled here. Your sister and Amy have trudged all around the main streets with Mr Manning, asking everyone if they have seen Olivia. The Magistrate has just left. Full of apologies—as if it is his fault that this has happened in his town. He undertook to ensure that the word is discreetly spread among all his acquaintance.'

'What did he make of the ransom note?'

'He said we'd best pay the ransom and hoped that would lead to Olivia's return.'

'Is that what you want to do?' It would not suit Jem to be idle, when at this very moment someone might be doing unspeakable things to Olivia. He ran his fingers through his damp hair, trying and failing to distract himself from his own thoughts.

'I would pay anything to have her back again. But there is not much we can do until sunrise—apart from speaking to the elusive Abe.' Adam's tone was grim. 'Tomorrow, we need to make enquiries in the town itself.'

Jem nodded. He could see the strain on Adam's face—concern that was mirrored in his own. Harry looked equally distraught. 'What should we tell the ladies—and Manning?'

'They know about the note. I do not believe they need the details of her abduction, though.'

'Definitely not!' Harry shuddered. 'God! I'd much rather be back on the battlefield than stuck here, helpless, while Olivia—' He broke off, overwhelmed.

Jem averted his eyes from his friend's anguish, desperately trying to keep control of his own emotions. Each minute, each *second* that she was in danger, was agony. How the hell were they to get through the next six hours until sunrise?

* * *

'You're a damned fool! I told you she should not be harmed!' The voice, terse, and angry, penetrated through the fog laying on Olivia's mind. It sounded vaguely familiar.

'You told me to knock her out so I didn't get caught. I did what you said.' Another voice, sullen and flat. Olivia struggled to wake up. This was important! Various smells assailed her nostrils including onions, smoke and, strangely, potatoes! Was she dreaming?

'I did not intend for you to hit her on the head so hard that she was left unconscious for hours. And she is soaked and freezing! What were you *thinking*?'

'It was raining. I cannot stop the rain.'

There was an exasperated sound. 'Put a blanket over her. I shall return in the morning.'

'When are you going to pay me?'

'When your work is done. She is no good to either of us dead. See that she survives, or we will both hang.'

'You never said nothing about the gallows!' The dull voice finally held some animation. 'An easy job, you said.'

'Yes, it should have been easy, but you have made a complete mull of it! If she dies, they will never rest until they hang us. So make damned sure that she lives.'

Yes, thought Olivia. *I need to live. There is someone I must see again*...

The dull voice replied, but Olivia was already drifting again. Once more, the blackness closed around her.

Before the sun had risen, the weary group reassembled, bleary-eyed, in Huddleston's parlour. The landlord and his wife, along with both servants, were doing all they could to support the 'unfortunate young lady's' family and friends. They were already bustling about, lighting candles, stoking the fire and cooking breakfast. Adam had spoken to Abe last night and that young man had sworn blind he knew nothing of notes, or abducted young ladies. He had been plucking chickens in the scullery, he said, at the time the note was discovered. Adam was not satisfied, but had to retire, frustrated.

Lizzie and Amy, who had helped each other dress, swore they had not slept so much as a wink. Jem, with his army background, had fared a little better. Billeted with Manning, he had avoided conversation with the man as they had prepared for their beds, but he had been surprised to discover that Manning had tossed and turned for an age. Finally, just as Jem had been drifting off, Manning had risen from his bed and quietly left the room. He was gone a good half-hour and returned smelling of cigar smoke. Jem was surprised that Manning cared enough for Olivia to have it affect his ability to sleep. Having pegged the man as an out-and-out loose screw, he was surprised to discover that Manning might have some redeeming qualities. Or perhaps the man was simply so fond of his cigars that he could not survive long without one. Jem shook his head cynically. That was the more likely explanation.

Today's plan was to knock every door in Farnham, seeking information, while waiting for further contact from the kidnappers. They all agreed that the time for discretion was past and worried that they might lose their best chance of finding Olivia if they were too slow to act. Adam was ready to pay whatever ransom was demanded, but the longer Olivia was missing, the more anxious they were becoming.

Huddleston advised them on the layout of the town and its outskirts, sketching them a rough map. Lizzie and

Amy were determined to be involved, so Jem offered to accompany them, while Harry, Adam and Manning each undertook to cover different parts of the town.

George Manning was all energy. 'I shall do these two streets as well,' he offered, pointing to Bear Lane and Park Row. 'I shall go down this way—' he pointed to the map '—and come back via Park Row.'

'Good. Let us be at it then.' Adam spoke briskly. 'We shall meet back here by eleven. I shall let Joseph know where to find me, in case another note arrives.'

And so it was that, on a dull day in early summer, with a chill in the air and droplets of yesterday's rain adorning the branches and fences like watery jewels, the people of Farnham were awakened by a polite but persistent knocking on their doors. It began soon after dawn and the townspeople were astonished to find an earl, and his friends and brother, beseeching their assistance.

They were variously shocked, upset, or impressed by the news that a ruthless kidnapping had taken place in their quiet little corner of Surrey. No, they had not seen anything out of the ordinary. Yes, they would visit the Goat's Head if anything occurred to them.

Jem knocked on door after door, told the summary story time after time and asked the same questions. Lizzie and Amy then filled in any needed details and engaged the tenants while Jem assessed their reactions to the news. He could have sworn that every one of them was as surprised and shocked as they made out. Olivia, it seemed, had vanished into thin air.

Olivia awoke slowly. This time, though, she awoke properly. As consciousness gradually returned, she carefully catalogued her ills. The headache remained, but had subsided to a dull thudding. Her mouth was dry and tasted foul, but the gag had been removed. Her damp clothes clung to her, but a thin blanket was over her and she was no longer shivering. In fact, she realised, the space she was in was fairly warm. She opened her eyes. Darkness.

Gingerly, she moved. Bringing her hands up, she gently explored the wound on the top of her head. A large lump and her hand came away sticky with half-dried blood. Cleaning it automatically on her damp dress, she pushed the blanket down to her waist and tried to sit up. Immediately a wave of nausea and dizziness overwhelmed her. Bringing her knees up to her chest, she clasped her arms around them and sat like that, breathing slowly.

Memories came flooding back to her. Crossing the stable yard to return to the coffee house. Hurrying because it was just starting to rain. The agonising blow to her head and the blackness overwhelming her.

And now she was here—though she had no idea where 'here' was. Why had someone done this to her? What did they want? Would she ever see her loved ones again? Immediately, a procession of faces paraded through her mind—Adam. Harry. Great-Aunt Clara. Charlotte. Juliana. Lizzie.

Jem.

Her heart missed a beat and she felt a pain that was like a blow to the stomach. These were the people who were important to her.

In her mind, she saw their faces, one after another. Would she ever see them again? Her family would be frantic with worry. And to think that she had wished to be away from them!

Regret flooded through her. Right now, she would give anything to be safe at home in Chadcombe. Hot tears stung her eyes. Oh, why had she only realised now how important her family were? How much she was loved? Now, when it might be too late to do anything with her new knowledge.

The dizziness and nausea was subsiding, so she slowly raised her head. *There!* A glimmer of light—straight ahead, along the floor. She put her right hand on the floor—where she felt something hard, and round, and small. She brought it to her nose. A potato! Dropping it, she felt the area to her right. Dozens of them, all piled up on top of each other. She was in a potato cellar! Something elusive stirred in her memory, then slipped away. *Two men talking?* No, it was gone.

Crawling slowly on hands and knees, she moved towards the glimmer of light—it was obviously the door. She reached out and touched it. Solid wood, smooth and somehow reassuring. Warily, slowly, she stood, all the while leaning on the door with both palms. Breathing carefully, she waited for the new bout of dizziness to ease. She laid her forehead on the door and, just for a second, imagined leaning on someone like this and feeling strong arms close around her—

Stop! She refused to allow the thought to develop. *Concentrate on what is happening now!* She spoke fiercely to herself within her mind. *Use your strength and your determination to try to get out of here and then you will see them again. All of them.*

She explored the surface of the door. The hinges were on the left, so she spread her hands to the other side. There was the latch, which was of course designed to be worked from the other side. There was no keyhole, for who would ever need to lock a potato cellar?

She worked at the simple latch until, on the sixth attempt, it finally popped open. Sliding her fingers around the edge of the door, she eased it open, wishing that the hinges were not so loud!

Her heart was pounding loudly. Someone had injured her, abducted her and placed her in an unlocked cellar. It made no sense. They must be confident that she would not escape, which meant that either they were waiting nearby, or she would find her path blocked further on.

Warily, she peeped around the door. The light was muted and came from above. There was a narrow corridor leading to a stairway and the door at the top of the stairs was closed. Beside it, a grimy window admitted dim daylight. No one was there. Closing the cellar door behind her, she stepped quietly into the corridor.

'That's the last one.' Three hours had passed and Jem, Amy and Lizzie had completed the streets they had been assigned. Jem checked his watch. 'Half-past ten. We have some time left. Let us go this way and see if we can help Manning with Bear Lane and Park Row. He took those two on as extras.'

'Good idea,' agreed Lizzie and they walked together to Park Row. The houses here were mostly fairly new—built in the recent wave of prosperity brought by the hop trade.

'Oh, look!' said Amy suddenly as they turned into Bear Lane. 'It's the tavern where we passed the other day!'

Jem stopped walking and ran a hand along his jaw thoughtfully. 'This is one of the few establishments in this town that might be described as "not respectable".'

'True,' agreed Lizzie. 'But why do you think that might be significant?'

'Well, if you are ruthless enough to violently abduct a young lady and keep her from her family and friends, are you not more likely to have connections in a place such as this?'

'Possibly,' replied Lizzie dubiously. 'But villainy does not walk down the street proclaiming itself evil and calling it out to the world. The abductor may look and talk like other men—and so may be no more likely to frequent this tavern than any other.'

Jem shook his head. 'I know you are right, but I must try everything. I should like to go in and talk to the men in the taproom. Perhaps they might know something that respectable households don't.'

'Very well,' said Lizzie. 'It will no doubt be an interesting experience.' She visibly braced herself, as if going into battle. 'And you are right, we might discover something.'

Olivia advanced stealthily along the corridor. There were two other cellar doors, one of which was ajar. She peeped inside, but saw nothing of interest, save a few pieces of broken furniture. She moved past, then suddenly reconsidered. Tiptoeing back into the open cellar, she picked up a piece of wood that had at one time been a chair leg. As a weapon it was not much, but it immediately made her feel better.

She had just reached the bottom of the staircase when she heard a man's voice. It was too far away to make out his words clearly, but his footsteps were approaching!

Panicking, Olivia ran swiftly back to the open cellar. As she dived inside, she heard a key turning in the door at the top of the stairs. So she *had* been locked in! She hid behind the open door, raised her chair leg and waited. Her heart was pounding furiously, her palms were sticky with sudden sweat and her breath was shallow, quick and extremely noisy to her own ears.

Thankfully, the person descending the stairs was making a lot of noise. In a deep voice, he was muttering something and the sound was accompanied by the clank of a metal bucket that he must be carrying, as well as very noisy, heavy footsteps.

As he passed her door, Olivia held her breath. She could now make out what he was saying. 'Get potatoes. Check on the girl. Get potatoes. Must keep her alive.'

Again, a vague memory came to her, of that same voice, talking about the rain. He had been there, last night! He was her abductor!

She would be discovered in seconds. At least the potato cellar was dark and, she noted, there was no change in the light as the man passed the door. She hoped this meant he had no candle and might waste precious time searching for her in the dark corners.

Timing her move as best she could, she waited until he was past the door and then moved swiftly and as quietly as she could towards the stairs.

Chapter Eleven

'Girl!' the bellow came from the potato cellar. 'Where are you? Don't hide—you have to stay alive, so I won't kill you.'

Olivia resisted the temptation to look back. Her heart was pounding so hard that she could barely concentrate on her steps. One hand held her skirts—the last thing she needed was to trip or stumble. With the other hand she clutched her chair leg.

'Girl! Where are you?' She heard a loud clanking as he dropped the pail. There was a pause.

'Girl! Stop!' Now the bellow was in the corridor. The time for stealth was past—he had seen her! The wave of fear which engulfed her was intense. Her knees suddenly felt soft and her grip on the chair leg loosened. Somehow, she kept climbing the stairs, but more slowly. The chair leg clattered to the floor and bounced loudly down the stone steps. She could now hear the man's footsteps, running along the corridor. He would reach her in seconds.

Nearly there! The door was still lying open, suspended over the top step. And the key was in the lock!

She had a split second to decide. Keep running, or try

to close the door? If the door did not lock on her first attempt, he would have her.

She decided. Reaching the top step, she grabbed the door handle with her left hand and pulled it with her as she stepped out. The man let out a huge roar of protest as he realised her intent. She got a brief glimpse of his face—pink and furious—as she pulled the door closed. She turned the key.

'I am not sure this was a good idea,' Lizzie murmured.

The landlord, who had recognised them as wealthy customers immediately, came bustling forward. 'Ah, m'lord, m'ladies! Might I serve you some refreshment?'

Loath to correct the unnecessary and inaccurate titles, Jem decided to just smile politely. 'Thank you. A beer, please, and tea for the ladies.'

'Of course—you shall have them directly!'

Rubbing the settle with the corner of his grubby apron, the landlord bade them sit. They did so, Jem placing his hat on the table in front of him. He saw Amy jump when the landlord suddenly bellowed, 'Will! Will! Where is that boy?'

A young boy appeared from a door at the back of the room, looking frightened. His eyes grew big and round when he saw Jem. 'Will!' the landlord barked. 'Go and tell Sally to make tea for the young ladies and tell her to put it in the china cups. And come straight back when you have done it!' Will nodded, and disappeared again through the far door.

Bustling across to the taps, the landlord drew a decent-looking mugful of beer, which he then placed in front of Jem.

'You will no doubt have heard about our misfortune,' ventured Jem, watching the man closely.

'I have and it is shocking!' said the landlord. 'I don't hold with no violence,' he said. 'Never have. And taking a young lady like that—' He shook his head in disgust.

Jem refrained from pointing out that the bruises he had seen covering the small child would be described as violence. 'So you have not heard any information which might help us recover her?'

'Nothing.' The landlord leaned closer and spoke in a hushed tone. 'And I usually know about everything that is going on. But this? Not a word!'

He straightened, spying Will, who had just returned. 'Did you tell her?' Will nodded furiously. 'Now, go and help in the kitchen. How is that stew coming along?' He ushered Will towards the back door. A sudden impulse made Jem speak.

'Just a moment.'

The landlord stopped, his hand still resting on Will's shoulder. 'Yes, sir?'

'Might I have a word with the boy?'

'Of course you might!' The landlord attempted a smile, revealing a set of teeth in various shades of yellow, brown and black. 'Will, you mind your manners, now! Don't let him give you no sauce, now, Sir,' he told Jem. 'These parish boys oft times forget their place.'

Will approached them, looking anxious, while the landlord retreated behind his taps. Jem gave the child what he hoped was a reassuring smile. 'Will, were you the boy I saw outside this tavern the other day?'

'Yes, sir.'

'Do you remember the other young lady who was with us—the one with dark hair?'

The boy nodded.

'She has disappeared and we want to find her again. Do you know anything about that?'

'No, sir.' Will was wide-eyed and anxious, but seemed to be telling the truth. Jem's heart sank with disappointment. He was hoping against hope that a boy like Will, all eyes and ears, might have seen or heard something.

'Ah, not to worry. Never mind.'

'I'm sorry, sir. If I'd seen your young lady I'd tell you. But I ain't seen nothing.'

'Tell me, Will, do you like living here?'

Will shrugged. 'Sometimes. There's always stew and bread, sometimes I get bits of chicken and ham when there's some left over. And sometimes Gunn lets me look after his horse. I know it's got a peculiar-looking face and all, but I like it better than Gunn does.'

Jem stilled. His body prickled all over with sudden awareness. 'What's peculiar about Gunn's horse's face?'

'It's brown and white, see, and its face is mostly white, but it's got these two brown patches over its eyes that look like—'

'Eyebrows!' finished Jem.

'Yes!' Will's face lit up. 'Have you seen it, sir? You don't think it's peculiar, do you?'

'Not at all.' Jem's heart was beating quickly and he could see Lizzie looking at him curiously. Using all his self-control, he kept his voice natural. 'Tell me, does this Mr Gunn have a cart?'

'No. Well, yes, but it's Carson's cart,' he said with a nod towards the landlord. 'Gunn owns the horse, see, and Carson owns the cart. They always argue about it, cos Gunn says he's allowed to use Carson's cart to do jobs of his own, cos Carson gets Gunn's horse to pick up his stuff.'

'Jobs of his own... I see... Tell me, where does Gunn live?'

'Here. There's an old building out the back. Used to

be a house. Now it's more like a stable. Gunn stores stuff in the cellars and sleeps up above.'

'Does he really? And where is Gunn right now?'

'He's out back. Sally needs potatoes for the stew. He's gone to get some from his cellar.' Will leaned forward, tapping his temple with his finger. 'He's enormous, but he's not right in the head, you know.'

Jem could barely contain himself. He managed to sound reasonably composed as he patted the boy on the shoulder. 'Thank you, Will. That was very interesting. Now, I need to speak privately with the ladies for a moment, so I would like you to stand over there, and then I want you to show me Gunn's cellars. Is that all right?' Will nodded, and walked across to the fireplace. Carson, who had been watching the exchange with keen interest, did not call him.

'What's going on?' hissed Lizzie. 'Is Olivia in the cellar here, do you think?'

'It's possible. There was a horse and cart like the one Will described outside the coffee shop yesterday.' Amy gasped. 'The question is, does Carson know about it? And Sally? Or—assuming Olivia is actually here—is Gunn working alone?'

'There's no way of knowing.' Hope blazed in the ladies' eyes. Jem recognised it, for he was feeling the same desperate hope in his own heart. They had to be wary though.

'I am going to see if she is there. Be careful—especially with Carson!' He stood.

'Never mind us—*you* should be careful! Should we fetch Adam and Harry?'

Jem nodded. 'If I do not return in ten minutes, get out of here—make any excuse you like—and go fetch them!'

Lizzie looked frightened. 'Very well. But I don't want you to take any—'

'Tea, my ladies!' It was a woman who must be Sally, holding a tin tray containing two china cups. Her heavy perfume wafted over Jem and he had to stop himself from allowing his revulsion to show on his face.

'Thank you,' said Lizzie. 'Might we have a word with you?' She patted the space next to her.

Sally looked pleased. 'Of course you might! Though I think I know what it is you wish to discuss. At least three people have told me about the disappearance of the young lady!' She sat, rearranging her voluminous skirts and leaning forward slightly so as to give Jem a better view of her bosom.

Sally dropped her voice, speaking conspiratorially to the ladies. 'There is something I should like to say to you. But it is…er…rather delicate…' Her voice tailed off. She looked at Jem who excused himself and walked towards Will. Straining his ears to unashamedly eavesdrop, he heard some of Sally's question to Lizzie. She was asking if there was any possibility that Olivia had eloped.

He almost laughed. There was no possibility whatsoever, as he well knew. Olivia had showed no partiality for any man, including himself. He frowned. That wasn't true. She had shown partiality for Manning, but she certainly had not eloped with him!

Crouching down beside the boy, who looked rather frightened, he spoke kindly to him. 'You have done nothing wrong, Will. In fact, you have been most helpful. Now! Lead me to Gunn's cellars!'

Olivia stood, swaying slightly, beside the locked door. Her abductor was tugging on it and banging it loudly with his fists, but the door remained closed. She looked about her. She seemed to be in a dilapidated one-room cottage. There were signs that someone lived there—a grimy pallet lay in one corner, there was an old chair and a table with a candle and a beer mug on it, and a coat hung over the back of the chair.

Why had he done it? *Money*, she thought. He was probably trying to extort payment from her family for her return.

She did not know how long the door would hold against Gunn's attacks. He was a huge man and probably very strong, and the door was likely a hundred years old. She must escape as quickly as she could! Somehow, though, she was struggling to move.

Her spirit was strong, but it was clear that her body was still feeling the effects of the blow to her head, followed by getting soaked to the skin. Instinctively she was aware that if she tried to move too quickly, she might end up fainting and completely losing her chance to escape. Fighting her instinct to run, she walked slowly and carefully through the cottage.

The door lay open and she paused there for a moment, scanning her surroundings. The cottage stood in a small yard behind a two-storey building, with other buildings all around. There was a stable to her right and she could see the rear of a brown-and-white horse inside. Across the yard, directly in front of her, was the door to a large building and nearby an archway leading to the street. To freedom.

To her horror, as she stood there, the back door to the building opened. Her mind had now become overwhelmed with fear and so she found herself unable to think, or move, or act. Escaping from the cellar had taken every ounce of strength from her. She was done.

In dull shock, she saw the small boy from the other day come through the door. He was speaking to someone behind him. 'It's just across the yard, sir.' Then he frowned. 'What's that awful banging and yelling noise?'

Olivia gripped the door frame with both hands. She had been so close to escaping!

'Olivia!' Jem's voice reached her ears and reverberated through her body, mind and heart. The boy was ignored as Jem bounded across the yard. Olivia's heart leapt as she tried to take in what was happening. *It was Jem!*

Reaching her, he scanned her face, then opened his arms and enveloped her in them. Taking in the clean smell of him and the warmth of his chest against her, Olivia sighed in relief. Her head fitted neatly in the hollow of his shoulder and his strong arms were encircling her protectively. Through his clothes, she could feel the rapid pounding of his heart.

Jem! While she would have been delighted to be rescued by anyone, the fact that it was Jem seemed, in that moment, perfection. Needing to see his face, she lifted her head and looked at him. His expression was a mix of anguish, elation and relief. He gazed into her eyes, then, with a strangled sound, bent his head and kissed her.

Chapter Twelve

Olivia was lost in wonder. Jem's lips were firm and warm and were creating the most pleasant sensations she had ever experienced. Desire exploded in her body, surprising in its intensity. She returned the kiss with enthusiasm and instinctively pressed closer to him. He groaned against her mouth, and his arms tightened even more around her.

How long they kissed, Olivia did not know. The world around them faded to a far distance. The only reality was Jem and the fact that he was kissing her. Now he was planting tiny kisses all over her face, her cheeks, her forehead, her closed eyelids. He paused and she opened her eyes. What she saw in his gaze made her heart swell. He was looking at her as if she was precious to him. She had never known such happiness as in that moment.

'Olivia!' he murmured. 'Oh, Olivia! I thought you were lost, gone for ever! I worried that I might not ever see you again!'

Olivia found her voice. 'I confess I worried the same thing. When I woke in that cellar, I did not know what would become of me.'

Jem lifted his hand and gently stroked her face.

Olivia turned her head to lean into his caress. His hand strayed to her chin and he tilted it up for her to receive his kiss. This time the kiss was feather-soft, reverential. She opened her eyes again. Slow smiles grew on both their faces.

An almighty crash distracted them both. 'If he isn't careful, he'll break his hands on that door!' said Olivia testily, then laughed slightly at the absurdity of it all.

'What have you done with him?'

'I locked him in,' said Olivia proudly.

'You did *what*?' Jem looked astounded. 'You locked him in? But how? I mean—I'm told he's enormous!'

'He might be enormous, but he isn't very clever, is he?' As she spoke, a wave of reaction overcame her and, once again, the world turned black.

Jem caught her as she fell. 'Will!' he called out. 'Bring the other ladies! Now!' He looked around for somewhere to place Olivia, but there was nowhere. He certainly wasn't bringing her back into the cottage where she had been held. So he carried her towards the tavern. Olivia's face was white as paper and she felt light and insubstantial in his arms.

Lord, he hoped that nothing serious ailed her! At first glance, he had seen that her hair was filled with dried blood. From his army days he knew that even small head wounds bled profusely, but knew also that they could be fatal. Was he to find her, only to lose her again? His blood ran cold at the thought. As he reached the back door Will was already there again, Lizzie and Amy running behind him. Sally was following, too, her face creased with what looked like genuine puzzlement.

'Oh, Jem, you have found her! How wonderful!' Lizzie's voice was replete with relief.

Jem could not respond—all his attention was focused on Olivia. He brushed past the women, into the back hallway of the tavern. He looked at Sally. 'Lead us to a private parlour!' he barked.

Will dived around Jem and opened a door further down the hall. Jem carried Olivia inside. Placing her gently on a couch, he knelt down beside her. Smoothing a loose curl back from her face, he looked at her anxiously. Strangely, his brain would not tell him what he must do next.

Vaguely, he became aware that Sally was talking. There was a great deal of emotion in it, but the essence was that she had no idea that the young lady was there and that perhaps she had accidentally got locked in somewhere.

Unexpectedly, it was Will who challenged this. 'Gunn locked her in his cellar. She said so.'

Sally gasped 'No! I never thought he would do something like this!' She clasped her chest dramatically. 'To think we have had such a viper in our bosom! But, are you sure, Will? We all know that Gunn is beef-witted, so maybe he locked her in by accident. Oh, the poor young lady!'

Jem, concerned that Olivia was showing no signs of revival, took charge. 'Lady Olivia has collapsed. We need a doctor, urgently. And someone must fetch her brothers.'

'Of course, of course! Carson shall fetch the doctor, and Will—go you to the Goat's Head and fetch the lady's brothers!' She left in a flurry, ushering Will before her.

Amy collapsed into one of the chairs, overcome with emotion. Lizzie, looking determined, dropped to her knees beside Jem. Picking up one of Olivia's hands, she rubbed it gently. 'All will be well, Jem. You have found her and she will be well.'

He nodded, outwardly calm. But his heart was pounding and all he could think of was the ordeal Olivia must have suffered. He could see her head wound. What other damage had that monster, Gunn, inflicted?

'Lizzie.' He spoke quietly, for her ears only. She sat back, the better to see him. 'Gunn had Olivia in that cellar in his cottage all night. He may have done unspeakable things to her.' His voice faltered. Lizzie, realising what he meant, gasped. He saw all the colour leach from her face.

'Oh, Jem, no!'

He gripped her two hands in his own. 'We must consider the possibility. As well as needing the doctor to see to her head wound, it might be helpful if a woman were to ask her certain questions.'

She nodded. 'I understand that. But I am not a married woman, so—' She broke off, faltering.

'Perhaps Charlotte or Juliana could do it?'

'Yes—of course! I shall mention it to them.'

Silence fell. Jem, having spoken his worries aloud, now began to think through the implications of what he had just said. What if, in fact, Gunn had attacked Olivia in that way? The rage which coursed through him at the thought was like a wall of fire.

By God, if Gunn has harmed her so, then he will not live long enough to face trial!

Deliberately, carefully, he damped down his anger. It would not do to focus on it right now. Distantly, he could hear Gunn continue his shouting and thumping on the door. The priority was to see to Olivia.

Turning away from Lizzie, he looked to Olivia again. She looked calm, restful. It would be easy to pretend that she simply slept and that all was well. *Lord*, he thought, *how beautiful she is!* It was hard to imagine that anyone could deliberately harm her.

She had just been through a terrifying ordeal. Somehow she had found the strength to not only survive it, but to escape her prison and even defeat her captor. Jem was accustomed to appreciating her lively mind, her kind heart and her beautiful face. Now he also had direct evidence of her strength and courage. Surely there was no woman in the world like her!

Another thought came to him. That kiss! At the time, he had acted purely on instinct. Seeing Olivia in the cottage doorway, alive, had been the miracle he had been praying for. Overwhelmed by relief, he had not been thinking straight and so had kissed her. Repeatedly.

Part of him gloried in the memory. The intense desire he felt for her, fuelled in that moment by her enthusiastic response to him. The sensation of her body pressed close to his. The taste of her. He would relive it many, many times in his memory.

But, now that his brain was beginning to function again, he realised that kissing her had been a huge error of judgement. All of the reasons why he had not pursued her four years ago remained. She was sister to an earl. Her brothers trusted him to behave honourably towards her. She now saw him as a friend. And now he had risked that friendship, through his base impulses.

But she responded to you, an inner voice urged. *Perhaps she, too, has wished for something more than friendship.*

As tempting as it was to believe this, he dared not and so reluctantly dismissed the notion. The truth was that he had swooped on her at a time of great vulnerability. Escaping from an ordeal, his was the first friendly face

Olivia had seen. Of course her reactions would not be normal!

His mind made the logical jump—he had abused her! By taking advantage of her at such a moment, he had betrayed her trust and his own code of honour. A gentleman did not do such things.

Part of him knew that his mind was overset, his thoughts chaotic after the events of the past day and particularly the past half-hour. But as his mind spiralled into dark thoughts of what Gunn might have done, compounded by confusion and guilt, he could not stomach his own thoughts. Rising from the floor, he lurched for the door and made his way to the yard, where he was violently sick. Thankfully, Lizzie and Amy did not follow him.

Gunn continued to shout through the locked door. 'Let me out!' he pleaded. 'I cannot bear being trapped!'

The irony was too much for Jem. Entering the cottage, he marched straight to the locked door and spoke to Gunn through it. 'Then you should have known not to trap the young lady!'

Silence. Hoping he had given Gunn food for thought and resolving to question him as soon as Adam and Harry got there, Jem left him and returned to the parlour. Lizzie was still by Olivia's side. 'I fancy she is not so pale as when you first laid her here, Jem.'

Jem studied Olivia's face. In truth, there did seem to be a hint of natural colour there. Releasing a breath that he had not known he was holding, Jem nodded.

A moment later, he raised his head to listen. There were voices in the hallway. A moment later, the door opened, admitting Adam and Harry, and behind them, Manning.

'Olivia!' Harry rushed straight to her side, taking her

hand and rubbing it against his cheek. 'Wake up, little sister!'

Adam, looking pale and forbidding, took the time to shake Jem's hand. 'Thank you for finding her, Jem.'

Jem found that he couldn't speak. His throat had closed over, it seemed. Instead, he simply nodded grimly, brushing away Adam's thanks with a wordless gesture.

Amy and Lizzie were now hugging, both crying openly.

At least women are allowed to do so, thought Jem. *This was an ordeal for all of us.*

Sally and Will then arrived, Sally looking ashen and rather distressed. 'The doctor will be here shortly,' she said. 'In the meantime I have brought some hartshorn.' Leaning over Olivia, she held the salts beneath her nose.

The hartshorn had an immediate effect. Olivia moaned and turned her head away. A moment later, her eyes fluttered open.

At this, Manning, who had been loitering near the door, swooped forward. 'My dear Lady Olivia!' he said intently. 'Fear not! You are safe now!' His expression was one of anguish.

Her brow creased. 'Well, of course I am safe,' she replied tartly, 'for I have locked my captor in his own cellar!'

The contrast between Manning's dramatic tone and Olivia's prosaic one struck them all forcibly and they laughed. That the laughter was heavily tinged with relief was obvious to them all, apart from Manning, who frowned and retreated to his place near the door. He and Jem briefly made eye contact and Jem could not but feel a brief moment of satisfaction.

Olivia tried to sit up. Sally helped, while Lizzie and Amy dashed forward to sit on either side of her, admonishing her to 'take it slowly' and 'be careful'.

Sally, looking uncertain, spoke to Olivia. 'So it *was* Gunn, then, who imprisoned you? You did not simply get locked in by accident?'

'I certainly did not!' retorted Olivia. Jem was relieved to see her in fine fettle. 'He hit me over the head in the coffee-house yard and locked me up with his potatoes!'

'But why?' said Sally. 'Gunn gets in fights now and again, but—forgive me—he has never been one to show much interest in young ladies, never mind abducting one for his own purposes.'

Olivia looked confused. Seeing it, Jem dared to hope that perhaps, Gunn had not made any attacks upon her person. He exchanged a relieved glance with Harry.

Adam replied to Sally's question, clearly judging—as Jem had—that the woman genuinely knew nothing about Olivia's kidnapping. 'Last night we received a note demanding payment in exchange for Olivia's safe return.' He drew it from his pocket and showed it to Sally.

She frowned. 'But Gunn cannot read or write!'

There was silence as this sank in. 'Then he was not acting alone!' Harry stated what was obvious to all of them. 'Olivia, did you see or hear his accomplice?'

Olivia shook her head. 'I want to say no, but there is something at the edge of my memory—something about Gunn getting paid.'

'So he was hired by someone else.' Adam pocketed the ransom note. 'I think I am going to have a word with Mr Gunn!'

As he spoke, the door opened again, this time admitting Carson and a kindly looking middle-aged man. Carson went straight to Jem. 'M'lord, I wasn't telling no lies before! I had no idea that Gunn did this! Will tells me he locked the lady in the old cottage cellars, but I swear to you, I had no idea!' He indicated his companion. 'I went for Dr Frame here like I was asked. I only hope the young lady is well!' He looked at Olivia. 'I hope you are well, m'lady!'

Olivia, ever polite, confirmed that she was feeling perfectly well, a statement belied by her pale face, bloodied hair and the fact that she was, even seated, swaying gently. This was enough for Dr Frame to take control.

'There seems,' he said casually, 'to be an enormous number of people in this room.'

Everyone started at this and began talking at once. They indicated they would leave immediately and Carson and Sally spoke of brandy for the shock. Gradually they all filed out, except for Lizzie and Amy, who asked to stay if Dr Frame did not object.

Jem could not resist one last look at Olivia as he left the room. She was sitting perfectly peacefully, her hands in her lap, welcoming her friends' offers to stay. That he should see her so safe and calm, when he had feared her dead, was truly a miracle.

Closing the door behind him, he followed Harry to the taproom, which was unexpectedly busy. The news of the lady's discovery was spreading in the streets outside and curious locals were drifting into the tavern, keen to gawp and exclaim.

Ignoring the locals, he and Harry found Adam and the three of them held a brief assembly. They all agreed quickly that Sally seemed not to have been involved, but they were highly suspicious of Carson.

'Let us go and question Gunn, then.' As they walked towards the yard, Jem was conscious that Olivia's brothers had automatically included him in their discussions and plans. No one had even thought of involving George Manning. He had not covered himself in glory during this episode.

Harry drew his pistol. Seeing it, Jem nodded approvingly. As they crossed the yard, Jem realised that the noise had stopped. Was Gunn still reflecting on Jem's words to him? Was such a man even capable of reflection?

As soon as they entered the cottage, he saw it. Exclaiming, he ran towards the cellar door, which was lying open. Of Gunn, there was no sign.

He kicked the door in frustration. 'Damn it to hell! We had him and now he is gone!'

'The door is intact,' Harry pointed out. 'Which means someone unlocked it from the outside to let him out. Carson, perhaps?'

'Gunn cannot have gone far,' said Adam. 'His horse is still in the stable, so he is on foot.' Quickly, they hurried through the arch to the street beyond. It was almost noon and the street was busy with people going to and fro about their business. Jem counted three alleyways that were immediately within view. Gunn could be anywhere.

They split up and searched for around half an hour, then returned to the tavern yard, frustrated. 'We need to work out who his accomplice is,' said Harry. 'In my opinion, Carson is the most likely.'

'Is it possible that Will opened the door for him?' pondered Jem. 'He is used to obeying Gunn and may have been in fear of a beating.'

'We should ask him,' agreed Adam. 'But first, I want to see this cellar.'

Jem took Gunn's tallow candle from the rickety table and lit it, following the others to the cellar door. The key was still in the lock. Adam pocketed it and they went downstairs.

They checked all three rooms, staying longest in the potato cellar. There were no signs of Olivia's presence, save a bloodstain on the floor and a grubby blanket. Of her captor, there were no clues whatsoever. The cellar was tiny and there was, of course, no natural light. Jem could not imagine how Olivia must have felt, imprisoned in this hole.

As they returned to the cottage, Jem felt forcibly what a blessing it was to have the freedom to see daylight and breathe fresh air. That Gunn should have imprisoned Olivia! Rage rose in him again. Glancing at the others, he could see the same fury and determination on their faces. Three men who cared for her. Three men who—

He refused to finish the thought.

'Nearly there now, Olivia.' Lizzie patted her hand. They had just entered the estate and would soon be home at Chadcombe. In truth, Olivia's head was pounding and the journey had seemed to take a hundred years, but she was glad she had persuaded Adam not to stay the night in Farnham. She was looking forward to sleeping in her own bed and it was important to reassure Charlotte and Great-Aunt Clara that she was well.

And she needed time to think. About her ordeal and escape, but also about Jem. She needed some time away from him—to understand herself fully and consider what might happen next. What did his kisses mean? Relief at her return? An impulse of the moment? Or was it something deeper?

And what were her own feelings? All she knew was confusion.

Jem was travelling in the other carriage, with Adam and Harry, leaving the ladies in the first coach. Olivia knew why. Female company would soothe her, they believed, but equally, she knew they would want to talk about what had happened. Olivia had seen the same grim looks on all three faces—a determination to locate Gunn and question him was uppermost in their minds. Olivia was glad to have such indomitable, capable men in her life. It allowed her to let go a little and trust that they would keep her safe.

George Manning had opted to stay in Farnham—his aim to uncover what he could of the mystery surrounding Olivia's kidnap. Olivia was grateful—both for his efforts on her behalf and for his absence. George's intensity and garrulity was not what she needed just now. Instead, she had Lizzie and Amy—both trusted friends of long standing. There was no need to worry with them. She could talk or be silent, even doze a little at times, and no one would think anything of it. But, oh! How she wanted to be home!

Chapter Thirteen

Finally! After two days of being confined to her chamber on the doctor's advice, Olivia was today free to go downstairs. In truth, she had needed the bed rest, for she had been more shaken by her ordeal than she had initially realised.

Priddy, Charlotte's personal maid, had been assigned to her comfort since she got home and Olivia had been glad of it. Priddy had spent an hour on the first night gently washing Olivia's hair, topping up her bath in front of the fire with buckets of warm water. It had been absolute bliss.

With two days to do nothing but sleep and eat, and sleep again, Olivia had had plenty of time for reflection. Charlotte, Juliana, Great-Aunt Clara and Lizzie had all taken turns to sit with her, until she shooed them away, saying that they were preventing her from falling asleep. She had spoken of her ordeal with each of them, though she was careful to shield Great-Aunt Clara from some of the more distressing details.

Both Charlotte and Juliana had asked her personal questions, aimed at establishing whether Gunn had assaulted her intimately. She was able to reassure them that she had no memory of an assault and that there were no physical signs on her body of any such attack. It had brought home to her, however, how vulnerable she had been during those hours and how death might not have been the worst thing that Gunn could have done to her.

Nightmares came frequently, as she relived the fear and distress she had experienced. They came when she was awake, too—intruding into her thoughts at perfectly random moments, assailing her with liquid coldness in her belly, trembling hands and images in her mind that she did not wish to re-experience. All she could do was endure and wait for it to pass. It helped to focus on how she had outwitted Gunn and escaped through her own endeavours. It made her feel less powerless.

She was aware of new feelings of gratitude for all the wonderful people in her life and for everything around her. She found herself making lists in her head of all the taken-for-granted wonders in her world—feather beds, fresh bread, slippers, feeling clean.

She added a few more. The view from her bedroom window. The sky. Her wonderful family. It was hard to believe that only two weeks ago she had been feeling so frustrated and bored, and ungrateful. She remembered flouncing into the morning room and distressing poor Great-Aunt Clara. What a spoiled brat she had been!

That was the day she had met George Manning. The day before Jem and Lizzie had arrived. Immediately, her thoughts turned again—as they had a hundred times—to the kisses that she and Jem had shared in the doorway of the cottage. Her heart leapt at the memory. Jem had kissed her. And what a kiss! In that one day, she had experienced the most frightening event of her life, and the most sensual.

Jem was not one to trifle with a young lady, she knew.

Therefore his intentions must be serious. And yet, she could not assume anything. Past experience had shown her that she could easily misread Jem. Four years ago, she had built her hopes up, had gone too far in her dreaming and had had her heart broken.

She must not act hastily. The kiss had happened in a moment of intensity, when he first knew that she was still alive and might have been an impulse of the moment. She would do well to guard her heart and not make assumptions about him.

Despite her self-warnings, knowing she would see him downstairs today had, she admitted, caused her heart to flutter a little. She had chosen the dress she would wear with great care. It was pale blue, trimmed with white embroidery, and had tiny seed pearls adorning the bodice. The colour accentuated her pale skin and calm grey eyes, and its masterly cut ensured it clung to her form in all the right places without being vulgar in any way. She remembered seeing admiration in Jem's eyes when he had first seen her wear it—admiration which she had told herself was nothing but friendly approval.

Priddy was dressing her hair, being careful to avoid brushing near the wound. It was healing nicely, but was still extremely painful when touched. Priddy bound her hair loosely in an elegant plait, which she arranged over one shoulder. It was rather a grown-up hairstyle for an unmarried lady, but, with her head wound, Olivia would not be able to wear her hair up for at least another few days. Olivia looked in the mirror. She liked it!

Thanking Priddy, who very kindly told her that she looked beautiful, Olivia left her chamber and went slowly down the main staircase. Priddy walked with her in case she should become poorly and watched her like a hawk as she descended.

In truth, Olivia did feel rather unwell. Her heart was pounding with a combination of the knowledge that she would see Jem in a moment and the after-effects of her ordeal. She held on to the banister, knowing that if she fainted now they would put her to bed for another week. One more step. And another. She faltered. Priddy took her arm and they descended the last five steps together.

The first footman was in the hallway. 'Look sharp,' Priddy told him tersely. 'Open the drawing-room door for Lady Olivia!'

The footman sprang into action, bounding ahead and opening the door. Careful to present the right image, Olivia thanked Priddy and stepped away from her before entering. It would not do to appear an invalid.

The drawing room was a large, airy salon, currently flooded with light from the three long windows in the far wall. Olivia had never before really *noticed* what a beautiful room it was.

And they were all there to welcome her. Her brothers and their wives. Darling Great-Aunt Clara. Lizzie. Jem. Olivia hesitated, feeling suddenly uncertain. They were all looking at her. It was as though everyone held their breath.

Breaking the momentary pause, Great-Aunt Clara bustled towards her and gave her a quick hug. 'Dear Olivia! It is so wonderful to see that you are on the mend. Come and sit, for you must not over-exert yourself!'

Juliana had now reached her, hugging her fiercely and winking encouragingly at her. The others came, too— Charlotte, now waddling uncomfortably with advanced pregnancy. Lizzie. Then the men. Adam, then Harry both approached to hug her, Harry making a jovial comment about her hairstyle.

'Oh, do you like it, Harry? Only, Priddy said I should not pin my hair up for another few days.' Olivia's voice sounded rather breathless to her own ears. *Be calm*, she told herself.

'It looks very grown up,' he replied warmly.

Finally, Jem was there. 'I am so glad to see that you are recovering. How are you feeling today?' He had taken her hand and was still holding it.

'Feeling?' She could not think. 'Oh, yes, much better.'

They were all watching—she could feel the curiosity burning into her. They were her family, but she was not used to being the focus of attention. Flustered, she withdrew her hand from Jem's. He stepped back.

Great-Aunt Clara, who had been hovering by her side during all the greetings, now ushered Olivia towards a sofa and bade her sit. There was another pause.

'Stop looking at me!' snapped Olivia. 'I am not going to break into pieces!'

They laughed then and the tension was past. Great-Aunt Clara sat beside her and talked to Olivia of little things—Amy's brother Charles had gone to visit a friend in Yorkshire and Charlotte was planning pigeon pie for tonight's dinner, and oh! One of Adam's dogs had had pups, which she would let no one near, but she had taken up residence in the stable loft, where Ned, the stable boy, usually slept, and so a space had had to be found for him in the servants' quarters. Ned was most put out and was determined to return to his loft as soon as the dog might permit.

It was delightful to sit in her own drawing room and hear stories like this again. The others had all broken into smaller conversations, too. It was just so—so *normal*. Then she glanced at Jem and the way she felt was anything but normal.

He was chatting to Harry and so she saw his face in profile. How handsome he was! She had always known it, but now his good looks were so much more meaningful to her. She looked at his mouth and remembered it on hers. Warmth flooded her belly and her pulse raced.

As if sensing her eyes on him, he glanced towards her. She averted her gaze, but too late! She knew he had seen her. Blushing, she fixed her eyes on Great-Aunt Clara, who was still talking.

'And the neighbours have been so civil and so concerned. We have had a visit from Mrs Turner, who came to fetch Amy. They are to call again later in the week and they can see for themselves that you are up and about.' She frowned. 'Although…perhaps you should go for a lie-down later. You are likely to tire quickly on your first day out of bed.'

Olivia felt a stab of disappointment. 'But I have chafed at being confined to my room!'

Charlotte took her hand. 'You are not confined and it is entirely up to you. But…' She hesitated. 'Mr and Mrs Foxley, and their guests, plan to call this afternoon. Now you know how much I love my cousin Faith—if it was just her, then I would have no hesitation. But all five of them are likely to arrive. Including Mr Manning and his sister, and my Aunt Buxted.'

'Ah, I see what you mean.' The thought of facing an interrogation by Mrs Buxted was rather daunting. 'Well, if I become tired, I shall simply excuse myself.'

'Dear, dear Lady Olivia!' Mrs Buxted held Olivia's hand in a vice-like grip. 'I was so upset when I heard what had occurred! Utterly hysterical, I tell you!'

Olivia was not sure how to respond. Murmuring a polite thank you, she gently extricated her hand. She had already greeted Mr and Mrs Foxley, so that only left the Mannings. Miss Manning offered a gloved hand, murmuring simply, 'Most dreadful.' Olivia was relieved that the woman had not made more of it.

George Manning was last to address her. He lifted her hand and kissed it, then held on to it. 'I am so glad you are well. I cannot tell you how anxious I was during your disappearance.' His brown eyes seared into hers, his expression one of absolute sincerity.

Conscious that people might be watching, Olivia tried to remove her hand, but his grip tightened. He lowered his voice, so that only she might hear. 'Lady Olivia, I was distraught. I barely slept that night. Knowing that you were in danger—' He broke off, but not before she had seen tears form in his eyes. Olivia was a little taken aback. Men did not usually appear so emotional. He must have genuinely been concerned. Berating herself inwardly for her uncharitable thoughts, she put her other hand on top of his.

'Thank you, Mr Manning. I truly appreciate your concern.'

She frowned. Something strange had happened. George was just as handsome, just as charming as he had been, yet Olivia felt exactly *nothing* when she looked at him now. In fact, she was struggling to understand how she had been attracted to George. So much had changed, so quickly.

Adam came to shake George's hand and welcome him back to Chadcombe and so, with seeming reluctance, he let Olivia go. They all stood around engaging in informal chats, until the tea arrived.

Surprisingly, Jem chose to sit with George. Olivia remembered the antagonism between them, made worse, she sensed, by Mr Manning's having irritated the other men during her kidnap. Under cover of nibbling on some cake, she tried to hear what they were talking about.

'I was with the Light Infantry, under Colborne,' George was saying.

'Ah, the Light Bobs! You saw plenty of action that day then.'

Waterloo! They were talking of their time in the army. Straining her ears to try to hear more, Olivia was distracted by Mrs Buxted, who came to sit beside her.

'Now, dear Lady Olivia, you must tell me everything!'

Olivia inhaled and promptly choked on a cake crumb. By the time she had coughed and recovered, and taken a drink, Mrs Foxley had come to join them.

'My dear Faith, I was just asking dear Lady Olivia to tell me all about her dreadful, dreadful ordeal.'

Olivia sent Faith a wordless appeal. Faith looked evenly at her. The exchange was entirely missed by Mrs Buxted.

'Well, Mama,' said Faith, 'I'm sure it is best for Lady Olivia not to speak of such things!'

That was exactly what Olivia needed. 'Thank you for your concern, Mrs Buxted…' Olivia smiled politely to soften the blow of her refusal '…but Faith is right. I have been advised not to dwell on it.'

Mrs Buxted pursed her lips. 'Well, I'm sure I don't know about that! Still…' she brightened, as another thought occurred to her '…if you are resolved to put it behind you, I hope that means you will attend the Monkton Park ball in two weeks. It will be Faith's first ball as hostess and I am determined to make it a great success!'

Faith shook her head, her face creased with anxiety. 'Oh, no, Mama! You know we said we must cancel the ball, after what happened to Lady Olivia!'

Mrs Buxted's eyes widened. 'But Lady Olivia has decided to be well! She can have no objection.'

Olivia found herself, surprisingly, in agreement with Mrs Buxted. 'Faith, please do not change your plans on my account. Why, we so rarely have the opportunity for a ball here that I would feel very guilty if it were to be cancelled on my account!'

Faith looked dubious. 'It does not feel appropriate to be pressing ahead with plans for a celebration when you were so recently taken from your family in such a way!'

'But that is over now. I am well—or, at least, I will be well by then. Please do not cancel for my sake.'

'There you are, Faith, it is all settled!' pronounced her mama, with an air of finality. She raised her voice. 'Dear friends, after discussing the situation with Lady Olivia, my daughter has decided to go ahead with the Monkton Park ball!'

Faith gasped. There was a murmur of reaction around the room. Most people seemed pleased. Olivia quickly scanned the faces. Mr Foxley looked surprised—as well he might. *Oh, dear!*

Eventually, the visitors rose and made their farewells. George kissed her hand again and told her how much he was looking forward to dancing with her at the ball. Olivia was completely unmoved.

The next day, Olivia made the effort to come down for breakfast at the usual time. She had not slept well, her dreams punctuated by nebulous threats and feelings of fear and panic. Twice she had woken in alarm, with vivid nightmares where she was running from an unseen pursuer. Knowing it was pointless trying to sleep again immediately afterwards, she lit her candle and read for a while, till her eyelids drooped and she felt she had a reasonable chance of dropping off.

Ideally, she knew she should stay in bed and sleep again until she felt rested, but the opportunity to spend some time in company was too important to miss. So she donned a simple white muslin dress with a pink ribbon, grabbed an Indian shawl and went downstairs. She was becoming quite accustomed to wearing her hair down and had plaited it herself this morning.

'Good morning.' Jem was tucking into some eggs and ham, but rose when she entered the room. Adam was the only other person there, apart from the footmen, who were busy bringing dishes and serving the food. Adam remained seated—there was no formality among family members. Olivia waved Jem to sit. 'Do, pray, stay seated. You should not stand on ceremony with me, Jem!'

'Yes, Jem,' agreed Adam. 'Why, we should make you an honorary Fanton!'

He was jesting, but Jem's smile in reaction was strangely rueful. Olivia looked at him in puzzlement as she took the seat opposite him. He looked fine—looked ravishingly attractive, in fact, although there was a small crease at his brow.

He glanced at her. 'Did you sleep well?'

About to lie, she saw his raised eyebrow and thought better of it. 'Not really—though it was better than the previous two nights. I only awoke twice. How about you two? I am aware that, although I was at the centre of the drama, this has been difficult for everyone.'

'I slept quite well,' said Adam, wiping his mouth with his napkin, 'once I got to sleep. I tossed and turned for a while, imagining what I would do to Gunn and his unknown master if I could get a hold of them.'

'I know what you mean,' agreed Jem. 'I have the soldier's trick of being able to sleep in any situation, but I confess that when I am awake my thoughts often turn in the same direction.'

'I have decided to stop thinking about Gunn,' said Olivia. She frowned. 'I feel that, when I think about him, it makes him more important than he is. For me, it is better to think about the good things—that I escaped and that we are all safely together again.'

Jem's eyes smiled at her. 'You are right—that is the most important thing. But I should still like to know who was working with Gunn and where they both are now. Have you remembered anything else?'

'Unfortunately not. But—there is something I wondered about.'

The footman served her some toast and buttered eggs, just the way she liked them. She thanked him absent-mindedly. Adam and Jem were waiting for her to elaborate.

'So, you know that we are due to visit the dressmaker in Farnham on Thursday, for the final fitting for our ballgowns?'

'We can get the dressmaker to come here instead,' said Adam kindly, 'if it would be easier for you.'

'But that is not what you are going to suggest, is it?' asked Jem, his eyes narrowing.

She shook her head, grateful for his insight. 'I want to go back to the tavern.'

'But why?' Adam looked astounded.

'I think it would help me,' she said simply. 'The whole thing passed in such a blur, I can hardly recall anything.' Jem raised an eyebrow and she felt herself blushing. Was he, too, remembering the kisses they had shared? Dropping her gaze to her food, she continued without looking at either of them. 'And I might remember something that is useful in helping us work out who was behind it.' She looked up. 'I did wonder if it might be Carson.'

'Why?' Adam was watching her intently.

'Gunn works for him, so it seems the most logical possibility. And when he came into the cellar that last time, he kept saying, "Check the girl. Get potatoes." As if they were part of the same instruction.'

Jem shook his head slightly. 'Carson seemed genuinely not to know anything when I questioned him. And I can often spot a liar.' As he spoke, a new expression came over his face, as if something new and blindingly obvious had just occurred to him. Adam saw it, too.

'What is it, Jem? Have you just thought of something?'

'Yes, but nothing to do with Carson. Something else entirely.' He frowned. 'I hope I am wrong, but…'

'Yes?' Adam was clearly intrigued.

'Oh, nothing. Just a passing thought.'

Her brother eyed him keenly, then nodded, seemingly content to trust Jem to reveal his thoughts at another time. 'Now, about Farnham. Are you sure, Olivia, that you want to do this?'

'Quite sure. I survived the journey back to Chadcombe, with the immediate aftermath of my abduction still affecting my heart and head. I am a hundred times better now than I was then.'

Adam shook his head. 'I think that you are not so well as you believe yourself to be. Would you wait until next week and go then?'

That was a fair compromise—and was presented as a question, rather than an order. Was Adam finally allowing her to make her own decisions—even when he

did not agree with her? 'Very well. We shall need to let
Amy know and send a note to the dressmaker.'

Adam had no interest in the details. 'Excellent.' He
pushed his chair out and rose. 'If you will excuse me,
my steward awaits.'

After he left, Olivia and Jem continued their breakfast
in companionable conversation, the presence of the servants having a calming effect on Olivia's nerves. They
were not alone—had not been alone since that kiss in
the cottage doorway.

Finally, after what seemed like an eternity, they both
finished their meal.

He looked at her. Olivia held her breath. 'Are you
well enough to take a turn about the gardens today?' he
asked, his tone light and nonchalant.

She forced herself to speak calmly. 'Of course. I shall
meet you in the hall in a few minutes.'

The day was cool, so Olivia donned her warm redingote. Picking up her bonnet, she placed it carefully on
her head. Her wound was healing nicely and, although
it still hurt a little, the bonnet was too pretty to be dispensed with. She tied the ribbons under her right ear and
checked herself in the mirror.

She could see both excitement and anxiety in her
eyes. How many times had she put on a bonnet to go
walk in the gardens? Yet never before had she felt like
this!

He kissed me! she told herself in the mirror. She
smiled at her reflection, before adopting a stern look
and wagging her finger at her own image. *Now, do not
assume that he will do it again! Just because you are
about to be alone with him...*

Oh, she knew that she ought to be careful, but

strangely, the thought of being alone with him caused such giddiness that her sensible self was entirely vanquished. She felt like she was eighteen all over again.

Chapter Fourteen

Although the day was cool and breezy, there was no sign of more rain. They turned towards the rose garden, chatting idly about trivial things.

'Lady Shalford has missed breakfast again, I noticed.'

Olivia frowned. 'Yes, her baby will come in the next couple of weeks.'

'Are you worrying about her?'

'Charlotte has, as you know, lost three babes so far, so we are all a little worried.'

'Perfectly understandable.' His instincts told him there was something more. 'It seems to me that you are, perhaps, more worried about her than anyone else is.'

She looked at him, then seemed to come to a decision. 'It is true that the others are reassured—they think that the risk of losing the child has passed, but—' She bit her lip.

Jem waited.

'My mama died in childbirth and her baby, too. No one would tell me what happened, but I remember well the grief and the fear, and how everyone was changed by losing her. I worry that something terrible will happen to Charlotte.'

His eyes softened. 'I cannot offer you any comfort, much as I would wish to. We all know that tragedies sometimes happen during birth.'

'But what if she needs me to be strong? And what if my fears make me weak? I should hate to let her down.'

'I think you should see yourself as I—as we all see you. During your recent ordeal, you were stronger than any young lady could be expected to be. Why, you could not even wait long enough for someone to rescue you, you insisted on freeing yourself from captivity!'

She shook her head. 'It is different, somehow. When I think of childbirth, I freeze inside. I fear I will be of no use to Charlotte when her time comes.'

'I believe you are much stronger than you think.'

She shook her head, but did not argue.

Although pleased she had confided in him, Jem was at a loss as to how best to reassure her further. How could she not see how strong and capable she was? He felt unusually hesitant. Strange that she unnerved him more than anyone ever had.

Underneath their conversation, part of him was still wondering what she thought now about the kisses they had shared. Yes, she had responded at the time with great enthusiasm but, he reminded himself sternly, she had just escaped from the cellar and had been overjoyed to see a friendly face. He could not assume that she held him in any particular affection—had she not made it crystal-clear that what she sought from him was friendship?

And then there was George Manning, who had, he judged, already succeeded in dazzling both Olivia and Lizzie. He had noted Olivia's continued conversations with Manning, seen how she had smiled at him.

He had to face facts. The man was clearly in pursuit of her.

Is he a liar? thought Jem. *As my instincts tell me? Or is it simply that I dislike his interest in Olivia and have allowed that to colour my opinion?*

He almost felt ashamed of his own uncharitable thoughts. Almost. Was it not his duty as a gentleman to look after the young ladies, including his own sister, and protect them from a Captain Sharp? If Manning was, in fact, not what he seemed, then, as a good brother, he should find him out.

He had always had an instinct for spotting a liar. At breakfast this morning, when he should have been considering whether Carson had been involved in Olivia's abduction, instead he had suddenly realised that there was something about *Manning* that did not ring true.

Up until now, he had been distracted by the fact that he disliked the man and the way he had been wheedling both Olivia and Lizzie—ammunition enough, were it needed, to hold him in disdain. But this was something more. He now had the feeling that Manning's charm was a calculated act and that he was up to something.

He shook his head ruefully. Manning wanted Olivia. It was clear as day. And that fact alone meant that Jem was unable to be objective about him. He must be careful not to paint the man a villain just because he wanted Olivia's interest in him to end.

'You are very quiet.' Olivia's voice was small and uncertain. Her hand still rested in his arm and Jem realised with surprise that they had walked all the way to the end of the rose garden.

'Forgive me!' he said. 'I was wool-gathering.'

'About anything in particular?' She would not meet his eyes.

Oh, Lord! Once again, he reminded himself that this was the first time they had been alone together since he had kissed her. She was probably feeling uncertain and conflicted—especially given her interest in Manning. He made haste to try to reassure her.

'No, just nonsense. I apologise if I seemed distant. I… er… I think I must travel up to London as I have some matters of business to see to.'

'Oh.' She sounded disappointed. 'But you will be back in time for the ball?'

'Of course. It would not be the same unless I can dance with you, my dear friend.' He glanced at her. She looked confused and unsure. He frowned. 'Though— only if you wish to dance with me.'

'Of course I do!' Her voice trembled.

'Olivia! Are you unwell?' He was immediately concerned.

'No— Yes. Yes, I think perhaps we have walked enough for today. Do you mind if we return to the house?'

'Not at all!' Oh, he was a selfish swine! He had ignored her the whole way through the garden and not even noticed that he was tiring her out. He looked at her again. She was pale and her jaw was set. Filled with remorse, he kept up a stream of small talk all the way back to the house. Olivia answered in monosyllables and was clearly struggling to maintain her end of the conversation. Eventually, as they reached the gravel path outside the front door, he subsided into silence.

Entering the hall, he waited while the housemaid removed her boots and replaced them with satin slippers. 'Excuse me,' she said calmly. 'I think I shall rest for a while.' As she turned away towards the staircase, he could tell by the stiffness in her posture that she was using every ounce of courage to behave normally.

Damn it! This was not the Olivia he knew. His Olivia

was confident, sunny, compassionate, outgoing and self-contained. The emotional wounds from her capture were clearly still raw and he had added to her distress with his unthinking abstraction. He could have hit himself.

He remained in the hall for a few moments, absent-mindedly co-operating with the footman who was removing his muddy boots. Once shod appropriately, he paused for a moment, deep in thought, before coming to a sudden decision and swiftly mounting the stairs.

Lizzie was not impressed with his persistent knocking on her door, claiming that it was the middle of the night and that her brother of all people should know better than to wake her before noon. He finally impressed upon her that the situation was urgent and so she admitted him.

Normally, he would have teased her for her sleepy grumpiness, but he was in no mood to do so. That awoke her more effectively than anything. She listened carefully, then chased him away, stating that she would go to poor Olivia immediately.

For the next hour and more, he was unable to settle. Knowing that Olivia was in distress, he himself was plagued by restlessness and agitation. He stalked from room to room, irritating numerous servants who were attempting to do their work, until finally, he settled himself in the parlour nearest the stairs, put a book in his hand for cover and waited.

Olivia reached the sanctuary of her room and immediately engaged in a healthy bout of tears. Her bonnet and redingote were flung to one side, without any care or thought. She grabbed some clean handkerchiefs from a drawer and threw herself on the bed, sobbing as she reacted to the most distressing encounter she had ever experienced with Jem.

Throughout their walk, he had been distracted and distant. He was leaving to go to London. He had called her 'my dear friend'. He had done or said *nothing* to suggest that he had ever kissed her, or ever would again. Indeed, he had barely looked at her, seemingly lost in his own thoughts. In another gentleman, this behaviour would have been considered rude.

This was exactly how she had felt four years ago, when he had disappeared with such coldness, such suddenness. And she had actually hoped for more kisses! It had clearly been the last thing on his mind.

Once again, she had foolishly allowed her stupid heart to read too much into his actions. And once again, he was disappearing.

His behaviour could mean only one thing. He regretted kissing her. He was trying to get their friendship back to its previous rhythm. He did not want her. *Just like before.*

Though he had certainly seemed to enjoy those kisses at the time! As she had. Once again, she allowed herself to relive those blissful moments. Once again, she felt a wave of desire and excitement. This time, though, it hurt to remember.

And that he would break his stay, halfway through his visit, to go to London! She was not convinced there was any business to attend to. He had received no letters recently and if it had been a necessary trip, planned from the beginning, surely he would have mentioned it before now?

It did not make sense that he could have some matter of business that was so urgent that he must leave now. No, it must be to do with what had happened between them. He wanted to put distance between them, enabling them to start fresh as friends, and his going away and coming back would allow him to do that.

But how could she turn back the hands of time? Only a few days ago, she had been feeling reasonably relaxed and outwardly calm in Jem's company. Now, the thought of seeing him again terrified her. How was she to behave normally and talk with him as usual, when inside she would know that she was falling for him and that he did not want her?

Although she valued his friendship, it was no longer enough.

How am I to be friends with you, Jem, she thought, *when I want more? How am I to deny the fact that I want you to kiss me and hold me in your arms, and look at me with adoration in your eyes? How am I to act as I ought, and pretend that I am well, when inside I am crying?*

In truth, she was not sure their friendship could now survive. She tried to imagine being in his company as she had this morning. She had even confided in him—told him of her worries for Charlotte and of her own, hidden fears.

But everything had changed. Now she felt the pain of loss—the loss of something she had never owned, would never own. Once again, she was that eighteen-year-old girl, heartbroken at losing him. But she felt the loss more keenly now, as the four years without him had made it clear that no one else could compare. This was why no other man could affect her deeply. It was clear as day. Jem was why.

The tears flowed again. Friendship? *Friendship?* She could not do it! She did not know how she would even manage to *speak* to him without crying—and she did not normally cry.

Part of her was aware that she was being self-pitying and weak, so she admonished herself, wiped her eyes and blew her nose.

Suddenly she stilled. Had that been a knock on her chamber door? *Lord!* Whoever it was would have heard her distress!

The knock came again. Embarrassed, she leapt up, dashing away her tears with the back of her hand and straightening her crumpled dress.

'Olivia! Please may I come in?' It was Lizzie.

Olivia opened the door. There was a brief pause while they just looked at each other. Olivia noted the signs that her friend had not long risen from her bed—Lizzie's hair was not yet up and none of the sleeve buttons on her dress were fastened. It looked as though she had dressed herself—and in some haste.

'Oh, Olivia!' Lizzie was all sympathy and Olivia's fragile defences crumpled again. Clearly her current state was perfectly visible to her dear friend. Lizzie hugged her and Olivia cried anew. It was only when a housemaid passed the open door—the girl's eyes carefully averted—that Olivia had the presence of mind to step out of Lizzie's comforting embrace and close the chamber door.

'What is it?' Lizzie's face reflected concern—she almost looked as though she might cry herself. 'Has something occurred?'

Then, a strange thing happened. For the first time in their friendship, Olivia knew that she could not be truthful with Lizzie. Jem was Lizzie's brother. And Lizzie had no idea of Olivia's true feelings for Jem—thank goodness! In an attempt to make things right, Lizzie might betray Olivia's secret to her brother. Olivia shuddered at the very thought.

'Olivia! What ails you? Please tell me!'

Olivia shook her head. 'There is nothing to tell.'

Nothing that I am free to tell you, she added silently.

'Today has been a perfectly normal day. Nothing un-usual has happened.'

Except that I have feelings for your brother, and he does not want me. The tears welled up again and Lizzie hugged her once more.

'Oh, you poor thing! It must be the wound to your spirit caused by that monster, Gunn!'

Olivia could not speak—she was too busy crying into the fine cotton of Lizzie's morning dress. Lizzie sim-ply held her and maintained a flow of comfort, inter-spersed with criticisms of Gunn's actions, intelligence and parentage.

After a little while, Olivia became calmer. The tears subsided and she was left with a numb emptiness. Noth-ing mattered. It was a blessed relief from her earlier pain.

She and Lizzie were now seated together on the edge of Olivia's bed.

'Thank you,' she murmured.

'It is of no matter,' said Lizzie tremulously. 'Though I hate to see you like this. Why, where is my strong Olivia, who laughs her way through adversity?'

'She went away,' said Olivia, with a half-laugh, half-sob. 'Lord, I do sound positively Gothic!'

Lizzie squeezed her hand. 'I do hope she will return, for there is a ball to prepare for and a certain handsome gentleman to dance with!' Lizzie's tone was gently teas-ing and Olivia was confused.

Did she mean Jem?

'I am sure he will visit from Monkton Park again in the next few days.'

Suddenly, her meaning was clear. And Olivia had not

even remembered the man's existence! All her thoughts now were for Jem.

'I do believe I ought to step back and allow you the full right to flirt with Mr Manning,' said Lizzie, considering. 'After all, you have been through such a difficult time—you deserve all the joys that can be given you.'

'Oh, no, Lizzie!' Her friend looked surprised at Olivia's vehement tone. 'I mean—you must continue to flirt with him if you wish.'

'But why? He is handsome, for sure, but my heart is untouched. I do not mind giving him up—you know we have never fought over a man. Why don't we talk about the Monkton Park ball and think about who we shall dance with?'

Jem! Olivia resisted, forcing her mind back to the topic of George Manning. It was disappointing that Lizzie was not even a little bit in love with him—but understandable, since she felt exactly the same way herself.

Lizzie was looking at her curiously. Olivia needed to be careful. Lizzie must not guess the identity of the man that Olivia longed to dance with! An idea came to her—something guaranteed to divert Lizzie's attention.

She forced a smile. 'In that case, Lizzie, since your heart is untouched, I shall tell you something. George Manning kissed me!'

Lizzie shrieked in delight. 'No! When?'

This was more like it. As she told Lizzie the tale of the kiss on the stepping stones—which felt as if it had happened to another Olivia, in another life—she felt her more normal self begin to return. And, she thought, it would do no harm to let Lizzie think that George meant something to her. The secret of her true feelings must never be known.

Lizzie was every bit as intrigued as Olivia hoped. By the time they had discussed George and his unexpected kiss, the upcoming ball and the dancing lessons they had promised to Amy, an hour had passed. Olivia felt much better and said so, and Lizzie gave her a brief hug. 'Good! For I have not yet breakfasted.'

'Oh, no, Lizzie! You should have told me!' She glanced at the small clock on the mantel. 'You must be famished! It is nearly time for nuncheon. Shall I help you with your buttons and your hair, then we can go down?'

Lizzie assented and, as they descended the stairs twenty minutes later, Olivia told her of the plan to return to Farnham for the final dress fitting. 'But—will you be well enough?' Lizzie's brow creased. 'I mean, just now…' Her voice tailed away.

'I shall be just fine,' said Olivia confidently. Inwardly, she knew that Gunn and his cellar held no terror for her. Not compared to the devastation she was feeling at losing Jem all over again.

Losing him?

But, she reminded herself, *he was not mine to begin with. He never was.*

Jem watched Olivia surreptitiously, as he sat across from her in the carriage. He spent half his life, it seemed, watching her surreptitiously. Since her abduction, at least he had the comfort of knowing that if anyone spied him, they would assume it was simply well-meaning, friendly concern for her welfare. And he *was* genuinely concerned for her welfare. Despite her confident statements, she had to have been affected by Gunn's violent attack on her and coming round to find herself imprisoned in the dark. He was deeply concerned that returning to the tavern was an unwise idea.

Outwardly, she looked perfectly composed. The six of them were in Adam's (admittedly spacious) new carriage—Olivia, Amy and Lizzie in the facing seats, and he, Adam and Harry in the backwards seats opposite. Both Adam and Harry had insisted on coming, despite Olivia's protestations that lightning would never strike twice in the same place, and that the chances of Gunn or anyone else attacking her today were infinitesimal.

She was wearing a pale green dress, now covered by a fashionable spencer. He had greeted her at breakfast and complimented her. She had brushed away his words gaily, seeming to barely register them. He suppressed a sigh. Her outfit was now completed by delicate kid gloves and a pretty bonnet. She looked stunning and every inch the self-contained, confident younger sister of an Earl.

Lizzie and Amy wore similar, fashionable clothing, but he had eyes only for Olivia. At least today he could enjoy her company without the attentions of George Manning. He had noted that, thankfully, neither Lizzie nor Olivia had mentioned their planned trip to Farnham when Manning had called yesterday, bringing flowers for Olivia from Monkton Park. Olivia had exclaimed over the flowers and passed them to a housemaid, asking that they be displayed in a vase in her chamber. Jem had felt decidedly resentful—after all, Manning did not own Monkton Park and had not the right to take any credit for the beauties of its flora.

He searched Olivia's face. There was no sign now of the vulnerability he had seen as they hurried back from their walk last week.

After she had disappeared upstairs that morning, he had remained restless and ill at ease until finally, he had heard Lizzie and Olivia's voices on the stairs. They had been discussing the plan to return to Farnham to see the dressmaker and he had been relieved to discover that Olivia had looked and sounded perfectly well.

As she does today, he thought, glancing again at her tranquil, beautiful face. They were now on the outskirts of Farnham and the ladies were chattering excitedly about seeing their dresses. Was Olivia's gaiety a little forced? Attuned as he was to her, he could not help but feel that something was not quite right. She seemed fine, on the surface, but he had the persistent feeling that there was something big, and important going on inside her. Was he imagining it? Knowing what she had been through, he almost expected it.

Of course, it might *not* be the ordeal with Gunn that was preoccupying her. Lizzie had provided him with information that hinted in quite another direction, information that should not have shocked him, yet he had felt the impact of it like a blow to the stomach.

Manning had kissed her.

Anger and jealousy had flooded him at Lizzie's words—though his sister, ironically, had shared Olivia's secret in an attempt to reassure Jem that Olivia was recovering.

'She was most excited at his kissing her, Jem.' Lizzie had spoken earnestly to him. 'No, don't frown. I am perfectly serious! Yes, her tribulations from her abduction are real, but I do see her recovering.' She had paused and a furrow had appeared on her brow. 'I hope that Mr Manning is not trifling with her, though. The last thing she needs now is a wounded heart.'

'And is she—do you think that her heart is engaged?' Jem had had to force himself to say the words in a normal tone.

'I cannot say.' Lizzie had tilted her head to one side. 'I

did think so, when she was telling me of his kiss. And I have never known her affections to be seriously engaged before. Yet—and I did find this confusing—she did not seem particularly disturbed by his company yesterday. Do you think she is particularly drawn to him?'

'I confess I have seen signs of partiality at times.' It had galled him to admit it, but he had been unable to deny the memories that assailed him. The way she had placed her hand so warmly on Manning's arm the first day he had called after her abduction. And further back—during that dinner at Monkton Park, when it had bothered him to see their two heads close together. A hard knot had developed in his chest that night—a knot that had remained in him, night and day, ever since.

And now, sitting in the carriage looking at her, he was unable to prevent himself from again remembering that Manning had kissed her and that Olivia—according to Lizzie—had been excited about the kiss, or possibly excited *by* the kiss. The thought of Manning's mouth covering Olivia's made him feel sick. He did not dare to imagine further intimacies.

In what way had Olivia been excited? he wondered. Was it simply a girlish thrill at having a well-travelled man of fashion show interest in her? He had noted the way the young ladies giggled and flirted with Manning, how they gave each other speaking looks when he was announced as a visitor. They had clearly decided to find him interesting. That did not mean, however, that there was any depth or serious intent on Olivia's part.

He forced himself to consider another possibility. It might have been the sort of excitement associated with the bedchamber. The sort of excitement that had flooded through him when he had held Olivia in his arms and explored her mouth with his. An intense, carnal, sensuous excitement.

He was no stranger to lust and had enjoyed liaisons with various barques of frailty since reaching manhood, but had been surprised how lust had combined with warmer feelings during his kiss with Olivia to create a maelstrom of sensuous wonder.

When one has waited four years for a kiss, he told himself wryly, *it must of necessity be a more intense experience.*

It need not mean anything more than that.

But in that moment, feeling her enthusiastic, passionate response, he could have sworn that she had felt it, too. She had responded to him measure for measure as they kissed in that doorway, oblivious to all else. Had her kiss with Manning been equally sensuous, equally passionate? Was she simply exploring her sensuality with both of them, enjoying a sense of awakening to new experiences?

Perhaps Olivia was even falling in love with Manning. His chest clenched in reaction to the idea. He had forced himself to ask Lizzie. 'Do you think,' he had said casually, 'that Olivia has developed a *tendre* for Manning?'

His sister had been unable to offer him any reassurance. 'In truth, I cannot read either of them,' she had concluded. 'It may simply be a flirtation, or it may be that something more serious is building between them.'

Something more serious. Lizzie's words came back to him now and he felt the same stabbing sensation he had felt before. What if, in fact, Olivia *had* developed feelings for Manning? He wanted her to have everything she desired, of course he did. He just struggled to imagine that Manning would care for her happiness.

Really, he thought with renewed anger, *Manning took*

a shocking liberty by kissing her. Although, he conceded ruefully, it was no more than he had done himself. *Ah, but I care about her*, he thought fiercely. *Manning does not. There cannot be true feelings on Manning's side. He is simply not capable of it.*

A new thought struck him. What if Manning was simply playing games? What if the man hurt Olivia?

Jem's jaw set. *If that man dares to cause Olivia any pain, why, I will—*

'Jem! Quit scowling and pass me my reticule!' Lizzie's voice brought him back to reality. The carriage had pulled up in the stable yard of the Goat's Head and the ladies were being helped out of the carriage by the groom. Grabbing the reticule from the seat opposite, he jumped down from the carriage.

Chapter Fifteen

The tavern looks different, thought Olivia. Although it had been less than two weeks since her abduction and escape, it felt like a hundred years. In her memory, the tavern had been dark, gloomy and forbidding. Today, in the bright daylight, it looked like any other rundown tavern in any of a hundred towns. She felt strangely disconnected from it, as if there were, somewhere nearby, *another* tavern that looked a little like this one, but bigger, and darker, and scarier. The ladies had gone ahead to the dressmaker's, but she had insisted on accompanying Jem and her brothers back to the tavern.

She was intensely conscious of Jem. Her feelings for him, once acknowledged, seemed to have entirely taken possession of her. They were sited somewhere between her chest and her stomach, she decided, and burned like a brazier within her. She was alive when he was near and anxious—in different ways—whether he was near or not.

Drawing her attention back to the present, she realised that the men had paused to allow her to lead the way. Avoiding the front door of the tavern, they walked under the archway and through the yard. The cottage was unlocked. Silently they continued inside, through the untidy room to the cellar door. Jem's expression was grim, his mouth set in a hard line as he prepared to re-enter the place that had been Olivia's prison. Seeing it, Olivia knew she could face the cellar again. This time, she would not be alone. Her brothers were with her, and Jem.

Adam took the key from his pocket and unlocked the door, while Harry lit a candle. In single file, they walked down the dusty stairs, along the corridor and into the potato cellar.

It was a tight squeeze. Harry held the candle high so that they could all see the space.

'Damn it!' said Adam. 'It is even smaller than I remember. What sort of creature locks a lady in a hole like this?'

'A coward,' said Jem, his voice taut with anger.

'I opened the latch from the inside,' said Olivia, remembering her terror as her fingers once again ran over the mechanism. She moved to the corridor, almost dreamily retracing her steps. 'I hid behind that door. I found a chair leg—I was going to hit him with it. Then I heard him pass the door and I knew I had to make a run for it.'

'However did you do it?' Adam sounded grim.

'I did it because I had to,' Olivia said simply. 'One does not know what one is capable of, until the moment when you are forced to act.'

'Soldiers know,' said Jem. His voice sounded flat, as if he was struggling to suppress emotion. Olivia's heart swelled at this evidence of his compassion. He cared about her, she knew he did. Just not enough.

'I was just thinking the same thing,' said Harry. 'Soldiers do know. Young ladies, however, should not be forced into such knowledge.'

'Let us get out of here,' said Adam roughly. 'We've seen enough.'

Silently, they followed Harry up the stairs.

'The coat has disappeared.' Harry was indicating the chair. 'Either Carson has purloined it, or Gunn has returned for his things.'

'He took his horse, too.' They all turned around sharply. It was Will, in the doorway, sporting a new bruise on his left cheek. Olivia heard Jem gasp. He stepped forward and spoke kindly to the boy.

'When was Gunn here, Will?'

'Dunno.' He looked wary. He was clearly frightened.

'Very well. When did you notice the horse was gone?'

'Dunno.'

Jem spoke quietly to him. 'Today? Last week?'

Will just stared at him. Jem crouched down beside the child. 'Will, do you remember me?'

Will nodded. 'Of course I do! You found the lady—' he indicated Olivia '—who was in the potato cellar. And you—' He broke off, looking from Jem to Olivia and back again. With sudden alarm, Olivia realised the child was about to mention the kiss he had witnessed in this very spot!

'Yes, well,' said Jem quickly, 'that's enough. You do remember me. And you know that I mean you no harm.'

Will eyed him evenly. Olivia, feeling as though she and everyone else were holding their breath, almost sensed the moment when the boy decided that he trusted Jem. He nodded slowly.

'Yes.'

'That's right. And now I need your help.' The boy nodded again. 'We want to find Gunn and to work out who was paying him to kidnap Lady Olivia. You are not in trouble—not in any way.'

Will tilted his head to one side, considering, and then the truth came out in a rush. 'Carson said I should have been listening, should have come to get him. But I couldn't, I swear! He'd have done for me! And he took his horse.'

This was not particularly clear. Jem, with endless patience, kept his voice low and measured. 'You knew he would come back for the horse.'

The child nodded again. 'He always said how it was his own horse, not Carson's. But he didn't care for it— not like I cared for it! I love horses, me.'

Olivia felt a lump in her throat. Will sounded upset at the loss of Gunn's strange-looking horse. Moving towards the child, she, too, crouched down beside him.

'Will, can you tell me how this happened?' She indicated the bruise on his cheek. Here was definitive evidence that Will was being abused.

'Carson made me sleep out here, waiting for Gunn. I was supposed to come and get him when Gunn came.' He indicated the pallet in the corner of the room. 'I woke up one night and Gunn was already here, in the dark. He was saying things to himself—he was angry.'

Jem and Olivia exchanged a worried glance. 'Did Gunn beat you?'

Will's eyes opened wide. 'No! I was too afeared to move! He'd have killed me for sure! He took his coat and then went out for the horse. He didn't see me. I was as still as a stone.'

Olivia's heart melted. 'Oh, you poor thing!' She knew from direct experience how it felt to be in Gunn's power. The child must have been terrified. She put a hand on his thin shoulder. He winced. She removed her hand and exchanged a worried look with Jem.

Slowly, giving Will plenty of time to resist, Jem

moved the fabric of Will's thin shirt off his shoulder, revealing another, very large bruise. He swallowed. 'Are there any more?'

Wordlessly, Will lifted his shirt. His torso was a mess of bruises, of varying sizes and colours.

'Who did this?' Jem's voice was hard. Olivia suspected she already knew the answer.

'Carson.' Will let his shirt fall back into place.

'Is Carson your father?'

'No. I'm an orphan and he says I'm lucky he gives me a roof over my head.'

'Why did he beat you? Was he involved in Lady Olivia being locked up?'

The boy shook his head vigorously. 'He beat me to tell him who Gunn was working with. I kept telling him I dunno! I dunno! He didn't believe me. Said Gunn was too stupid to do something like that by hisself.'

Jem straightened, giving a hand up to Olivia as he did so. 'He could be right there.'

'So he told me I wasn't allowed to sleep in the house again until Gunn came back. He wanted to find out from Gunn who was paying him. Said he didn't hold with fleecing the gentry. Too dangerous, he said.'

Adam intervened. 'What was Gunn saying, when he came in for his coat?'

Will's eyes widened, as he looked at Harry and Adam. The force of all those eyes trained on him seemed to flummox him.

He shook his head. 'Nothing. I dunno.'

Olivia laid a gloved hand gently on the boy's arm. 'Be easy. You do not have to answer any more questions.'

'No. I want to help.' His small face creased in concentration. 'It was a vicar or priest that done it, he said. He was going to find him in the park and make sure he gets paid. He said it was supposed to be easy and a swell keeps their word.'

'Which was it, a vicar or a priest?' Adam asked.

Will's voice rose shrilly. 'I dunno! One of them church coves! I dunno who they all are!'

Olivia wrapped her arms around the child. 'Hush! You do not have to tell us anything more.' Gently, she smoothed the hair back from his brow. 'You are a brave lad.'

Her heart melted as she embraced Will's small thin body. She could not bear to leave him here, with Carson.

Over Will's shoulder, her eyes met Jem's. She murmured his name, her voice a plea.

He nodded grimly.

'Good day, good day to you!' Carson was making his way across the yard, wiping his hands on the corner of his grimy apron. He bowed to them all, before enquiring generally as to their state of health. They all murmured appropriate platitudes.

He turned to Olivia. 'And how is the lady? Quite recovered, I hope?'

'Much better, thank you,' Olivia confirmed shortly.

'Good, good.' He rubbed his hands together and turned to Adam. 'My lord, I assure you again that I had nothing to do with this. Since it happened I have been doing my damnedest—pardon the language, my lady—doing my *best* to discover who Gunn was in league with. But I have run aground and finished short of a leg! Even the boy has seen nothing.'

Jem looked grim. 'Er...about the boy—might I have a private word with you?'

Carson grimaced. 'If he has been giving you sauce, I am sorry for it. I shall clip his ear later!'

'I haven't given no sauce!' said Will indignantly,

flushing with anger. 'I have been only polite and answering questions.' Olivia was encouraged to see that,
so far, Carson had not broken Will's spirit.

'You're giving sauce right now!' retorted Carson.
'How many times have I told you not to speak unless
your betters ask you to?'

'I told you—I just answered their questions!'

Carson's anger visibly rose. 'Come here, boy!' he
roared. Will blanched, but stood his ground.

Jem's jaw hardened. 'As interesting and enlighten-
ing as this conversation is, I believe I had a prior call on
your attention, Mr Carson.' His tone was that of a man
bored beyond endurance, but the expression in his eyes
was implacable. 'Shall we?' He indicated the rear door
of the tavern.

'Yes, yes, of course!' Carson bowed deeply. 'Apologies, but he tests my endurance every day. This way,
sir!'

Olivia watched Jem walk away—that strong confident gait that she had seen him build and regain after
his terrible injury.

While her brothers discussed the various churches,
vicarages and rectories that lay within the area, she stood
silent, looking around Gunn's grimy cottage again. She
now remembered it more for Jem's kisses than Gunn's attack on her. Jem had—quite without realising it—helped
her vanquish the memory of the potato cellar.

By the time Jem returned, Adam and Harry had decided that, after escorting Olivia to meet the other ladies
at the dressmaker, the gentlemen would pay courtesy
calls on the various men of the cloth in the local area.

'I know it is unlikely,' mused Harry, 'that any of them
are involved or know anything about Gunn, but it is
worth trying.'

'Perhaps,' speculated Adam, as a new thought struck him, 'one of them may be *now* aiding Gunn, without realising that he was involved in such a heinous deed.'

Olivia was not listening. 'Jem! What has happened?'

Jem was approaching them with a wide smile on his face and a decided air of satisfaction. 'I have succeeded,' he said, 'in persuading Carson to make over Will's contract to me.'

Olivia clapped her hands. 'Oh, how wonderful, Jem!'

Could this man be any more magnificent? He had, with one bold move, rescued Will from a lifetime of drudgery and beatings.

Will looked confused, so Jem addressed him directly. 'That means, Will, you will now work for me.'

'Not Carson?'

'Not Carson.'

Olivia saw disbelief, then joy, come over the boy's face. 'Work for you, sir? I should say so! But—what would you like me to do for you?'

'I had a notion,' said Jem, 'that you might like to help with my horses.'

Will's eyes opened wide. 'You own more than one horse?'

Jem nodded. 'I do. I currently own ten horses—four carriage horses and a string of hunters. There is also my sister's mare.'

Adam laughed. 'Why, Jem, you have more horses than I do!'

Will ignored this. 'And can I look after *all* of them?'

'You can.' Jem laughed lightly, clearly enjoying the boy's awed tone. 'When we return to my home, you will live with the grooms and stable boys and you can learn how to be a stable boy.'

'Be a stable boy!' breathed Will. 'An actual stable boy!'

'Only if you work hard. And you can learn how to read and write, too.'

Tears started in Will's eyes. 'My mam taught me, a little bit, before she died. I should like to learn more, though.'

'Good.' Jem's voice was a little choked. It was all Olivia could do to stop herself from hugging him, right there in front of everyone. He cleared his throat. 'You will have to follow the orders of my head groom, who is currently staying in the mews at Chadcombe.'

'Chadcombe!' Will's eyes opened wide. 'I heard of Chadcombe. They say it is bigger even than the royal palace and that an earl lives in it!'

'Correct—that would be the Earl of Shalford.' Jem indicated Adam. Olivia suppressed a giggle—she was really enjoying the way Jem was managing the situation.

'Delighted to make your acquaintance,' said Adam. Will's mouth fell open.

'Allow me also to present to you,' continued Jem, 'the Earl's brother, Mr Harry Fanton...' Harry clicked his heels together and tipped his hat to the child. 'And his sister, Lady Olivia Fanton.'

Olivia, enjoying the game, dipped a slight curtsy to Will. As Jem introduced himself, she could barely hear him. Her heart was swelling with pride. Jem looked at her briefly and she, unable to dissemble, smiled tremulously at him. He smiled back and they enjoyed a moment of perfect harmony.

'Lords and ladies and all—I cannot take it in!' Will did indeed look rather bewildered.

Jem blinked, as if recalling himself to the present. 'Will, go you and pack up whatever belongings you have. Say goodbye to Carson and Sally, then come straight back here.'

'Yes, sir. Right away!' The child shot off through the tavern door like an arrow, whooping in delight.

'How much did you have to pay Carson?' asked Harry drily. 'I bet he fleeced you for an amount far above the true cost of the contract.'

'It was worth it,' said Jem. He glanced at Olivia. 'It was worth every penny.'

Chapter Sixteen

'And will the waltz be played, Faith?' asked Olivia.

The ladies had retired to the drawing room at Chadcombe, allowing the men to enjoy their after-dinner port. The Monkton Park party had joined them for dinner, as had Amy Turner.

'Of course it will!' Mrs Buxted answered for her daughter. 'For what is a ball nowadays without a waltz? I must say that in my day it would have been considered not at all the thing—don't you agree, Miss Manning? But in these enlightened times it is considered perfectly acceptable even for unmarried maidens to be seen twirling around a room in a man's arms!'

'I find it unexceptional,' said Miss Manning, in her usual colourless tone.

'So there you have it, Lady Olivia! You may twirl around the room in the arms of Mr Manning—or any other young fellow that catches your eye!' Mrs Buxted laughed loudly at her own wit. Olivia gritted her teeth and said nothing.

'I am sure my brother would be delighted to waltz with Lady Olivia,' said Miss Manning, smiling at Olivia. Strangely, this did not ease Olivia's discomfort.

Miss Manning had been curiously friendly towards Olivia tonight, singling her out for attention and conversation. She had even asked Olivia about her abduction and recovery.

'You are a strong young girl—I am sure it did you no harm to have such an adventure!' she had opined.

This was a novel approach to the subject and one that Olivia had not heard before. Everyone else had talked of 'ordeal' not 'adventure'. But then, Miss Manning was an unusual person. Despite this, Olivia was rather thrown by the woman's words.

'Apart from the blow to the head and the terror, do you mean?' she had said tartly, without thinking. Miss Manning had raised a cool eyebrow. 'At the time, I certainly did not see it as an adventure.'

'And now?' Miss Manning's gaze had been curiously intent.

Olivia had considered this. 'I am not sure,' she had said with honesty. 'I remember the fear and the horror, but I also feel proud that I managed to extricate myself.'

'Ah, yes,' Miss Manning had replied knowingly. 'They told me that you had given Gunn the slip. Such a pity that George never got the chance to rescue you— he was distraught with worry, you know! But the whole thing does sound remarkably Gothic!'

'Indeed! I thought so myself. But the heroines in novels do not find themselves shivering with the cold and drenched to the skin. The novelists fail to include that part.'

'I understood that your captor had covered you with a blanket,' Miss Manning had said.

Really, the woman had seemed determined to trivialise her ordeal! Olivia had found her irritation increasing. 'A blanket is not much use when you are already soaked. It took me the best part of the day to feel warm again.'

'Women in novels are often relieved and grateful when the hero rescues them. I do recall…' her tone changed, a strange jocularity entering her voice '…that you were recently wishing to be rescued by a dashing hero!'

Olivia had looked blankly at her. What on earth was she talking about?

'Our conversation, while walking at Monkton Park? I distinctly recall you saying that you should enjoy being rescued by someone dashing and heroic.'

Olivia had frowned, Miss Manning's words reminding her of her flippant comment. 'I did say that—how foolish!'

'Is it foolish to see that someone cares for you, or that a man would want to rescue you when you were in danger?'

Miss Manning was looking closely at her. Conscious that her face might betray her true feelings, she had simply said, 'No. That is not foolish at all.'

Miss Manning had patted her hand. 'Good girl,' she had said, as if satisfied about something.

Looking at George's sister now, Olivia was still at a loss to explain her behaviour.

'I do hope,' said Adam to Amy, 'that you will now feel able to take your place on the dance floor at the Monkton Park ball?' They had all spent a couple of hours practising dances together, while Charlotte played the piano and Adam turned pages for her.

'Oh, yes!' said Amy warmly. 'I feel much more ready for it! Thank you to all of you for doing this and to you, Charlotte, for playing for us for such a long time.' She turned to Jem. 'And thank you to the best partner I could ever have. I am sorry that you have been burdened with me tonight, but I do feel much more confident now.'

When they had cleared the furniture back in readiness for the first cotillion, George Manning had immediately claimed Olivia's hand and, as the others had paired up, Jem and Amy had ended up dancing together. Jem was endlessly patient with Amy and her confidence had bloomed as the evening went on.

'Let me assure you, Miss Turner,' said Jem, with a bow, 'that you are certainly not a burden and I have thoroughly enjoyed your company this evening.'

Amy blushed and stammered, while Lizzie caught Olivia's eye and gave her a meaningful look. Olivia knew exactly what she intended—she had noted, as they all had, Jem and Amy's enjoyment of each other's company.

Olivia's heart sank. She looked blankly back at Lizzie, unwilling to acknowledge a reality she was not willing to face.

Amy and Jem.

Jem and Amy.

No! It could not—must not—be!

Jem untied his cravat and threw it on to a chair. One shoe, then the other, were flung across the room with great force—the second almost hitting the unfortunate footman who had just entered his chamber to help him undress.

'I shan't need you,' Jem told the footman curtly. The man backed out with a bow.

Manning had known exactly what he was at. He had positioned himself ready to take Olivia's hand as dancing partner as soon as the opportunity arose, thwarting Jem's plans in an instant. Of course, Jem had managed to remain outwardly calm—to do otherwise would have been insulting to young Amy—but inwardly, he was seeth-

ing. Manning had thrown him a self-satisfied smile at
one point, making his blood boil. And seeing the man's
playacting with Olivia—the shameless compliments and
hand-kissing—was sickening.

Manning had been blatantly ogling her, too, Jem had
noted—particularly during the waltz, when he had made
the most of his proximity to Olivia to direct his gaze to
her bosom as she whirled around in his arms. No one else
seemed to have noticed, including Olivia. Thankfully
the Monkton Park party—and Amy—would all leave
in the morning. How he would otherwise have endured
another day without hitting Manning, he did not know.

'Will you walk with me?' Jem gave her a crooked
smile as he asked the question. They had just finished
breakfast, and the others were dispersing to their various
business. Today was the first day that Olivia had breakfasted downstairs since that disastrous morning when
she and Jem had last walked together. Knowing it was
cowardly, she had nevertheless decided that breakfasting
in her room was preferable to having her heart bruised by
his friendly cheerfulness—or, worse, by that abstracted
distance she had felt on their last walk together. The fear
that he was interested in Amy had made it even worse.
She had avoided breakfast with the guests yesterday—
no one had thought anything of it.

Today, though, Jem was to take his leave of them,
travelling to London on his mysterious business. Since
it would be her last chance to walk and talk privately
with him until his return, Olivia had chosen to be brave
and come out of hiding. And, to her relief, he wanted to
walk with her.

No one would realise, she hoped, that her decision was
entirely based on Jem's departure. Charlotte had chal-

lenged her just yesterday about missing breakfast and advised her to return to normality as soon as she felt able.

'My babe will come soon,' Charlotte had said, lightly, 'which means that I myself might miss the family breakfast for a time. That is a shame, for I confess I do enjoy our shared breakfast. It is a Fanton family tradition that I wholeheartedly endorse.'

Olivia had squirmed uncomfortably, loath to admit that she, too, loved the tradition—especially with Jem's presence. She loved the thrill of seeing Jem again after a whole night of thinking of him, dreaming of him and, sadly, crying over him.

'When will your baby come, Charlotte?' she had asked, genuinely interested, but also hoping to divert Charlotte from pressing her on the breakfast issue.

'I have no idea!' Charlotte had replied frankly. 'It must be soon, but it cannot come soon enough, for I am so ungainly and uncomfortable that I struggle through each day and night at present.' She had patted her stomach lovingly. 'The midwife says all is well and that these painful tightenings I am feeling mean that my time will soon be here.'

'Does the doctor not attend you?' Olivia had asked curiously. Each time she thought about Charlotte's upcoming trial, cold fear pierced her belly.

'He does, but he has commended me to Mrs Logan, the midwife, whom he says is a person of superior understanding. She has helped hundreds of babies into the world and, he says, has more knowledge in her hands than he has in all his books.'

'How wonderful!' Olivia had exclaimed, unwilling to let Charlotte see how terrified she was by the notion of childbirth and her fear that Charlotte or her babe—or both—might not survive. 'I had heard that doctors and midwives do not always work well together and that mid-wives usually look after the village women, with doctors or accoucheurs serving ladies.'

'We are lucky hereabouts,' agreed Charlotte. 'The doctor says he trusts Mrs Logan to call him if needed. But when my time comes, it will be Mrs Logan that I shall send for first.' She had smiled contentedly. 'Great-Aunt Clara is continually apologising that she will not accompany me in my labour. She says it will distress her too much and that she should be a burden. I have assured her that Juliana has already offered to be my comfort and so she is satisfied.'

Olivia frowned. Charlotte had not, it seemed, even considered asking *her* to be there when the baby was coming. She sighed inwardly. Although fearful for Charlotte, she nevertheless wanted to be included. She had hoped that, since her kidnap, the family might have begun to see her differently. Yet Charlotte's decision suggested that, despite everything, the others still saw her as a girl, to be sheltered and protected from any-thing…anything *real*.

Charlotte had eyed Olivia keenly. 'Anyway,' she'd said, 'I recollect we were discussing your absence from breakfast. I do hope you will consider rejoining us to-morrow.' Olivia had shrugged uncertainly. 'And besides,' Charlotte had added with a twinkle, 'I am quite certain that Jem is missing your walks together.'

Olivia had given an unladylike snort in response and refused to be drawn. Hopefully Charlotte had not meant anything particular with that remark! But today she had come down for breakfast.

She smiled now. 'I'd love to, Jem,' she said, feeling as though it was the most honest thing she had said to him in days.

Chapter Seventeen

The Monkton Park party had, thankfully, only stayed one night. Much as she loved Faith, Olivia had been relieved to wave them all off yesterday morning after the dancing. Normally, she enjoyed having visitors, as it broke the tedium. But these days, she would gladly welcome that tedium. There was, it seemed, a lack of time to think! Jem and Lizzie were still here, of course, and Charlotte's father, Sir Edward, had arrived to await the birth of his first grandchild, but they were like family. They added to her life: they did not take anything away.

Then there was Amy. Olivia sighed as she donned stout kid boots for her walk with Jem. Amy was a dear friend, but, after the dancing, Olivia had found it hard to be easy with her. She had been relieved when the Foxleys had offered to take Amy home on their way back to Monkton Park yesterday morning.

Olivia knew—of course she did—that Amy had done nothing wrong and that her friend would be horrified if she knew how Olivia was feeling. She just couldn't help it. The thought of losing Jem was tormenting her.

I have no right to Jem's regard, Olivia reminded herself. *He is free to bestow it wherever he wishes. Amy is free to admire Jem as much as she wants to.*

Tears started in her eyes, but she refused to allow them to flow. Jem would not trifle with any young lady, she reminded herself. Although he had broken her heart four years ago he had not done so knowingly or callously.

She could not fault his behaviour back then. He had never, by word or deed, suggested that he had wanted to marry her. She had taken too seriously the admiration she had seen in his eyes when she was eighteen. She could not trust her reading of him—she had been disastrously wrong before. So how was she to work out why he had kissed her in the cottage, or whether he had feelings for Amy? She could only be with him, one last time, before his departure. She tied her bonnet firmly under one ear, lifted her chin, and went downstairs.

As always, Jem's heart leapt as he watched Olivia descend the staircase. He was becoming accustomed to the sensation. Of course she looked stunning—she always did.

She slipped her little hand into the crook of his arm and they stepped outside, turning immediately, by unspoken agreement, towards the rose garden. They chatted—a little awkwardly—of everyday things. Of Will and how well he had settled into his new role of assisting the grooms. Of little Jack coming out in spots, necessitating the sudden removal of Juliana and Harry to their own home. Of the dancing practice and how Amy had, over the course of the evening, developed great confidence in her ability to master the intricacies of the steps. He fancied that Olivia's demeanour became a little strained at this point. Was she recalling her evening dancing in the arms of George Manning?

'…in time for the ball?' Olivia's voice drew him back to the present. He looked at her blankly, having momentarily lost the thread of the conversation. 'Or will your business keep you in London beyond next Tuesday?'

'I do hope to return for the ball,' he said, 'though I cannot guarantee it.' In truth, he was not sure how and when he would manage to find out more about Manning. He simply knew that he had to try. He had already sent off letters to a couple of key contacts, asking subtle questions and indicating that he would shortly be in town if they wished to meet with him. If there was scandal, he was more likely to unearth it face to face.

Inwardly, he had abandoned the pretence that any of this was for Lizzie's sake. It was now clear that Manning was fixated on Olivia—to the extent that, according to Lizzie, the man's cold fish of a sister was dropping not-so-subtle hints of approval in Olivia's direction. Marriage seemed to be on *her* mind, at least. Whether her brother was of like mind, no one seemed certain.

Jem, of course, was not related to Olivia and, as such, had no right to investigate Manning on her behalf. But he had spoken to Harry of his concerns and Harry had encouraged him to investigate further. He felt that he was fumbling in the dark, unsure where he was going, knowing only that he was compelled to search and explore, and attempt to discover what was real and what was false.

So, he would leave Olivia to the tender flirtations of George Manning simply in order to try to establish the truth about his rival. In his absence, Manning would no doubt haunt Chadcombe, doing his best to fix Olivia's interest.

His mind was filled with memories of the kisses they had shared outside Gunn's cottage. Had Olivia enjoyed them? Would she miss him, he wondered, when he left for London?

No sooner had the thought entered his mind than, shockingly, he spoke it aloud! He had been encouraged, he realised, by the fact that she had reacted with a frown to his hint that he might not be able to return in time for the ball. 'Why, Olivia, will you miss me?'

'Of course I shall!' she retorted immediately. 'I mean…' She faltered. 'I expect to see you there and that finally we might dance together.' She was blushing slightly, as if unsure of herself. Strangely, that was what encouraged him to hope there was more to her words than a friendly offer of a dance.

Quite before he knew what he was doing and certainly without conscious thought, he stopped right there in the middle of the rose garden, drew her into his arms and kissed her thoroughly and passionately.

She froze for an instant, then responded with an ardour similar to her feverish response to his previous kisses. Jem was overwhelmed with the strength of his desire for her. Lost to all reason, he kissed and kissed, and kissed her again. When he came round, as if from a dream, he found that they had moved to sit on a curved stone bench and that Olivia was cradled on his lap. Not that there was anything dreamlike about the raw fever between them. Her hands were on his back, pressing him closer, and her mouth sought his as if she were dying from the same hunger that afflicted him. It was quite the most wonderful thing that had ever happened to him. Heart pounding, he groaned and returned her latest kiss, losing all reason again as he succumbed to the miracle that was unfolding between them.

It was unclear to him how long they kissed. All he knew was that, eventually, they paused to look at each other and smile, then kiss again, this time softly, gently, tentatively.

'Olivia,' he murmured against her mouth, feeling her smile in response.

'Jem,' she returned softly. 'You are kissing me.'

'Yes, I am. Is that a difficulty for you?'

'Not at all. In fact, it is an exceedingly pleasant experience.'

'For me, too. Shall we, then, do it again?'

For answer, she took his face in both hands, swooping on his mouth with a confidence and enthusiasm that both exhilarated and thrilled him. His hands stroked her back, while his heart soared with the realisation that this was *Olivia*, in his arms as if she belonged there!

Swift footsteps sounded on the gravel path, running, and getting closer. Just in time, he and Olivia separated— she jumped up and feigned interest in a nearby statue of Poseidon, while he extracted his watch swiftly from his pocket and pretended to study it. An instant later, the runner was upon them.

It was Will, his young face creased with anxiety.

'What is amiss, Will?'

'It is the lady!' the boy gasped. He bowed to Olivia, who had turned to face him. 'The *other* lady, I mean. Her baby is coming!'

Chapter Eighteen

Mrs Logan, the midwife, was plump, short and kindly, with a lined, weathered face and deep blue eyes that twinkled with warm intelligence. By the time she arrived—Joseph, the head groom, having fetched her in the curricle—Charlotte had been escorted to the rooms she had selected and prepared for her confinement. Olivia had taken Charlotte's arm and tried to help her up the stairs, until Charlotte protested testily that she was not an invalid and was perfectly capable of walking un-aided. Olivia had bit her lip and said nothing, but when they reached the inner chamber had asked Charlotte if she should leave or stay.

'Oh, please stay, Olivia!' Charlotte laid a hand on Olivia's arm, her expression pleading. 'You are truly a sis-ter to me, so I would love for you to keep me company—if you are willing? And you know that Juliana is gone home to nurse little Jack through the chickenpox, so I need you, sincerely.'

How on earth was she to support Charlotte in Juliana's absence? Juliana was herself a mother—the mysteries of birth were known to her. And what if Olivia's fear should paralyse her at the wrong moment? Or if some-thing went terribly wrong and she was there?

Her shoulders drooped as the enormity of her task sank in. For all her resilience during the kidnap, all her assertions of maturity, all her wishes that others should treat her differently, perhaps she truly was not as ready for life as she had thought.

She had wished to be Charlotte's companion during her confinement. Now that the opportunity had been given to her, the responsibility of it was terrifying.

Mrs Logan entered the chamber without fuss and, ignoring Olivia and Charlotte's personal maid, Priddy, who was to be Charlotte's other birthing companion, went straight to Charlotte, who was at that moment leaning over the back of a chair, rocking gently from side to side.

'Now, then, Lady Shalford, it's Mrs Logan, the midwife, here to tend you.' She placed her hand comfortingly on Charlotte's back. 'That's it, my love, just you keep moving like that.' She left her hand there, making soothing noises, and Olivia almost felt the slight air of tension leave the room.

She and Priddy locked glances, both smiling tensely. Priddy was, like her, unmarried and had also never seen a babe born before. She had been Charlotte's maid since childhood and cared deeply for her mistress. While they both loved Charlotte dearly, they had been at a loss as to what to do for her. Mrs Logan's arrival had changed everything. Olivia's feelings of inadequacy remained, but the fear was a little diminished.

Charlotte sighed, straightened up and opened her eyes. 'The pains are getting stronger and lasting longer, I think. Oh, I am glad that you are here, Mrs Logan!'

'You are doing beautifully, my lady,' said the midwife reassuringly. 'Just you do whatever feels right—walk or sit, lean or kneel on the floor. But, would you be more comfortable in just your shift?'

'Oh, yes, please,' said Charlotte.

Relieved to have something to do, Olivia and Priddy helped Charlotte undress, while Mrs Logan went around the chamber, subtly changing it to create what she called a proper birthing room. She closed the heavy curtains, leaving the windows ajar, and set out bunches of lavender around the room. On one of her previous visits, she had arranged with the housekeeper for clean linen, soap and plenty of old sheets. The sheets she laid on the floor, creating a completely new atmosphere in the room. It felt a little like a cave now, with the dim light, a low fire in the hearth and soft sheets on the floor. If it was a cave, Olivia thought, it was the nicest, cosiest cave imaginable. The midwife removed her own shoes and signalled to Olivia and Priddy to do the same. Barefoot, they all walked quietly on the soft flooring. Mrs Logan kept her tone low and reassuring and Olivia and Priddy took their lead from her.

And so began the longest day and night that Olivia had ever known. Charlotte was amazing, remaining calm and composed through the hard work of wave after wave of pain. Mrs Logan created an atmosphere of quiet and calm, punctuated only by Charlotte's moans and their words of encouragement to her.

After the first few hours, Olivia realised that she was less frightened—not because anything had changed, but because everything was *unchanged*. Unending pains for Charlotte. Olivia and the other two women being with her, comforting and soothing her. Mrs Logan had brought her knitting.

If she is calm, thought Olivia, *then there is no need for me to be afraid.*

Night came and the temptation of sleep. Olivia felt guilty about her struggles to stay awake. How could she sleep, when Charlotte was suffering so? She fought it, determined to stay by Charlotte's side.

As time ticked by during that long, long night, Olivia slowly became conscious of a strange feeling—something she had never felt before. She frowned as she tried to work out what it was.

Looking at each of the others in turn, and recognising how focused everyone was on Charlotte, she suddenly saw it. She felt *proud*. Truly, she felt privileged to be part of this—as if she, in supporting her sister-in-law, was herself finally stepping across a doorway into true womanhood. Not because she wished to do so. Because she had already done it.

Late into the night, Mrs Logan insisted that Olivia and Priddy take breaks. 'We will need you later,' she said. 'Best to save your strength.' When Charlotte nodded furiously, Olivia and Priddy reluctantly agreed. They took turns to nap a little on Charlotte's armchair. Mrs Logan, though, was tireless, explaining in a low voice that she'd developed the knack of staying awake all night through many years of being with women.

At some point deep into the night, the room was quiet and Olivia felt able, for the first time in many hours, to think about Jem.

Her heart skipped as she recalled the passionate kisses they had shared that morning. Her nerve endings tingled and she sensed her breathing become quite shallow as she closed her eyes, immersing herself in the memory of those amazing kisses.

Surely, she thought, *the kisses meant something to him, too?*

She tried to consider this rationally. Jem was not the

sort of man to trifle with a lady. He was a true gentleman and surely would not…

Rationality departed almost immediately, overwhelmed by a wave of emotion.

Maybe, she thought, *is it possible, that he is seriously interested in me, too? Oh, if only it could be so.*

Remembering her worries about Jem and Amy, she now felt much more confident that his relationship with Amy was innocent after all. He simply had too much integrity to kiss her so passionately if he was also flirting with another lady.

Or was she assuming too much? Men saw these things differently, she knew. They were encouraged to flirt and to kiss, and to take opportunities whenever they arose— though mostly with women who were not of the *ton*.

Men were not judged if they were known as flirts, or even rakes. Ladies, on the other hand, could be judged as being 'fast' simply for flirting too noticeably with different men, or for wearing the wrong dress, or associating with the wrong people. If society's leaders had seen her behaviour with Jem in the rose garden, she would probably be ostracised.

It would be worth it! she thought fiercely. *Even if I never saw him again. Just to have had those moments, those shared kisses… It is worth any sacrifice.*

He was gone now, she knew. Confined to Charlotte's chamber, she had not been able to go down to say goodbye to him. But she had heard the carriage being brought round and voices from below had reached her ears through the open window. Lizzie. Adam. Jem. Then the carriage departing.

The yearning for him had been intense in that moment, as she had pictured him hugging his sister, gripping Adam's hand in farewell and, perhaps, wishing she could have been there to say goodbye to him, wish him well on his journey. He would have plenty of time to reflect during the long trip to London. Would he think of her? Truly, she knew not. All she could do was hope and think of him. At least she had these new, wonderful memories to cling to. She hugged them to herself, revelling in the way she felt.

Lady Shalford's timing could have been better, thought Jem ruefully, as he settled back in the carriage, having given a final wave to Lizzie and the others as they saw him off. Olivia had been responding with a thrilling enthusiasm to their kisses when they were so suddenly interrupted. What might have passed between them, he wondered, if Olivia had not been called away at exactly that moment?

Not for one second did he regret kissing her. Yes, it would have been helpful to talk to her about their kisses and find out once and for all what she felt for him. But he would not trade those precious moments for anything.

Knowing how frightened she was of Charlotte's upcoming confinement, he had felt proud of her composure as she had rushed to the house to support her sister-in-law. He had been honoured that she had confided in him—surely that meant something?

Before leaving, he had asked Lizzie for her sketchbook. Without asking permission, he had carefully removed her best sketch of George Manning. Beneath it was a stunning drawing of Olivia. Wordlessly, he had taken that one as well.

'Why on earth are you taking my drawings to London?' Lizzie had enquired.

'I want to show my friends how good an artist you

are, of course,' he had replied with a wink, then breezed out before she could question him further.

In truth, he had not needed the sketch of Olivia. Well, not for his business in London, which would be focused entirely on investigating George Manning. However, having the drawing of Olivia would make his separation from her a little more bearable.

She was, after all, the woman he loved.

Adam would be worrying about Charlotte. He would be unable to settle, Olivia knew, until the baby was safely born and he had confirmation that all was well. He was probably frantic with concern—especially given Mama's death and the troubles Charlotte had had with previous pregnancies. Olivia prayed again that both she and her child would survive the birth.

Olivia reflected anew on her brothers' marriages. Both had married for love—a fact that was evident to her every day. Charlotte knew without questioning how much Adam loved her. Olivia was confident that it was helping to sustain her through this long labour.

Her mind leaped forward to a time, perhaps only a few years hence, when it could be she herself having the baby and Jem waiting anxiously for news of her. *Oh, to have his child!* A little boy with the same crooked smile, or a daughter with Jem's deep blue eyes and serious nature. She hugged the images to herself, ignoring the small voice warning her that her imaginings could yet lead to heartbreak.

Some time very late in the night, things changed with Charlotte. Her pains were constant now, with only very brief breaks in between, and she seemed to be struggling to manage them.

'I cannot do this,' she muttered. 'It is too much and I have no strength left.'

Mrs Logan was unperturbed. 'You *can* do it,' she insisted, 'and what is more, you are already doing it. You'll see, it won't be long now. You are so strong, so brave.'

Olivia moved to sit beside Charlotte and took her hand. Suddenly, Charlotte stopped rocking and uttered a loud, strangled growl. It quite startled Olivia who looked to the midwife for reassurance. Mrs Logan nodded in a satisfied way. 'That's it, my lovely. Your baby is moving down and your womb is pushing now. Keep making that beautiful sound—it means all is well.'

This went on for some time, while outside birds began to stir and chirp, heralding the dawn of a new day. Suddenly Mrs Logan spoke to Charlotte in a loud, compelling voice, quite at odds with the soothing tone she had used up to now.

'Now, my lady, it is time. Will you kneel, or do you wish to stay where you are?'

Charlotte opened her eyes. 'Advise me, Mrs Logan. What is best?'

'There is no best, my lady. It is entirely up to you. So long as you don't lie down, like some of these newfangled doctors insist on, all will be well.'

Charlotte did not respond. Olivia felt her grip tighten and the extraordinary noise began again. 'Good, good... Wonderful!' soothed Mrs Logan. 'That's it, my lovely.'

Once it passed, Charlotte opened her eyes again. 'I have to kneel!' she said urgently. Rising as she spoke, she whirled round, catching her shift and holding it above her knees. She then knelt on the pile of linens, resting her elbows on the sofa. Just in time, for another wave came over her, and the strangulated groaning sound came again.

Responding quickly, Olivia and Priddy dropped to their knees on either side of Charlotte. Olivia wiped Charlotte's face with a cool damp cloth and Priddy murmured words of encouragement. Mrs Logan then tapped Olivia on the arm.

'Now, miss,' she said calmly, 'I would like you to receive the baby.'

'Me?' Olivia's jaw dropped.

'Yes. I will guide your hands.'

Olivia gulped, nodded and knelt behind Charlotte. Her heart was pounding in her chest. Lord, what if she dropped the child? *I can't do this!* she thought, panic taking hold of her. Yet something about Mrs Logan's calmness, and the bond that had grown between them all during this long, long night, steadied her. Stilling her fevered brain, she focused again on Charlotte. Within only a few more pushes—Mrs Logan urging Charlotte to go slowly, slowly—it was done. With a wet slither, the baby emerged and Olivia passed the baby to Charlotte.

'A boy!' said Charlotte, delight on her face. Olivia's throat closed with emotion.

'And a strong, healthy boy, too!' affirmed Mrs Logan. 'He is a good size and has come out pink and moving nicely. Well done, my lady!'

Charlotte beamed at her child, the pain of just a moment ago now seemingly gone. 'Hello, beautiful boy,' she crooned. 'I am your mama!' She reached for the baby's little hand and he immediately gripped her finger tightly. 'Look!' she said to the women, 'See how strong he is!'

Tears were running down Olivia's face. 'Oh, Charlotte, you were amazing!' She hugged her gently, careful not to squash the baby.

They sat like that for a few moments, Charlotte exploring her son's tiny fingers and toes, kissing his head and generally feeling quite delighted with herself—as well she might. Olivia could barely take her eyes off them. She felt so proud that she had been part of this.

Mrs Logan was busy, gently drying the baby and covering him with a clean soft cloth, without disturbing his first embrace with his mother. She asked Charlotte if she felt like pushing again.

'No,' said Charlotte, 'why, must I push again?'

'The navel string—the baby's life cord has stopped beating and has almost finished its work. See?' She indicated the cord, which now looked quite thin, white and empty—a dramatic change from the fat and throbbing blue-grey rope of just a few minutes ago. 'That means the afterbirth will come soon, but there is more blood than I would like.' She rested her hand gently on Charlotte's stomach. 'Hmmm…' She rose decidedly. She rose decidedly. 'My lady, listen to me carefully. You are bleeding, and your womb is dormant. We need to encourage the afterbirth to come out. Put the baby to the breast and let him suckle, and I shall give you an infusion.'

Bleeding. Charlotte is bleeding! Olivia froze, paralysed with fear. *This is how Mama died.*

She had not remembered until this very moment, but now snippets of overheard whispers came back to her.

Bled out.

She had never understood those words. Now she did. Mama had bled to death after the baby had been born. And now it was happening to Charlotte!

Mrs Logan glanced at her keenly. 'Lady Olivia, I need your assistance.' Leaving Priddy to speak to Charlotte, who was obediently drinking the infusion, the midwife drew Olivia over to the fireplace. 'All will be well, miss.' Olivia looked at the midwife, realising that her own terror was apparent. Mrs Logan remained calm—and it was clear did not want Charlotte to be distressed.

The midwife looked steadily and calmly into Olivia's eyes until the horror inside began to ease. She nodded to Mrs Logan to indicate she had herself under control.

'Now, please fold these towels for me,' said the midwife. Olivia could not speak, but took the pile of towels and mechanically began folding them. Mrs Logan touched her hand briefly, then went back to Charlotte's side.

The infusion took effect after another few minutes. Charlotte groaned as a new wave of pain came over her.

'Take the baby,' the midwife instructed Olivia. Charlotte held the child out and Olivia came forward and gently cradled her nephew.

Was he doomed to grow up without a mother, as she had been?

Panic threatened to overcome her again, but suddenly, she felt the babe curling one tiny hand around her finger. He gripped it tightly. She looked into the child's dark blue eyes, and was reminded of Jem's words of encouragement.

Jem believed in her, so she could believe in herself.

Her own fear was irrelevant here—her responsibility was to Charlotte. Pressing a soft kiss to her nephew's head, she crouched down beside Charlotte. 'Your son is eager to return to his mama,' she said. 'You are already a wonderful mother, Charlotte.'

Charlotte opened her eyes and reached out for Olivia's hand. Olivia took it, and for a moment they looked at each other. Olivia could now see fear in Charlotte's eyes, but she ensured that her own mind and heart were filled only with calm confidence. Charlotte seemed to sense it. Her breathing slowed a little, she nodded, then she pressed her chin down to her chest and pushed with the tightening.

Within a short time she had expelled the afterbirth, and soon afterwards, Mrs Logan announced that the bleeding had subsided to her satisfaction. Olivia released her breath. Charlotte was truly safe!

Olivia's mind was racing. She had experienced so much today. The ordeal at the tavern had started it and now this. She felt changed, made new. She could almost sense the anxieties of girlhood flutter away and wither. Supporting her sister-in-law, seeing her strength, and working together with the other women to help Charlotte safely birth her child, had given Olivia an unexpected yet potent appreciation of the power of women.

It was the same power, she realised, that had helped her through her own ordeal and afterwards. Gunn was huge, muscular and powerful, yet she had bested him. Her thoughts were whirling around without anchor or logic, but beneath them there was a newfound wisdom, a certainty that she had lacked before.

She had huge admiration for her sister-in-law and a sneaking suspicion that the midwife had just saved her life. Mrs Logan had begun to tidy her belongings into her bag, so Olivia went across to speak to her.

'What was the medicine you used?' she asked tentatively. 'In the infusion, I mean.'

Mrs Logan looked at her keenly. 'That was ergot of rye,' she said. 'It can awaken a dormant womb and cause it to tighten. It can stop women from bleeding out after the birth.' She looked at Olivia directly, then spoke quietly. 'I was here, the night your mother died.'

Olivia gasped.

Mrs Logan kept her voice low. 'The doctor and I did all we could, but we could not save her.' She stared re-

flectively into the fire. 'I will never forget it.' She shook
her head decisively and turned back to Olivia. 'I swore
it would never happen to me again. So I wrote to every
midwife and doctor I knew of, to find out what they do
in such cases. Some of them had no answer, save to call
the priest, but two granny midwives suggested ergot.
I've used it ever since, though in very small amounts.
Thankfully, it has always worked.'

'Yes, but what is it? What is it made of?' asked Olivia.
This medicine could have saved Mama. She could barely
take in what Mrs Logan was telling her.

'It is a spur that grows on rye. It is dangerous when
too much is taken, but in tiny amounts, it can be helpful.' She took Olivia's hand. 'I am so sorry that we could
not save your mama, but what I learned from losing her
has saved many women since.' Olivia nodded. Strangely,
it made sense. Mama's death had saved other lives—
including Charlotte's.

Mrs Logan squeezed Olivia's hand, then returned to
the new mother. 'Now then, my lady, would you like
some tea before we allow that husband of yours to see
his son?'

Adam! He would still be worried. 'Charlotte, can I go
to him, to tell him all is well?'

'Oh, yes, Olivia, please do. Tell him to come directly.'

Olivia bent to kiss her cheek and to gently stroke her
new nephew's soft face. 'I shall.'

Olivia stepped outside the chamber. The house was
still quiet, it being too early for the servants to be up and
about, but at least one servant was awake. Olivia had forgotten about the housemaid stationed outside Charlotte's
chamber. As soon as the door opened, the girl jumped
to her feet, ready for orders, an apprehensive look on
her face. 'Some food for the new mother, please,' said

Olivia with a smile, 'and for us as well—it has been a long night!'

'Yes, my lady, right away!' said the girl, with a relieved smile.

'Where is my brother?' Olivia asked.

'In his study, my lady. He has been there all night, I understand.' The maid curtsied and disappeared towards the servants' stairs.

Olivia went directly down the main staircase to Adam's study. She entered without knocking, keen to give him the good news immediately. He was slumped in a high-backed armchair by the fireplace, his cravat lying in a crumpled heap on the floor and an empty bottle of brandy at his elbow. His head was leaning against the back of the leather armchair and he had clearly fallen into a doze. Opposite him, in a parallel pose, was Charlotte's father, Sir Edward.

Stirring already, Adam rose from his chair as soon as he opened his eyes. Seeing his anguished expression, Olivia made haste to reassure him. 'All is well,' she said. 'Charlotte was amazing and you are a father.' She beamed at him, loving the way the fear left his face, to be replaced by incredulous joy.

'Truly?' His voice was gruff from emotion, alcohol and lack of sleep.

Olivia nodded happily.

'Congratulations, my boy!' Sir Edward, wearing a similarly relieved expression, rose to shake the hand of his son-in-law.

'And to you, Grandfather!' Their grip lasted longer than normal, both men seemingly struggling to contain their emotions.

'You can go up and see her and the baby.' Olivia spoke softly to her brother, her voice shaking a little.

Taking two quick strides towards her, he enveloped

her in a fierce hug. 'Thank God!' His voice cracked with emotion. 'I have been imagining the worst!' She hugged him back, feeling gratitude for the hundredth time for being part of such a family. Was it even possible that she had been feeling so restless, so ill at ease with her life, just a few short weeks ago?

After he had gone, Sir Edward accompanying him, Olivia slumped into Adam's armchair, tiredness finally washing over her.

What a day! It had been almost a full twenty-four hours since she had braved family breakfast and been rewarded with not only a walk with Jem, but passionate kisses! Then to have accompanied Charlotte through the birth of her child. She had much to think about, but, it seemed, no brain with which to do so. Food, then sleep, she decided, wrenching herself out of Adam's chair.

Chapter Nineteen

Jem strode up Horse Guards Parade, keen to press ahead
with the business of the day. During his three days in
London, he had been frustrated with the lack of information on George Manning—*though that in itself tells
a tale*, he thought grimly. Town was still busy—most
families having not yet retired to the country or one of
the spa towns for the summer—and there were quite a
number of Jem's set in London. Yet none—not one—
seemed to know George Manning or his sister. It was as
if the Mannings had appeared, like ghosts, in the park
on the day that Mrs Buxted befriended them.

Having also failed to find any trace of them in Mr De-
brett's book, Jem was now working on the assumption
that they had never lived in England at all. He recalled
Lizzie and Olivia being impressed that the Mannings had
lived and travelled in various parts of Europe—he was
frustrated with himself for not listening more carefully.
Even then, if they had moved in the first circles as they
claimed, someone would know them, surely?

He himself had spent time in Brussels before and after
Waterloo—though, afterwards, he had been confined to
his bed with his injury. He could not recall having met

Manning at any of the social events attended by the officers, yet Manning had specifically told him that he had fought in the great battle.

The Major will know, Jem told himself, as he followed a young clerk to his old commander's study. Major Cooke was a fount of knowledge and was renowned for his ability to ferret out information. Jem had written to him in coded terms about his concerns—he and Major Cooke had an understanding forged in the corridors of the War Ministry and the battlefields of France. Jem trusted him.

'Captain Ford—that is to say, *former* Captain!' Major Cooke rose to greet him, pumping his hand vigorously, a great smile creasing his lined face. 'Well, and how do you?'

Jem exchanged the usual pleasantries, enjoying being back in the building where he had first served in the Army and with the man he had first served. *In fact*, thought Jem, somewhat ruefully, *were it not for the Major putting me with Harry—then a captain in need of an ensign—I might never have met Olivia and might not now be investigating George Manning!*

As soon as Jem was seated, the Major, never one for prevarication, came straight to the point. 'This chap you wrote to me about, this George Manning—where did you encounter him?'

Jem hesitated.

'A delicate matter, perhaps?' asked the Major, one eyebrow raised.

Carefully, Jem explained about Monkton Park and the Buxteds, but did not openly refer to Olivia. He did, however, mention that he himself was spending the summer at Chadcombe with his sister.

'So that's it!' said the Major. 'Dangling after her, is

he?' Jem returned a non-committal response. 'Well, any-way. I looked him up.'

Jem leaned forward in his chair. 'And?'

The Major grimaced. 'I could not find him.'

Shock washed over Jem. It was true, then. 'So Man-ning is a fraud?'

Major Cooke shook his grizzled head. 'Perhaps, per-haps not. Believe it or not, some of the records from 1815 are incomplete. If he was one of the volunteers who signed up after Napoleon escaped from Elba, we may not have his details recorded fully. There are quite a few—and as you know, Jem, it frustrates me to no end—where there is only an incomplete record—registration but no payment for soldiers who died or successfully deserted, payment but no registration for those who made their own way to the battlefield out of patriotism or a hunger for glory. He may have been one of those.'

Jem's heart sank. For a moment, he had thought him-self the victor in this subtle battle of wits with Manning. 'I see.' It was time, he thought, to play his final card. 'I did wonder,' he said slowly, 'if you might have encoun-tered him—I know it was four years ago, but you have a great memory for faces and he is quite distinctive.'

He took from his pocket Lizzie's sketch of Manning, carefully unfolded it and passed it across. Major Cooke scrutinised it closely, then started. 'By God, it's that chap!'

'You do know him!'

'Tall chap?' asked the Major. 'Handsome, all tan and teeth?'

'That's the one,' Jem replied. *All tan and teeth…* That was a perfect description.

'I do remember him,' said the Major. 'Signed up as a volunteer in Brussels the day after we got there. I thought he was after the glory myself—a bit soft. Never been in battle. Much like you at the time, young Jem.'

'Yes, yes. I know. Green as grass, I was. But what of Manning? I don't remember him at all.'

'No reason why you should. As I recall, from the minute we arrived in Brussels, Captain Fanton had you both volunteering for every duty he could find! I barely saw either of you, except to give you new orders. No, it's the name that threw me. I don't think that was his name—or perhaps I never heard his name.' He eyed the sketch again. 'So he survived, eh? I wonder how he got on in battle?'

'I have no idea,' said Jem. He was still coming to terms with the fact that Manning, it seemed, had fought at Waterloo after all.

'Well, if you have a few hours to spare, we can trawl through the records again—now that I know the date he signed up!'

'Yes, sir!' said Jem smartly and they both grinned.

Five days. Olivia sighed and came away from the window. Five days since she had seen him, since they had walked in the rose garden. Since he had kissed her so unexpectedly, so vigorously.

She sat at the little table in her room and gazed at her reflection. He filled her thoughts at every moment—and not always in a pleasant manner. Oh, yes, there were the times when her heart raced and her nerve endings tingled as she relived those precious moments in the garden and the other kisses, in Gunn's cottage. Those were breathtaking, wonderful memories, and she revelled in them. But, rather like a poem one had heard too many times, or the many beautiful paintings that she walked past on her way to dinner and took for granted, the memories were beginning to lose their potency and sharpness. Like delicate fabric, they had begun to fray and fade with time and over-use.

I am being silly!

Yet, after only five days, she felt creeping doubts slide into her heart. They were whispers only, but she heard them. They said things like, *You are making too much of these kisses*, and, *His intentions are not serious.* And the longer he was gone from her, the more she doubted.

What right had she to assume Jem's intention was anything other than pleasant kisses? Why, George Manning had kissed her just a month ago and she had no notion of serious intent on his part!

That kiss on the stepping stones had been so long ago, it seemed now. She tried to recall the details— George's mischievous expression, the smell of maleness and smoke emanating from him, then the kiss itself. Knowing it was wrong to do so, yet she could not help but contrast the feeling she had had when kissed by each man. Mr Manning had caused a reaction, yes, but she rather thought now that it had been partly fear, mixed with elements of feeling flattered and a very large dose of irritation. There was no comparison with what she felt when Jem kissed her.

Once, when she was fourteen, she had tried to land a fish that Harry had caught in the home lake. He had warned her not to lean over too far but she, stubbornly, had insisted and had toppled over the side of the small boat. As the water had closed over her head, green and cold and everywhere, she had lost track of her body and her limbs, flailing around in panic with no sense of up or down, sight or sound.

Harry had been smart enough to reach down and grab her by the left leg, hauling her back out without the need to dive in after her straight away. 'Well, it was obvious where you were, you know,' he had said when she had railed at him for not rescuing her *properly*. 'You were thrashing around like a leviathan and the lake is only a couple of feet deep in that part.'

She smiled now, remembering the outrage with which she had reacted to this sally, as she had sat shivering in the boat, coughing and spluttering. 'I knew when you were denouncing me so bitterly,' Harry had confessed afterwards, 'that you were perfectly well and that the damage was limited to a ruined dress and some very fetching weeds in your hair.'

Her smile faded as she realised why the memory had come to her now. When Jem kissed her, she had that same sense of losing all awareness, of being tumbled in a maelstrom of feeling. Only this time, it was *passion* that took her so entirely away from the everyday, prosaic world. *Now* she knew what the great writers spoke of, what the poets sang. This was what love and passion truly felt like. It was, in fact, a little like drowning. And it was *real*.

She had often wondered if it happened in real life. From the outside, she could see devotion in some of the couples around her—Adam and Charlotte, the Foxleys, Harry and Juliana. Did they, too, feel this passion? Did they lose themselves in each other?

No. She frowned. That was not quite right. She did not lose herself when Jem kissed her. In fact, she could not remember another time when she was more alive, more gloriously *herself*. She was lost in him, with him. Nothing else existed—not even time. She still had no real sense of how much time had passed while they had been kissing.

She sighed again. Yes, being kissed by George Man-

ning so recently only served to underline the contrast
with the whirlpool that Jem's embrace created. Thinking
further back, she remembered the chaste kisses she had
permitted Mr Nightingale—the poet—to plant on her
lips. Yes, her heart had sped and she had been flattered—
briefly—by his poetry and his devotion, but when he
began to turn a little possessive she had gently, following Harry's advice, withdrawn her favour.

But what does it mean? she wondered now. *My response to Jem is very different to George Manning or
Mr Nightingale. Why?*

Her heart immediately gave her the answer.

I love him.

Well, of course she did! It was obvious. Although
wary of him because he had hurt her before, it had not
prevented her own foolish heart from doing what it
wanted—which was to fall in love with Jem all over
again.

But could she trust him with her heart? She had never
truly trusted another man, apart from her own brothers,
and Jem was, she believed, cut from the same cloth as
them. The fact that he was also handsome and strong,
and had the most interesting taut and lean body, might
also have influenced her. Yet none of it gave her any clue
as to his intentions or his feelings for her. She trusted
him as a friend—but their shared kisses had changed
everything and she knew not what to think.

Picking up her embroidery bag, she went downstairs.
The drawing room was surprisingly quiet. Juliana and
Harry—who had returned to visit their new nephew now
that the worst of little Jack's affliction had passed—were
out walking, Great-Aunt Clara was having her usual
afternoon nap and Adam was closeted with his steward. Which left only Lizzie keeping Charlotte company,

as she sat nursing her infant. Charlotte did not even lift her head as Olivia entered, so intent was she on studying her child as he fed. Olivia smiled at Lizzie and went to her sister-in-law.

'He is so beautiful, Charlotte,' she said softly.

Charlotte looked up at her mistily. 'I was just thinking the same thing!'

'Do you need anything?'

'Only for everyone to stop fussing over me!' Charlotte smiled to take the sting out of her words. 'Between Adam and Papa, and Great-Aunt Clara and Priddy… I have had a baby, but we are doing just fine.'

Lizzie stood. 'There! I have completed it.' She showed Charlotte and Olivia her latest sketch. 'Charlotte and her baby as Madonna and Child—though nothing like the Old Masters, of course.'

'Oh, how beautiful!' Charlotte's face lit up. 'Thank you, Lizzie. May I keep it?'

'Really? Of course you may have it—though I do not claim any particular merit.'

'Nonsense, Lizzie,' said Olivia, 'Why, we all know your great talent for drawing. May I?' Lizzie handed her the book and Olivia flicked through the recent sketches. 'See? This is a sweet study of little Frederick Foxley. And there is one here somewhere of Mr Manning—I remember you showed it to me at the time and I declared it an excellent likeness. Now, where is it?' She flicked through a couple more pages and was a little surprised when Lizzie took her book back.

'Oh, it was not so great as you say, Olivia. But I am glad,' she rushed on, blushing slightly, 'that you like my sketch of you and the baby, Charlotte.'

'Indeed I do,' confirmed Charlotte.

There was a discreet knocking on the door and, on hearing Charlotte's invitation, Priddy entered.

'Oh, Miss Charlotte—my lady—there are visitors arriving and you should not be downstairs!'

'What visitors?' enquired Charlotte, slipping her little finger into her baby's mouth to break his feed. He sighed and settled back to sleep.

'It is the Monkton Park carriage, my lady,' confirmed Priddy, receiving the baby as Charlotte adjusted her clothing.

Charlotte grimaced. 'I confess I do not feel ready to face visitors just yet.' Unspoken, yet understood by everyone, the spectre of Mrs Buxted and her 'kindly advice' loomed over them all. 'I shall retire to the sanctuary of my chamber.'

Too late! Charlotte had not yet reached the door when it opened, admitting Mrs Buxted. Behind her, looking decidedly uneasy, was her daughter, Mrs Foxley.

Mrs Buxted erupted forward in a wave of effusiveness. 'Oh, my dear Lady Shalford! I said—did I not say, Faith?—that Charlotte would not be one to keep to her room for weeks on end! Depend upon it, I said, if we visit today we shall likely see Lady Shalford in her drawing room—this *very room*! But I am always right! Did I not say so, Faith?'

Faith opened her mouth to speak, but Mrs Buxted's attention had already moved on. 'And here is the dear little creature! What a sturdy-looking child!' She approached the baby with a great deal of energy and Priddy visibly stiffened. 'No, I shan't take him! Strangely, although I am the most doting of mamas, I never really took to them when they were very small like that. Henrietta is just the same—she has a veritable army of nurses looking after hers! Once they can converse and one's friends can ad-

mire their looks and their intelligence, then children become *much* more interesting. At this stage all they ever
do is cry and sleep—all rather tedious really!'

Olivia realised she was holding her breath. Thankfully, the baby showed no signs of waking, but Charlotte's brow was creased. Realising that something ought
to be done, she summoned her courage and spoke. 'Good
afternoon, Mrs Buxted, Faith.'

Lizzie curtsied and Faith, after murmuring her own
greetings, moved forward to share a gentle hug with
Charlotte.

There was no escape. Charlotte resumed her seat and
reached out for her baby. Priddy gently passed him to his
mother and retired to a hard chair in the corner, where she
sat knitting and looking fierce. Faith and Mrs Buxted sat
either side of Charlotte, to exclaim over the baby's size and
what they said was a clear resemblance to his grandfather.

Mrs Buxted then turned her attention to Olivia and
Lizzie. 'Well, and are you looking forward to the ball?'

'Indeed we are,' said Lizzie, 'only two more days to
wait! And Mrs Foxley has kindly invited us to stay the
night and to come early for dinner.'

Faith smiled. 'Well, of course I did. I could not have
my dearest friends travelling home in the night, when
I could so easily offer you hospitality. Miss Ford, will
your brother be there, do you think?'

Olivia's heart leapt. Just the *mention* of Jem did surprising things to her!

'He hopes to return in time,' confirmed Lizzie.

'I suspect that Miss Turner will feel much better if
he is there to dance with her,' said Faith with a smile.

Mrs Buxted tittered. 'I see a match there—Mr Ford
and Miss Turner. Such handsome children they will

make! Depend upon it, I am never wrong with these things!'

Olivia's fingernails were digging into her palms.

'Oh, no, Mama,' said Faith weakly. 'Why, he was simply being kind in teaching her the dances.'

Mrs Buxted snorted. 'When you have lived on this earth as long as I have,' she pronounced, 'you will learn to see the difference between a young man who is being kind and a young man in love!'

In love! The words seared into Olivia's brain, freezing all thought for a moment. Jem, in love with Amy! *But it was me he kissed*, Olivia reminded herself. *He would not pursue two ladies at the same time.*

'Charlotte, such a pity that you will miss the ball!' chuckled Mrs Buxted. She turned to the others. 'Of course Charlotte cannot go to the ball while she is still confined, though after that she will be free to do as she pleases!'

'I intend to live quietly here at Chadcombe for the foreseeable future,' Charlotte affirmed, lifting her chin a little.

'Hmm, well, you young things will do what you fancy, I suppose.' Mrs Buxted shook her head sadly. 'In my day we could not wait to be free of the confinement and take up our social lives again.' She eyed Charlotte piercingly. 'You have a wet nurse, of course?'

Olivia stiffened. This would be trouble!

'Actually, no. I am feeding him myself.' Charlotte's voice was clear and even.

'No wet nurse? I am astounded!' Mrs Buxted's eyes, always slightly protuberant, seemed to bulge out of her head. 'But—why?'

'It is my preference, that is all,' said Charlotte, shrugging. 'Faith, how are the preparations for the ball coming along?'

Faith responded and Olivia breathed again.

Such a pity, she thought, *that Jem is not here for this! For I would be sure to catch his eye and know that we are both thinking the same thing.*

There was an affinity between them, she thought now—a potent mix of friendship and attraction. And his kisses had given her a taste of such happiness she had only dreamed of.

'…was seen lurking near the river. I am sure it is nothing, but I have asked the grooms to do a thorough search.' Olivia's ears pricked up—what was Faith talking about?

'That is worrying indeed,' said Charlotte. 'I shall ask Adam to put our grooms at your disposal, in the hope that you might catch him. Is he a vagrant, do you think?'

'That is what is so surprising,' said Faith. 'The reports we have had have described him as a large man, with serviceable clothing—not a beggar.'

'Most strange,' agreed Charlotte. 'It may be someone visiting one of the farm workers, or seeking work.'

'You are most likely right,' said Faith, though her expression still showed concern.

'Well, I for one shall not rest easy until this man is caught and removed,' asserted Mrs Buxted with a shudder. 'Else we shall all be murdered in our beds—you mark my words!'

'Do please let us speak of more pleasant things!' urged Olivia. 'Like the ball, perhaps.'

This met with approval and the next half-hour was spent in relative harmony. As she chattered and expressed her excitement, underneath Olivia's feelings were confused. Jem might be back soon. Would he again be distant with her, or was happiness finally within reach?

Chapter Twenty

The first pale hints of morning seeped through the chinks in the hotel curtains. Jem stirred, turned over, then opened his eyes. Today, finally, he would return to Chadcombe and to Olivia.

Slipping his hand under the pillow, he drew out a piece of paper. The sketch of Olivia. Carefully, he unfolded it, gazing at her image for the thousandth time this week. How well he knew the curve of her cheek, the arched brows, that mischievous look that his sister had captured so perfectly in the drawing.

She was so damned beautiful! His feeling in this moment was not carnal, but something profoundly emotional. He was honoured to know her, grateful that he was in her life. He placed the sketch on the pillow beside him, knowing he had another hour to sleep before the hotel footman would wake him. He looked into her eyes until sleep overcame him once more.

'You look stunning, Olivia!'

Olivia summoned a smile. 'Thank you. And I must tell you that you look beautiful yourself, Faith. Thank you again for inviting us for dinner—on the night of your first ball, that cannot be easy.'

'Oh, it is nothing,' said Faith, airily dismissing what must be days and weeks of preparation with a wave of her hand. Like Olivia, Faith was also in blue—a dark blue silk with a paler blue overdress that emphasised her blonde prettiness.

Dinner had just ended and the ladies had retired to the drawing room to allow the gentlemen a brief post-dinner port. Brief, because the first guests would arrive soon and Faith and her husband would stand in the hall-way to greet them.

The house looked wonderful tonight. Faith had filled it with flowers and with greenery such as normally adorned the hall and dining room at Christmastide. The scent of cut flowers wafted through the drawing room and the air of serenity among the ladies belied the fran-tic busyness that surely pervaded the kitchens and the ballroom, where the final touches, Faith indicated, were even now being added.

'I shall go there shortly,' said Faith, 'to check that all is well. Do come with me if you wish!'

Olivia was happy to comply and so a little later they ex-cused themselves from the drawing room, where the men had now rejoined the ladies. As she made to leave, Olivia was hailed, a little unexpectedly, by George Manning.

'Lady Olivia! Are you leaving us? Why, I have not yet had the chance this evening to converse with you.' Un-like the previous occasion, tonight Olivia had not been seated beside Mr Manning for dinner. Not that she had minded—she had been perfectly happy to be seated be-tween Charles and the Reverend Fenwick.

Olivia paused. 'Oh! I am just going with Mrs Fox-ley to the ballroom. We shall return directly.' For some reason, the look in George's eye made Olivia a little un-comfortable—she had no idea why.

He bowed with a flourish. 'I pray you will return without delay. My heart cannot stand to be apart from you!' Catching her hand, he held it and kissed it, looking up at her as he bent over her hand as if to check her reaction.

Resisting the urge to pull her hand away, Olivia murmured something polite and joined Faith. How she wished that Mr Manning was less flowery in his flirtation with her! She did not for one moment believe that his heart was actually engaged—his eyes when he looked at her held nothing of truth. Only the game of praise and flirting, and empty compliments.

Not for the first time, she wished he were not so particular in his attentions. She knew that she had stopped flirting with him an age ago—indeed, it was hard to recall now how she had possibly ever been attracted to him. In comparison to Jem, he now seemed florid and insincere.

Once in the hallway, Faith opened her mouth as if to say something, then closed it again.

They made their way down the wide hallway to the ballroom. Around half the size of the Chadcombe ballroom, it was nevertheless a striking room, with space for the musicians at one end and a floor big enough to accommodate twenty couples. The musicians were already there, preparing their instruments and talking quietly together. To one side, a tray of glasses stood ready for the ratafia and punch that would be on offer when the guests arrived. The two doors leading on to the terrace were open to the evening sky. Olivia knew that, once the room filled up, the room would likely become unbearably hot, so easy access to the terrace and garden was vital. The near side of the ballroom was lined with large mirrors and, as she and Faith wan-

dered around, arms linked, they caught sight of their
own reflection.

I look sad! was Olivia's immediate thought. Schooling her features into a more appropriate expression, she
noticed Faith looking at her keenly.

'I remember,' said Faith, 'there was a ball at Chadcombe when we visited you five years ago. Much grander
than mine will be tonight. I still count it as one of the
happiest times of my life.' Olivia looked at her quizzically. 'That was the summer when I fell in love, and discovered that he loved me, too.'

'How wonderful!' breathed Olivia. 'Yes, of course it
was! Did you dance together that night?'

'Yes—the waltz. It was the first time I had danced it
at an actual ball and I was surprised when Mama failed
to comment at the time.' She reflected for a moment.
'Though I recall that her attention was fully taken up
by Charlotte dancing with Adam!'

'Did your mama not approve of Mr Foxley, Faith?'

Faith made a wry face. 'Not at all. I think she wanted
me to marry Harry!'

They both laughed at the absurdity. Faith was perfectly happy in her marriage and Harry and his Juliana
were blissfully content.

'I knew my own heart, you see,' said Faith softly.
'One cannot tell the heart what to feel. It loves where it
chooses and cannot be forced to love elsewhere.'

Tears started in Olivia's eyes. 'Oh, Faith, you are so
right. The heart knows its work and we can only be led
by its instinct.'

Faith squeezed her hand. 'Forgive me—I do not wish
to pry—but it seems to me that you are unhappy.'

Olivia nodded mistily.

'Oh, my dear!' Faith took her hand. Turning away

from the musicians, Faith led her on to the terrace. The red glow of sunset was fading, the sky paling to a blue-white vastness.

Faith addressed her directly. 'May I ask you one question?' Olivia nodded. 'Are you in love?'

For answer, Olivia burst into tears. The burden of hiding her feelings for so long could not withstand Faith's kindness. Wordlessly, Faith enveloped her in a soothing hug and allowed her to cry.

When she was able to speak again, it all came out. How her feelings had grown unexpectedly, out of what she had believed was friendship. How she had suddenly known it was love. How he had kissed her, but that she had no idea of his having any serious intent towards her. How she feared he was in love with someone else. How she had had no one to confide in, because she did not want his sister to know the truth. How she had loved him four years ago, but he had treated her as a school-room miss.

At this, Faith started. 'Four years ago? You knew him *four years ago*?'

They looked at each other, realisation slowly dawning on each of their faces.

'Then…' Faith spoke slowly '…you are not speaking of George Manning?'

'George Manning? *No!*' Olivia's shocked tone made it clear, she hoped, what she thought of that suggestion. 'How could you think such a thing?'

'I am so sorry, Olivia. But he is so gallant towards you and I should think that most young ladies would fall in love with him. I…' Her voice tailed off.

'Would *you* have fallen in love with him?'

Faith looked startled for a second. 'No.' She shook her head. 'No, I wouldn't. Even if I wasn't in love with my own dear husband. Mr Manning is too...' Her voice faded and a frown appeared on her brow.

'Too exotic and too smooth,' said Olivia bluntly.

'Yes—exactly that!' Faith placed a hand on her head. 'Olivia, I confess I have misjudged you. I assumed that as you are so young, Mr Manning's charm would have touched your heart.'

Olivia snorted. 'I might be young, but I hope my instincts are good.' Conscious that she sounded rude, she added 'I admire Mr Manning and I am impressed by his sacrifices in battle, but my heart, I assure you, is untouched by him.'

'Then—if it is not Mr Manning...'

Olivia waited, holding her breath.

'Not Charles—you still squabble like children...' She inhaled sharply and her eyes opened wide. '*Jem!* It's Jem, isn't it?'

'Hush!' Olivia glanced around, though nobody was in view.

Faith clapped her hands in delight. 'But this is wonderful! You and Jem will make a great match!'

Olivia placed her hands over Faith's, stilling her applause. She shook her head. 'But don't you see? There *is* no match. This is all in my head—in my heart. It is not real.' Tears welled up again. 'I have no notion of his loving me—Amy is the lady he is being linked with— even your own mama says so!'

'Tosh!' said Faith bluntly. 'My mama is not renowned for her insight, as you well know. And you have successfully hidden your feelings from all of us. Who knows? Perhaps Jem has as well.'

Olivia could not see any truth in this, but refrained from saying so. Behind Faith, a harassed-looking footman had appeared on the terrace. 'I think you are needed, Faith.'

Faith turned. 'The first of the guests must be arriving.' She swept Olivia into a quick, fierce hug. 'All will be well, Olivia. I promise.'

She left in a flurry of silk, leaving Olivia to walk slowly back to the drawing room. Jem had not come and he was probably in love with Amy anyway. This was going to be the worst ball ever.

'Faster!' Jem rapped the roof of the carriage with his cane. Now that he was nearly there, he was becoming increasingly impatient. Recalling his previous journey to Chadcombe, he was conscious of the similarities—and the differences. As they approached the last village, he outlined them in his mind.

Last time, he had anxiously looking forward to seeing Olivia again and telling himself that his thoughts of her had been nought but fantastical dreams. He had had no idea then that he had loved her, loyally and deeply, through four years of separation. Now, it was as clear to him as breathing.

He remembered their first conversation in the rose garden and his clumsy attempt to figure out if there was any hope of her returning his feelings. That plan had lasted no longer than it took to read her open, trusting expression. She had had no notion that he saw her as anything other than a friend.

But things are different now. A small hopeful voice spoke in his heart.

The kisses he had shared with her, her response to him, an indefinable feeling he had that she felt something for him—all these things did not constitute proof, but his instincts told him that it was at least possible. He smiled. He was looking forward to seeking opportunities to kiss Olivia again. The very thought of her stirred his senses in ways he could not have imagined.

He believed also that Adam, Olivia's guardian, had come to know him well these past weeks. He and Harry included him in all their conversations, joked with him in a relaxed way and seemed to trust him. Of course, he had not disgraced himself when Olivia was kidnapped. The fact that he had been the one to find her was nothing more than a lucky chance, but her brothers had expressed fervent gratitude towards him afterwards. In combination with his improved circumstances, the chances of Adam agreeing to a marriage between them seemed better than before. *If* that marriage was Olivia's wish.

Finally, the carriage entered the gates of Chadcombe, just as the sun was setting.

The one flaw in my plan, thought Jem, *is Manning.*

He frowned as he thought of his rival. The man had the looks and charm that many women went for and it was widely assumed that he was wealthy. But there had been—he refused to deceive himself—evidence that he and Olivia had been interested in each other. That was not true now. He found it hard to believe that Olivia was sharing similar passionate kisses with Manning as the ones she had bestowed upon him. It simply did not fit with what he knew of her. Therefore, he believed, there was at least a chance of him winning Olivia's heart.

If it weren't for Manning, Jem's path would be clear. He would propose to Olivia as soon as the opportunity arose—having kissed her thoroughly in the process. He shook his head ruefully. Manning or no Manning, that was still the plan—*must* be the plan. This time, he would not be deterred. He must speak his heart as soon as an opportunity presented itself.

The carriage came to a halt outside Chadcombe's portico and the groom jumped down to open the door and lower the steps. 'Call Will and have him walk the horses,' Jem instructed. 'I shall return just as soon as I have dressed in something more appropriate for a ball.'

The ballroom was full, the music sweet and the atmosphere filled with gaiety. It was clear to all present that the first ball in Monkton Park for many a year would be declared a success. Mr and Mrs Foxley were everywhere, seeing to their guests' comfort and amusement effortlessly and cordially. Olivia watched Faith finding partners for ladies who had not danced yet and stopping to chat to various guests as she worked her way around the room.

There were no dance cards, as the ball was a little less formal than the most extravagant of London affairs. Olivia was glad of it, as she had managed to avoid an invitation to dance from a rather inebriated middle-aged gentleman, who had eyed her figure most inappropriately. She had just managed to escape and was standing quietly with Charles and Amy, when she saw him.

Jem in his everyday clothing was striking and handsome. Jem in full evening wear in a candlelit ballroom, and with the added spice of not having seen him in a week, was simply gorgeous. Her eyes took in every inch of him—that wonderful, springy dark hair that she had caressed during their kisses, his handsome face, lithe body… She studied him hungrily, as her heart pounded and both anxiety and excitement danced in her gut.

Amy was talking—something about the music—but Olivia no longer heard her. Jem was here! He must have come straight from Chadcombe, even though he had been travelling all day. Such a wonderful sense of duty and commitment! He would be exhausted, she knew, so to even think about going straight to a ball said something about the man.

He was scanning around the room, looking for people he knew. She could tell the exact moment he spotted them. His eyes met hers and he immediately began moving through the crowd towards them. She reminded herself to breathe.

'Jem, old chap!' Charles pumped Jem's hand furiously. 'Didn't think you'd make it. There now, Amy, you can rest easy.' Amy blushed and stammered something. 'She's worrying over this damned waltz, Jem. I've told her I've no intention of dancing with my own sister, so you have rescued me in the nick of time!'

The musicians had indeed, Olivia realised with dismay, struck up the opening bars of the waltz—the only one to be played tonight. All around the room there was a flurry of activity as the gentlemen moved in pursuit of their preferred partners.

'Of course!' said Jem, smiling. 'I shall be delighted to partner you, Miss Turner—but you have nothing to worry about, you know.'

Amy gave him a friendly smile. 'Oh, no,' she said. 'Not *now*.'

Jem, finally, turned to Olivia. 'How do you, Lady Olivia?' His gaze was warm and intent, and it made something melt inside her.

'I am well, thank you.' Her voice was a little breathless. 'I am so glad that you returned in time for the ball!'

He laughed a little. 'My poor horses are not glad of it! I have sent them to Foxley's stable, with John Coachman and Will to rub them down and feed them. I do hope that Foxley has not changed his mind about having me as an overnight guest, for it would be cruel to put them out again.'

'I'm sure Will is happy to see you again. He missed you when you were gone.'

As did I, she added silently.

He grinned. 'Will is like a puppy, constantly at my heels. Can you believe he thinks me a hero? He insisted on accompanying me here tonight, quite against my wishes. I am not entirely sure how he managed it'

Amy perked up at this. 'But you *are* a hero! You rescued him from that awful man.'

'Not at all! I only did what anyone might have done.' He offered Amy his arm, bowed to Olivia and Charles, and led her to the dance floor. They looked good together, thought Olivia, in an attempt to be unprejudiced. Amy's blonde hair and beautiful pink and white dress was the perfect foil to Jem's dark hair and black evening coat.

She swallowed. The lump in her throat hurt and she was frightened that she might cry—right here, in the crowded ballroom. She loved Jem so much and could not bear the exquisite agony of being with him, yet not being his.

'Lady Olivia!' It was George—elegant, polished and smiling.

'Oh, Lord!' muttered Charles. Olivia threw him a cross look.

'Please say that you will dance the waltz with me, Lady Olivia! Mr Turner, I do hope that you have not cut me out, for there is nothing I would like more than to waltz with this beautiful lady.'

'No, no,' said Charles quickly. 'Not one for waltzing.'

Disappointed, for in that moment Olivia would have much preferred the comforting company of her friend,

Olivia nevertheless assented and allowed George to lead her to the dance floor.

Dancing the waltz with George was something of an ordeal. The waltz holds were more intimate and allowed for closer contact, and more touch, than any of the other dances. As a result of her conversation with Faith earlier, Olivia was feeling uncomfortable with George and worried that others might see her as having encouraged his attentions. She hoped that he himself understood that, if she had flirted with him at first, she had not meant anything by it.

'Are you well, Lady Olivia?' he asked her solicitously. He was so close that she could feel his breath, warm against her cheek. As they turned she glanced at him— and saw that he was studying the neckline of her dress with rather more interest than was appropriate. Her stomach turned in revulsion.

'Yes, quite well,' she lied, praying that the waltz would end soon. 'It is just that I am unaccustomed to the waltz and must concentrate. I do apologise if I am not good company.'

'Not at all. So that is it! I had thought that you would enjoy dancing.'

'I do, sometimes,' said Olivia, privately adding, *If I could dance with Jem, I would enjoy that*.

But Jem was paired with Amy. She had avoided looking directly at them, but caught a flash of Amy's dress from time to time out of the corner of her eye.

Finally, the trial ended. She curtsied to George and they walked off the floor together to where Harry and Juliana sat conversing with Foxley and Adam. Charlotte, of course, was at home with the baby. Jem and Amy soon joined them, as did Lizzie, who had also been dancing.

Jem was welcomed with genuine warmth and affec-

tion, Olivia noted. She was conscious of the compulsion
to keep *looking* at him and distracted herself by focusing
instead on whoever was speaking at any particular moment. Somehow, she got to supper time without having
to speak directly to Jem. It was shocking how shy and
unsure she felt around him tonight. In her head, she gave
herself a stern telling-off.

Supper was rather a crush, but George, who was constantly at her elbow, procured her some food. She was
too anxious to eat anything, but did not wish to draw
any comment, so after some time she set the plate down,
made her excuses and escaped to the ladies' retiring
room with a young lady of her acquaintance.

Thankfully, the room was fairly quiet. Olivia sank
with relief into a soft chair in the corner behind the door.

Her moment of peace was short-lived. A group of
three chattering matrons invaded the sanctuary, the
plumes on their feathered turbans nodding as they exclaimed and gossiped, and discussed the guests. Mrs
Buxted's penetrating tone pierced Olivia's ears and she
made a quiet but immediate escape before Faith's mama
spotted her.

Emerging into the hallway, she saw that George
Manning was hovering near the door to the ballroom—
possibly in an attempt to intercept her. For goodness
sake, why could everyone not leave her *alone*! Just now,
George was turned away from her, but he might see her
at any instant. Dashing across the hall, she opened the
first door she could find and dived in.

She was in luck. The room—a small parlour—was
empty. Sighing with relief, she wandered across to the
window and stepped behind the heavy curtains. As the
curtains fell back into place, the candlelit room disappeared and she gazed out at the night sky. A full moon

sailed serenely across the heavens and Olivia bathed in the peace and the profound silence for a moment.

She sighed. In a minute she would return to the ballroom. Supper must be nearly completed and the dancing would soon begin again. Although she had missed out on the waltz, she hoped that she would have the opportunity to dance with Jem tonight. It would be exquisitely painful, she knew, but it would be worth it.

She stepped back into the room, taken aback to see the door suddenly opening. It was George. She sighed inwardly.

'Ah, there you are, Lady Olivia! I thought I caught a glimpse of you coming into this room!'

Dash it! thought Olivia. *I was not quite quick enough.*

'I was hoping for an opportunity to speak with you.' He turned and closed the door, which immediately awoke Olivia's inner warnings. *Why had he done that?*

'Yes? Is something wrong?' Olivia's heart began to race. She felt deeply uncomfortable.

'No—at least, I hope not.' He gave her a wry smile. 'Not having been in this situation before, I have no idea what to expect.'

They were standing face to face and the door was on her left. Instinctively, Olivia took a step to the side and he moved to face her again. There! That was better. Now the door was at her back, with no obstacles in the way.

'What situation? I have no notion of your meaning, Mr Manning. Now, I believe I must return to the ballroom—'

He grabbed her hand, preventing her from leaving. 'Lady Olivia—wait! I must speak with you!'

She spoke coldly to him. 'Please release my hand, Mr Manning.'

He did so, looking shamefaced. 'I apologise—I was

overcome. I forget that you are so gently reared and deserve every consideration. I shall endeavour to contain myself.'

Olivia gazed at him in bemusement. What on earth was he talking about?

Her eyes widened as he dropped to one knee in front of her.

Chapter Twenty-One

He spoke earnestly. 'Lady Olivia, you are too kind-hearted to play games with me. You must know that my heart is yours, that I could love no other. Please tell me that you will be my wife!'

His *wife*? Oh, no! He must have thought that she was seriously interested in him. Lord, how foolish she had been! She had had no idea that he was in love with her. Despite her discomfort, she felt a twinge of sympathy for him. Now, how could she best reject him without hurting his pride?

He was looking up at her, his expression a mix of hope and confidence. 'I know I should have asked permission from Lord Shalford before speaking to you, but I confess I am overtaken with emotion!'

'Do stand up, Mr Manning,' she began prosaically. He did so, joy dawning on his face.

'Then—you will have me? My dear Lady Olivia!' Seemingly overcome, he drew her into his arms, his mouth swooping to claim hers.

'No—please!' she mumbled against his lips. How on earth had he interpreted her command as an agreement to wed him? Using her elbows, she tried to break free of his embrace, but he held firm. She twisted her face from side to side as he pursued her, trying to cover her mouth with his. He would not stop and she was becoming increasingly panicked. 'Stop! No!'

Then, wonderfully, she heard the sound of the door opening again—thank goodness. Whoever it was, they could hopefully rescue her from this distressing situation. As George's attention was also diverted by the door opening, she was able to turn her head. He tightened his grip on her—it was clear that he was not going to let her go, even if they were seen! Why would he do such a thing?

'Well! I had suspected this, but I am delighted to see it confirmed!' It was Miss Manning, smiling broadly, satisfaction in her tone.

Beside her, Mrs Buxted clapped a hand to her mouth. 'Well, this is shocking, and would never have been permitted in my day!' Seeing her friend frown, she made haste to add, 'Although one must of course make allowances for the natural feelings of two young people in love! Allow me to be the first to wish you happy.'

In horror, Olivia realised; Mrs Buxted thought that they were to be married! She glanced at George's face, which was alight with joy. 'Thank you, Mrs Buxted. I have only this moment secured her hand. As you might imagine, I am all happiness!' George released her, but only to snake his arm around her waist.

She stiffened, her mind still frozen in shock. *What was this nightmare?*

'Well, this is interesting…' Jem was in the doorway, leaning against the door jamb with his arms folded. 'Wouldn't you say so, my lord?'

Adam joined him, his face set. 'Extremely interesting, Jem.'

Olivia was confused. Everything was happening too quickly.

Now Harry appeared. 'What on earth is going on?' he asked sharply. 'And why is everyone standing in the corridor?' He ushered them briskly into the room and closed the door.

'Are we to understand,' said Jem, 'that you and Lady Olivia wish to marry?' His eyes bored into Olivia's. Beside him, Harry gasped.

Jem's gaze brought Olivia back to life. 'No!' she declared. George's arm gripped her more tightly. Taking her right hand, she knocked his away and turned to face him. Any sympathy she had had was now gone, dissipated by his manhandling of her. 'You did not wait for my reply. My answer is no.'

'But—' Miss Manning's voice was insistent. 'We have just seen you, embracing.'

'Most unseemly!' agreed Mrs Buxted. 'Kissing men that she is not even engaged to!' Mrs Buxted wagged a finger at her. 'You'll *have* to marry him now, Lady Olivia, or your reputation may never recover!'

Miss Manning and her brother exchanged a quick, satisfied glance. Olivia caught her breath. Had they *planned* this?

'Nonsense!' Jem stepped forward and laid a gentle hand on Olivia's arm. 'Are you well, Olivia?'

'I shall be,' she said, knowing he could feel her trembling. 'Mrs Buxted, I was not kissing anyone. I was trying to escape from a kiss that I did not want!'

Adam's jaw hardened. 'Manning!' he snapped. 'Is it your habit to kiss young women against their will?'

'Of course not! She wanted that kiss as much as I! And,' he added, with a sly look at Jem, 'it is not the first time we have kissed!'

Lord, she thought, *he is making it sound as though there was something going on between us!*

'Not true!' she retorted. 'I did not ask you to kiss me that time either! And just now you knew full well that I was trying to escape you!' She looked desperately to Jem and her brothers.

Adam nodded. 'I believe you.'

Jem concurred. 'I saw with my own eyes how you were struggling to be free, as we entered the room. I am surprised that these ladies—' he bowed to Miss Manning and Mrs Buxted '—did not also notice it.'

'It is very simple,' said Miss Manning, 'Lady Olivia heard the door opening and was embarrassed at being discovered as a wanton. Perfectly understandable'

There was a gasp of shock as everyone reacted to her description of Olivia as a 'wanton'. Olivia felt her face burn in embarrassment. She had allowed George to kiss her, on the stepping stones. And she certainly had behaved like a wanton with Jem. *Twice.*

'As Mrs Buxted says,' Miss Manning finished primly, 'we must make allowances for a couple in love getting carried away.'

Olivia felt as though the walls were closing around her. Must she marry George, to save her reputation? Adam's face looked as though it were carved from stone. Harry just looked confused.

She glanced up at Jem. Their eyes met and she tried to throw him a message of desperate appeal. He nodded and she felt marginally better.

With renewed vigour, Jem turned towards George. 'Tell me, what did you say to your sister, just before you entered this room?'

'Well, I…' George seemed confused. 'I simply…er… that is to say—'

'He told me,' said his sister firmly, 'that he was going
to ask Lady Olivia for her hand in marriage.'

'Yes! That's it! That's what I told her.'

Jem's eyes narrowed. 'And did you also ask her to
enter the room after a short interval had passed, bringing Mrs Buxted in an attempt to compromise Lady
Olivia's reputation?'

'Of course not!' George blustered, but a wave of ruddy
colour was spreading across his face. 'How dare you suggest I would do something so dishonourable!'

'I dare,' said Jem casually, 'because you have already
lied—to all of us!'

'Outrageous!' said George, but his eyes locked with
his sister's in mute appeal.

'How dare you accuse my brother of lying!' said Miss
Manning, her tone venomous.

Jem, without leaving Olivia's side, bowed politely to
Miss Manning. 'Unfortunately it is true. I have spent
the last week in London, discovering the truth about
your brother!'

Miss Manning grew visibly pale. 'What do you
mean?'

Jem stepped forward. Olivia put her other hand over
the place where his had been, to protect the delightful
tingle that was left there.

Reaching inside his pocket, Jem withdrew a note. 'I
found it interesting that no one I know is acquainted with
Mr Manning, despite the fact that he says he fought at
Waterloo. So I went to the War Office to find out.'

Harry stroked his jaw, his eyes dancing. He looked
like he was suddenly enjoying the situation. 'You spoke
to the Major?'

Jem nodded. 'He remembers George signing up.'

'Well, there you are then!' George erupted. 'Proof

that I told the truth!' He frowned. 'His name was Major Cooke, I think.'

'That's him,' Jem agreed cordially.

Olivia was totally confused. So far, Jem had only confirmed that George *hadn't* lied!

'The interesting part, though, was when we looked up the register. You see, there was no George Manning on the list.' He waited a moment, to let the full effect sink in. 'However, we eventually found an entry on the right date, for a—' he consulted his notes '—George *Mainwaring*. Can you explain that?'

George seemed incapable of speech. There was a brief silence. Jem continued to fix George with an intense gaze. Olivia's heart was thumping loudly in her chest.

'I can explain.' Miss Manning, a rigid smile on her face, stepped forward. 'It has all been a terrible misunderstanding. You see…' She paused and shook her head sadly. 'Our parents *were* called Mainwaring.'

'So why the deuce did you change your name then?' asked Adam in irritation. Unlike Harry, he did not seem as though he was being at all entertained.

'Ah. That would be a small matter of…er…' She was now wringing her hands together. 'That is to say, we were under pressure from some creditors and so we decided to have a fresh start. Mainwaring and Mannering and Manning are all the same name, you know. There was no harm in it.' Withdrawing an exquisite lace handkerchief, she dabbed gently at the corner of her eyes.

'No harm at all, my dear friend.' Mrs Buxted patted Miss Manning's hand consolingly. 'Why, anyone might find themselves in debt! And we all know your brother to have been one of the bravest at Waterloo.'

Jem shook his head. 'Mrs Buxted, I am afraid there is evidence that George did *not* fight at Waterloo.'

'Of course I did!' George spluttered. 'That is where
I was injured.'

Olivia was putting it all together in her head. 'Mr
Manning,' she ventured, 'you told me that you had rescued another soldier at Waterloo, after he had become
trapped under his horse.'

At this, Jem and Harry both started, then looked at
each other. Both looked astonished.

'Do pray continue, Olivia,' Harry drawled. 'This
sounds a most interesting story.'

Olivia frowned in concentration. 'Well, I cannot recall
the exact details, but he told me that a horse had rolled
on top of a soldier, leaving him trapped beneath it. Mr
Manning managed to pull him out, at great risk to himself, and almost died because of his bravery.'

George's eyes shifted downwards. 'Yes,' he confirmed. 'I do not often speak of it.'

'But you should!' cried Jem. 'Why, this is wonderful—
to have a true hero in this very room! Why, that settles
everything!'

Olivia's stomach lurched.

Jem brushed a tiny speck from his sleeve, adding casually, 'But, tell me, where *exactly* were you when this
happened? For I am certain that I heard some talk of this
particular act of bravery in the days and weeks after the
victory. But I cannot recall the precise location—was it
up on the ridge at La Haye Sainte, or on the plain below?'

'Er… I cannot be sure exactly. My injury…everything
was so confused…'

'Ah, yes, your injury. Broken arm, wasn't it?' George
nodded warily. Jem consulted his parchment again.
'But—can you explain to me how your injury was recorded by the Army doctor a full week before the great

battle? It says here that you fell from a horse during training and sold out *four days before Waterloo*.'

Olivia happened to glance at Adam. His eyes were gleaming with appreciation at Jem's revelation.

'Well, clearly, the records are wrong!' snapped George. He squared his shoulders. 'Emma, let us retire. This discussion is too upsetting for you.' He took Miss Manning's arm and they turned to leave.

'One moment!' Jem placed a hand on his brow, tapping his long fingers thoughtfully. 'A memory is coming back to me…something to do with a horse and a man trapped underneath… Now, what was that?'

George and his sister exchanged glances. George swallowed.

Olivia watched in bemusement. *What on earth was Jem up to?*

Harry had a mischievous look in his eye. 'La Haye Sainte, I think you'll find, Ensign. Just behind the ridge.'

'You are right, Captain Fanton!' Jem saluted smartly to his former commander, then grinned. 'If you hadn't pulled me out, I was done for!'

'And if you hadn't told Juliana where to find me on the battlefield, I'd not be here now.'

Olivia gasped. 'Then—Jem—your broken leg—?'

He gave her an expressive look. 'I am surprised you did not hear of it before. That horse was probably sixteen hands, if not more. I'm just glad that your brother here—' he jerked his head towards Harry '—was on hand to pull me out. It was half-covering my chest and I could not get a breath. Bravest thing I ever saw. He knew when he bent to help me that he would be leaving himself unguarded. And sure enough, a French cavalryman tried to take his head off.'

Harry rapped his knuckles against his own head.

'Takes more than a French sword to get through this skull,' he said proudly.

Olivia found her voice. 'Why has nobody told me this?' Harry had risked himself to save Jem's life. 'Harry, you are wonderful!' She hugged her brother tightly.

'Hey, steady on, little one!' he said gruffly.

Mrs Buxted looked confused. 'Then—it was a lie? All of it?' Her voice sounded small. 'Miss Manning? Emma?' There was a wounded appeal in her eyes.

Miss Manning's eyes narrowed. 'It was worth a try. You all have so much wealth, you have no idea what it is to scrimp and save, and make do! If he'd married the girl, we'd have been set for life! The sister of an Earl, no less! He'd only be forced to sleep with her once, to avoid an annulment. Then we'd be free to enjoy all that lovely Fanton wealth! It would have been worth all the sacrifices—including putting up with your incessant babbling!' Mrs Buxted gasped in shock.

'Then—it was all an act? You did not actually wish to marry me?' Olivia's voice shook a little. Manning's deceit was outrageous! She could not recall ever feeling so *angry*.

He smiled insolently. 'My taste does not run to aristocratic virgins, I'm afraid—even when they are as pretty as you!' Across the room, Jem's hand tightened into a fist.

'Come, George! We shall retire!' Miss Manning swept forward on George's arm, but Adam barred their way. 'You will both leave this house first thing in the morning,' he said softly, 'and you will never come back. And if one word of scandal involving my sister comes to my ears, then I will hunt you down. Do you understand me?'

'Oh, we understand,' said George bitterly, 'how you look down on such as us. Fear not, we shall leave as soon as possible.' Miss Manning, her lips closed tightly together in a thin line, kept her gaze on a fixed point somewhere over Adam's shoulder.

Satisfied, Adam stepped back and allowed them to leave. The door closed with a resonant click.

'Good work, Jem!' Adam placed a hand on Jem's shoulder. 'I am in your debt.'

'I had to know,' Jem replied. 'Once I'd got it into my head that there was something questionable about him, I could not let it go. It's why I went to London.'

'How did you know what he was up to in this room just now?' asked Harry. 'You were most insistent that Adam and I must accompany you immediately.'

'I didn't know for sure, but I have been watching him closely this evening and he seemed to be behaving oddly—hanging around the hallway, then suddenly dashing off to speak to his sister. She seemed most interested in whatever he was telling her and, as soon as he had gone, she approached Mrs Buxted in great haste. At that point, I decided to fetch you two and follow them.'

'I am so glad you did, Jem,' said Olivia, 'for Mr Manning would not let me go!'

His eyes searched her face. 'I am sorry if you have been hurt by this, Olivia. He is very charming and it would not be impossible to think that any young lady might resist such a handsome chap.'

'I assure you,' she replied earnestly, 'I have taken no hurt.' It seemed important that he knew. 'My heart was untouched by his charm. My only concern was how I might reject his offer without hurting his feelings.'

Something intense blazed in his eyes, briefly. 'I am glad of it,' he said gruffly.

'They *lied* to me!' Mrs Buxted, having had, it seemed, enough of being ignored, sank down on to a nearby sofa.

'I cannot *believe* I was so taken in! How could they
do such a thing? What sort of person would abuse my
friendship and my hospitality so?' She was beginning to
get herself worked up. Olivia, who had seen Mrs Buxted in full hysterics on more than one occasion previously, bit her lip.

Sitting beside her, she spoke softly. 'We were all taken
in. Miss Manning and her brother are clearly accom-
plished liars.'

Mrs Buxted seemed not to hear her and promptly
burst into noisy tears. Olivia looked round. 'Can someone fetch Faith? And we might need some smelling salts.'

Harry and Adam, already looking uncomfortable at
Mrs Buxted's distress, promptly left to discreetly fetch
a servant and their hostess. Jem stayed, his eyes on
Olivia as she tried to comfort Mrs Buxted.

After just a few moments, Faith bustled in, frowning.
'Oh, Mama, they told me you are upset. Hush, now, all
will be well!'

'They lied to all of us! Oh, Faith, I brought them to
your home. And they played us false!' Mrs Buxted was
genuinely distressed, though she was a little calmer now.

'I know,' said Faith. 'Harry has just told me. But,
Mama, it is not your fault. Why, we all trusted them!
Here, lie down and close your eyes.' Mrs Buxted did
so and, thankfully, after a moment her sobs subsided to
mere hiccoughs.

'At least we found out before they did any real harm,'
said Olivia, who was beginning to think it all over.
'Faith, did you know that it was Jem who exposed the
truth about George?' Jem's insight and persistence had
to be celebrated!

'All I did was to check his records,' said Jem, shrugging. 'It was you who revealed the lie about his so-called

heroism at Waterloo. It was lucky that you remembered his tale in such detail!'

Olivia dimpled at him. 'We make a good team.' She could not resist it.

'Indeed we do!' He smiled back.

Faith cleared her throat. Jem and Olivia both looked at her, startled.

'We must not let any breath of scandal come out about this. You two should return to the ballroom. Smile and dance, and be as you usually are. Then, if anything is said afterwards, people will say, in all truth, that all seemed well.'

'You are very wise, Mrs Foxley. Lady Olivia, may I have the next dance?' He bowed, the corners of his eyes crinkling in a hint of a smile.

She grinned, and curtsied. 'I should be delighted, Mr Ford.'

He offered his arm and she rested her hand on it.

Juliana bounced up to them as they entered the ball-room. 'Where have you been? You missed the first dance after supper—it was a quadrille. Faith, I must say your ball is wonderful!'

'Thank you,' said Faith. With a sidelong glance at Jem and Olivia, she added, 'I must speak to the musicians.'

Harry approached. 'Well, that was a good piece of work. Well done, Jem!'

'What have I missed?' asked Juliana, eyeing them all curiously.

'Dance this next one with me and I'll tell you,' said Harry, grinning.

Sure enough, the musicians were ready to play again. Jem offered his hand and Olivia took it. As they reached the dance floor she realised what Faith had done. The musicians were playing the tantalising opening bars of a waltz! The second waltz of the evening and totally un-planned. Faith had done it for them, she knew.

For me and Jem.

'A waltz,' murmured Jem, bending close to her. 'Olivia, have you any idea for how long I have wished to waltz with you?' Incapable of speech, she responded only with a smile. Her heart swelled.

Only an hour before, she had waltzed with George Manning. This waltz was as different as it could possibly be to that experience. This time, she was perfectly happy and in harmony with her partner. His closeness thrilled her and she quite enjoyed the notion that he would be presented with eyefuls of her cleavage as they moved through the figures.

And yet her feeling was not only physical. She felt as though she were floating, or flying.

Bliss, her mind said. *This is what bliss feels like.*

His hands in hers, or around her waist, the feeling of warmth from his body, his breath on her cheek. Why, it was a lot like kissing—but without the actual kissing! Now, finally, she realised why the older generation disapproved of waltzing. It was because you could feel like this!

All too soon, it was over. In a glow of happiness, Olivia and Jem sought refreshments, then sat chatting about everything and nothing. They were inseparable for the little that remained of the evening. Lizzie and Juliana, and Olivia's brothers came and went—sometimes they were in a group of six all together, sometimes just three or four, but always, Olivia stayed where Jem was and Jem stayed where Olivia was. By the time they were all retiring and the guests were gone, the incident with the Mannings seemed as though it had happened a week ago.

Jem kissed her hand goodnight and expressed the

wish that she might walk with him in the morning. The expression in his eyes was all that she had wished for. She floated up the stairs and to her chamber, only vaguely aware of where she was. She slept immediately and more soundly than she had for weeks. All was well. She just *knew* it.

Chapter Twenty-Two

Sometimes, when you first wake up, there is a moment of absolute stillness. The mind is not yet thinking or remembering, and the heart is resting, with no emotions to confuse the senses. In recent weeks, Olivia had come to appreciate this moment when it happened, as most of the time, she had been jolted awake by her own anxieties, fears, or dreadful memories, with no pause or boundary between sleep and worried consciousness.

This morning, it was different. She stirred, opened her eyes and stretched, savouring the perfect quietness of her own mind. Slowly, she became conscious of a wonderful feeling of anticipation—such as she used to feel when she was a child on her birthday, or at Christmas time. The birds were cawing raucously outside her window, waking her from a dreamless, restful sleep—just as they had the last time she had stayed at Monkton Park.

Monkton Park! A thrill rushed through her, as she remembered last night and waltzing with Jem. The way he had held her, had looked at her. The way she had felt… She hugged the memories to her, savouring each one. The blissful feeling was still there, and only a little muted since last night.

Restlessly, she tossed and turned, then, hearing some activity outside, she gave up trying to sleep and got out of bed. She rang for a maid, then, padding across to the window, drew aside the curtains and looked outside. Down below, a carriage was waiting, its paintwork a little worn in places. Olivia had not seen it before. A footman was busy strapping trunks to the rear and, as she watched, George and his sister walked towards the carriage. As far as Olivia could tell, only the servants were seeing them off—or, more likely, ensuring that they left.

Her hair had come loose from its plait and had fallen forward around her face. She reached up to pull it back— just as George looked upwards. The movement caught his eye and his gaze immediately went to her. His expression promptly changed from sulky to fierce and he said something to his sister. She looked up, sneered at Olivia and replied to him.

Shaken, Olivia stepped back into the safety of her chamber. She should not be surprised, she supposed, at their anger, yet she was. They had lied and cheated their way into Monkton Park and had tried to trap her into marriage. Yet *they* were angry with *her* that they had been found out!

She shook her head. Best to forget them—without ever forgetting the lessons she had learned from the acquaintance.

Sitting on the edge of the bed, she listened as the carriage moved away, then sighed with relief. They were gone.

The maid, when she arrived, informed her that the family and guests were all still abed. Knowing that she should still be sleeping, too, after such a late night, but unable to do so, Olivia got up.

I shall go for a ride, she decided.

It would be the best way to harness the restless energy within her and pass the time until she could see Jem again. With the maid's assistance she dressed quickly in her favourite blue riding habit, then went directly to the stables.

'I'm to accompany you, my lady,' said the groom. 'Mr Foxley was most insistent.'

'I see.' She did not normally ride with a groom at Monkton Park—the order was probably related to last night's drama.

But, she thought, *the Mannings are gone—and with them, any danger.*

'Thank you,' she said. 'However, I would prefer to ride alone.'

The groom looked alarmed. 'But, miss—I mean, my lady! The master was most insistent.'

'I can ride with you instead, on the pony!' Will's excited treble emerged from the hayloft. Olivia looked up to see his tousled head grinning at her. 'My master would wish me to accompany you, my lady.'

Unable to suppress a smile and warmed by the reference to Jem, Olivia relented. 'Very well. But I am going *now*, Will.'

'I shall take no more than five minutes to be ready, my lady! I promise!'

He was true to his word and, soon after, despite the dubious looks and worried mutterings of Foxley's groom, they trotted out together down the drive.

'Let us go to the gate, then round to the river, Will. Do not fall off!'

'*Pah!*' retorted Will in disgust. 'As if! This pony is not fast enough for me, but it is the only one that they will let me ride—yet.' He eyed Olivia's mount. 'She's a sweet 'un—I've seen John canter with her when she's exercising and she loves to run.'

'I know!' said Olivia with a grin. Suddenly, happiness bubbled over inside her. 'I have to gallop, Will! I shall wait for you at the gate.'

She gave the horse its head and they galloped down the drive. The drive was muddy after overnight rain and her progress was almost silent as she glided along the road, feeling again the sense of exhilaration that had woken her so early. Will, despite a valiant attempt to urge his pony into something better than a fast trot, was soon lost from view.

As she approached the gate, she was surprised to see a carriage, and people, up ahead. Pulling the horse up before she could be noticed, she took in the scene.

The Mannings' carriage was stalled just outside the gate, almost off the road, as if something had frightened the horses and they had bolted. Further progress was being impeded by a skewbald horse, with markings like strange eyebrows. A man was standing close to the horse—an enormous figure and one that was entirely familiar. Olivia's stomach clenched in fear.

It was Gunn—and he was holding a shotgun trained on George Manning! They had to have been here arguing for some time—it was almost half an hour since she had heard the carriage leave.

George was standing to the side of the carriage with his back to Olivia, and his sister was visible inside the carriage, her gaze fixed on the tableau of her brother and his adversary.

George and Gunn were deep in conversation, it became clear, about a matter of money.

'I care not,' Gunn was saying. 'I did what you told me and I am still waiting to be paid!'

'And you shall be paid!' said George smoothly. 'My

situation is a little delicate at present, but I shall be happy to sign you a note of promise.'

This suggestion did not, it seemed, meet with Gunn's approval. He raised the shotgun a little higher.

Open-mouthed, Olivia worked it out. It was *George* who had paid Gunn to kidnap her!

'You reprehensible snake!' she cried. 'It was you! You arranged it all!'

Despite the immediate threat of a shotgun pointed at his head, George immediately spun around. The startled look on his face gave way to calculation, then slyness.

'Well, well, it is Lady Olivia!' Walking forward and completely ignoring Gunn—who looked more than a little bemused at this turn of events—he took hold of the mare's bridle. 'This is most fortuitous,' he said softly. 'I do believe you may have just saved my life.' Without turning, he roared, 'Gunn!'

'What?' Gunn's expression was sullen.

'Luck is with you. We have been given a second chance to hold Lady Olivia for ransom. Come here!'

'No!' Olivia urged her horse to move, but George held fast to the bridle.

'Do not let her escape this time!' Miss Manning's voice, hard and shrill, added to Gunn's orders. Slowly, he began to lumber forward.

'Gunn!' said Olivia desperately. 'Do not be part of this! My brother will pay you to keep me safe from this man!'

'Do not trust her, Gunn.' George spoke with urgency. 'You have told me of your hatred for the gentry. Do not be fooled by her.'

Gunn was now beside her, huge and terrifying. Olivia trembled, finding herself unable to speak. All of her fears—the terror she had experienced—it was all real again.

'The gentry think only of themselves,' Gunn pronounced. 'How will I be sure you will pay me this time?' he asked of George.

'This time,' said George confidently, 'I *myself* shall ensure that she does not escape until her brother has paid me—paid both of us!' Gunn's expression did not change. 'It is our only prospect of money now.'

Miss Manning jumped down from the carriage. 'He's right,' she urged softly. 'We can demand a huge ransom this time, for they know we are serious.'

Gunn paused, considering. 'Very well,' he told George. 'But if we don't get the money, I will turn you in to the magistrate myself. Both of you,' he added, eyeing Miss Manning.

Wordlessly, he reached up and pulled Olivia roughly from the horse. She shrieked and struggled, but the enormous man seemed not to notice.

'Put her in the carriage!' Miss Manning ordered.

Gunn complied and, as he shoved her inside, Olivia caught a brief glimpse of the coachman, who was slumped on his seat, blood seeping steadily from a cut at his temple. Gunn must have hit the man hard after holding him up with the shotgun.

Shaken, and even more determined to escape before more harm could come to her, Olivia dived straight across the carriage and opened the other door.

'Why, thank you, Lady Olivia!' George blocked her exit with his imposing frame, pushing her back inside before climbing in. Miss Manning was behind her and together they forced her into a sitting position between them.

'I must say,' said George smoothly, 'I do admire your habit of riding without a groom!'

Will! Cursing herself for her stubborn foolishness, her

first thought was to protect the child. If he came upon them, he would likely interfere, in a misguided attempt to rescue her. And Gunn might shoot him! He must be almost at the gate by now. She bit her lip. Hopefully he would have the sense to hide.

Gunn finished tying his horse, and Olivia's, to the back of the carriage. Moving round to the driver's seat, he hefted the coachman down and carried him to nearby undergrowth, where he unceremoniously dumped the poor unconscious man. Olivia watched in open-mouthed shock. It was like a nightmare come to life!

'Oh, yes,' murmured George in her ear. 'It would be a mistake to underestimate our friend Gunn. He will do whatever he must. Now, just you sit still and do what you're told until we get our ransom, then you can go back to your brothers and that arrogant bastard!'

She glared at him. 'I am sure I have not the faintest idea who you mean.'

'Ha! Do you think me stupid? I saw you making calf eyes at the dashing Mr Ford. You must have enjoyed seeing him humiliate me. Well…' he rubbed his hands together gleefully '…now the tables have turned and you are quite in my power.'

Deliberately, he leaned forward and ran his finger down her face. Unable to help herself, she shuddered and flinched. He smiled—it looked like he was enjoying her distress.

'George!' Miss Manning's sharp tone called his attention. 'Tell Gunn to hurry and get us out of here!'

As she spoke, Gunn jumped up to the driver's perch and, a moment later, they were on their way. Olivia felt sick with terror. She closed her eyes and prayed, but she knew not how she could escape this time. At least Will was safe—and might raise the alarm more quickly than the Mannings anticipated. How long would he search for her when he failed to find her at the gate? How long after that before help could follow?

The answer came immediately. Too long. It was only three miles to the main road, after which there were any number of side roads and tracks where they might lose themselves for days. Once past the crossroads, the Mannings would have a head start that would make it difficult for anyone to trace them. Which meant imprisonment, messages about ransoms and possibly days of surviving George Manning's anger. For it was clear to her that this time, his motivation was not just ransom. It was vengeance.

Chapter Twenty-Three

Jem nodded at his reflection, then turned to Foxley's valet. 'Thank you, that will do.' He intended to be ready to walk with Olivia just as soon as she returned from her morning ride.

The servants had informed him that Lady Olivia had risen early and was riding. They had also confirmed, to his relief, that Mr Manning and his sister had already departed in their carriage.

Jem was conscious of a feeling of satisfaction. Manning had been exposed for the charlatan that he was and Olivia, seemingly, had *not*, after all, been in love with him. Indeed, she had seemed to put Manning out of her head after the distressing incident in the parlour and had spent the next two hours with him.

Their waltz had set the tone. In Jem's case it had brought him back to the feeling of harmony and intimacy he had shared with Olivia during their kisses. This time, though, there had been no interruptions to make him review and question, and doubt.

He knew without hesitation that Olivia saw him differently now. Gone was the friendly distance that she had offered him when he first arrived last month. In its place was a shared heightened awareness, fuelled by warm looks, as much touch as they could get away with in a ballroom and an awareness that she was as focused on him as he was on her. Finally, things would be clear between them. He meant to declare himself today—and he no longer worried about rejection. He simply *knew*, in his heart, that she felt as he did. He was also very confident that Adam would approve.

'No! I must see him! You must let me find him! Which chamber is his?' The sounds of an altercation came to his ears through the door. 'Sir! Master! Help! It's the lady!'

A terrible dread overcame him. He opened the door wide—to see Will, further down the landing, struggling with one of the footmen.

'Sorry, sir, I tried to stop him.' The footman was clearly embarrassed that a stable boy had penetrated the house and was attempting to enter a guest's bedchamber.

Jem ignored this. 'Tell me!' he commanded Will.

'It was Gunn—I saw his horse.' Will was breathless and clearly distressed. 'He has a shotgun. He put the lady in the carriage with the people who left early and they took her away!'

The footman was aghast. 'Which lady?' he asked, but Jem already knew.

Will looked directly at him. 'Same one as he took before. *Your* lady.'

Jem's blood ran cold. For a second, he could not think, or speak—just like last time. Then, his mind refocused, working much faster than usual.

He addressed the footman. 'Lady Olivia has been taken. Tell the gentlemen—her brothers and Mr Foxley. I shall go ahead and try to catch up with them.' As the footman ran off, calling the butler's name, Jem turned to Will. 'How long ago?'

'Not more than a quarter of an hour. I came straight here—though the pony was slow. The coachman is knocked out and lying in the bushes.'

'Well done, Will.' He dropped a hand on to the boy's shoulder. 'Now go and get the fastest horse in the stables saddled for me. And tell the grooms to go immediately to assist the coachman.'

'Yes, Master!' Will vanished at top speed, leaving a trail of mud, Jem noticed absently, all along the expensive carpet.

Turning to the valet, who was hopping from one foot to the other in great distress, he asked 'Where does your master keep his pistols?"

George and his sister were making plans. 'We simply need a barn where we can hide out for a few days, until they pay the ransom,' said George. 'We shall continue in the same direction as originally planned, then find somewhere along the way to hide.'

His sister wrinkled her nose. 'I suppose we shall be forced to live like peasants then, even if only briefly. If this stupid chit hadn't escaped the first time, we'd have had the ransom money already!'

She glared at Olivia, who refused to be daunted and glared back. Incensed, Miss Manning slapped Olivia hard across the face. 'Foolish girl! You are the cause of all our troubles! If you had stayed in that cellar like you were supposed to, or if you had agreed to marry George, we would even now have been safe. How dare you destroy all our plans!' She tried to slap her again—but this time, Olivia blocked her hand.

'You little idiot!' spat Miss Manning. Her expression was so filled with rage that Olivia, once again, was genuinely frightened. Bracing herself for another physical attack, she could not help cowering away from the woman, but thankfully, Miss Manning subsided. 'I shall not allow you to divert me. George, we shall need food and blankets, and something to tie her up with.'

'We must be careful about the ransom letter, too,' he added thoughtfully. 'We do not know the area well, it might be difficult to choose where they should leave the money.'

She nodded. 'First things first. Let us get safely hidden, then plan some more.'

Olivia was aghast. She could barely take it in. That they could just sit there, planning coercion and extortion, without any evidence of regret or even *awareness* of the evil of their actions! Despite her fear, she could not be silent.

'How can you do this? Gunn has hurt the coachman and you are kidnapping me! Where is your morality? Have you no conscience?'

George's lips thinned. 'You must understand, Olivia, that we would not do something like this unless we had no other choice.' His brown eyes pinned hers with seeming sincerity. Olivia was no longer fooled by it. 'You saw for yourself that Gunn intended to kill me,' he continued, seemingly oblivious to his own wickedness. She was not having it.

'Nonsense! There is always a choice,' she retorted. 'You could let me go, right now, and I will alert the magistrate about Gunn hitting that poor coachman. Just divert Gunn for a moment and I will jump out.'

Miss Manning laughed. 'What a ridiculous notion! No. We shall continue with our plan. As if a green girl could know better than us!'

Olivia looked questioningly at George, but could tell that he had not even considered listening to her suggestion. 'No. You will do what we want, or it will be the worse for you.'

Her mind was working furiously. 'Tell me something,' she said. 'When Gunn kidnapped me before, at the tea room, how could he have known that I would be there, unattended?'

'Ah!' said George. 'I had brought you to that very place, as I knew that the privy was across the yard. Gunn was told to wait in the stable and take his chance if it arose.'

'But—' Olivia was confused. 'It might not have been me. Amy or Lizzie might have needed the privy instead.'

'That is true,' said George, 'but the beauty of my plan was that it really did not matter which of you he managed to get—all three of you have wealthy relatives who would happily pay a ransom.' He looked infuriatingly self-satisfied as he said it. 'Getting *you* was a bonus!'

Olivia let this sink in. 'So you did not target me particularly?'

'Yes and no!' said Miss Manning, seemingly enjoying the opportunity to display what she probably thought was cleverness. 'Any of you would have served our purpose, but you were our preferred target. George was going to "rescue" you as soon as the ransom had been paid and use your gratitude as part of his courtship of you. That was, in fact, your idea!'

'My idea? What on earth are you talking about—oh!' She remembered the foolish conversation they had had about being rescued by a dashing hero. 'But that was not serious—you cannot think me so stupid and superficial that I would decide who to marry on the basis of his happening to find me first!'

'Actually, I do think exactly that!' said Miss Manning. 'You are what—nineteen?'

'Two and twenty,' said Olivia firmly.

At least while we are conversing like this, she was thinking, *no one is hurting me and I am also discovering something of their plans.*

'Precisely. Green, childish and unworldly. Most maidens would be swooning at the thought of marrying George.'

Not me, thought Olivia, but she bit the words back.

George laughed. 'My darling, clever Emma told me how you wished to be rescued and I fancied myself your rescuer. It is just the sort of thing silly young girls like you fall for.'

Olivia could hold back no longer. 'Except I didn't fall for it. Or you,' she said bluntly. 'But why do you call your sister "darling"?'

He gave a short laugh. 'Because,' he drawled, 'in truth she is not my sister.' He and Emma looked at each other.

Olivia could not, for a moment, understand this. She looked from one to the other and suddenly she *saw* what she had not seen before. '*Not* your sister? She is—*oh!*'

'Quite. Oh, your naivety is astounding!' He reached across her and lifted Miss Manning's hand to his lips. They looked at each other as he kissed her hand lingeringly. For the second time since they had abducted her, Olivia shuddered.

Her mind was reeling. What sort of man was he? And if Emma was his paramour, how come she would permit him to—?

'If he had married you,' said Emma, clearly reading her thoughts, 'he would only have shared your bed the one time to eliminate the possibility of annulment, as I said last night. It would have been worth it, for all we stood to gain.'

Olivia shook her head. She could barely take it in. She felt as though the ground were shifting beneath her, as if the world had suddenly turned to sand.

Yet she knew now exactly how strong she was. She had survived the ordeal with Gunn, she had learned of her own inner strength while supporting Charlotte and, somehow, she *knew* that she would survive this. Though waves of terror were threatening, so far she had managed to hold them off and keep her mind functioning.

A chance to escape would come, she thought. And she would be ready to take it. She had to—because a life with Jem was waiting for her. The thought caused belief to course through her. That was the prize. She was vaguely aware that, in her determination to make her own choices, to set her own path, the last vestiges of girlhood had left her. She was a woman, fighting for her future.

Forcing himself not to panic, Jem dismounted just outside the gate. According to Will, this is where Olivia had been taken. The carriage, and the people in it, could be none other than the Mannings.

Jem was berating himself. Why had he not worked it out? The previous kidnapping had been their first attempt to extort money from Olivia's family. He had suspected Manning was a liar—and had even felt guilty about holding such an uncharitable opinion. Last night the Mannings' plan to charm Olivia—or trap her—into marriage had further demonstrated their lack of integrity. Why had his mind not made the leap to the kidnapping—a hitherto disturbing, unexplained and altogether confusing incident?

Hell, damn and blast it! He could barely get past the image of Olivia, frightened and alone. In Farnham, he had done what was necessary to try to find her, but his brain—normally adept at seeing links and possibilities—had been lost under a wave of emotion.

It was the same now. Which is why he must not rush headlong into trying to find her. Remembering his futile trek through the hop lanes of Surrey, this time he would do better. He could afford to take a moment to search for information here, where she had been taken. He did not know what he was looking for—he had to be open to anything that might assist him.

There—was that blood on the ground? His stomach turned with anxiety. Had they harmed her? Dismounting, he led his horse to the dull red stain. Blood, for sure. His heart froze. A couple of feet away, more blood.

He followed the trail off the road, then lost it in the grass. Scanning around, he made for the undergrowth, leading his horse—which suddenly became skittish at something it could sense nearby. Then he saw something. A person, lying half-hidden under a row of hawthorns.

With a strangled cry, he dashed forward, Olivia's name on his lips.

It was not Olivia. It was an injured man, unconscious but breathing, and he was wearing the faded livery of a coachman. Of course—it was the Mannings' driver!

He gave a brief word of comfort to the man, but knew he could not tarry. The grooms would be here shortly and would carry the man back to the house, where he could be cared for.

He led the horse back to the road, pondering this. As he walked, he instinctively kept his eyes trained on the ground, seeking clues as to the driver's unfortunate experience and Olivia's abduction. The sun glinted off something ahead and he hurried to pick it up. A metal

button, like those typically seen on military uniforms.
It told him nothing—though something about it niggled
at his memory. Had there been yet another person there?
A soldier? Manning had no uniform, as far as he knew.
Nor Gunn. Absently, he stowed the button in his pocket,
then mounted his horse via a nearby tree stump.

His pause had taken no longer than two minutes. Now
time was of the essence. It would be difficult to catch
up with the carriage before the crossroad, but he had to
try. His Olivia as in danger!

'Gyah!' He spurred the horse and it responded, gal-
loping down the road with impressive pace.

As he rode, his mind was still working. Gradually,
resisting the diversions into blind panic, he pieced together the most likely circumstances—that Gunn had
ambushed the carriage, attacking the driver, then for an
unknown reason commandeered it…or that Gunn was
in league with the Mannings to kidnap Olivia again. But
how could they have known she would ride that way?
And why hurt the driver?

He could not imagine Olivia allowing them to take
her without a struggle. He hoped they hadn't hit her on
the head again. *Olivia!* His heart ached for her. Despite
himself, he could not help picturing her, being torn from
her horse by force and—

A thought struck him. Using precious seconds, he
slowed the horse to a canter. It would not do to over-
tire the creature anyway. Being careful not to drop it,
he fished the button out of his pocket and looked at it
again. This time, he recognised it. Not a military button, no. It was a button from Olivia's dashing, military-
style riding habit!

For some strange reason, this gave him hope. It was
a tangible link to her—an object that had been on her

person not long before. Reverently, he kissed it and replaced it carefully. She was alive—he felt it! Now, to
reach the crossroads in time!

Inside the carriage, a tense silence had settled over
them all. Olivia knew that she needed to think, to harness her energy and to plan. Perhaps her best option was
to stick closely to Emma.

Despite her loss of temper earlier, Olivia believed that
the woman was, in essence, a cold fish. She seemed to
care for nothing and no one save herself and George.
How could such a woman be reached?

Think! Olivia told herself.

She had had weeks of acquaintance with Emma.
There must be something that might divert or interest
her. Reviewing all the memories of her various inter-
actions with Miss Manning, she began to form a vague
plan. They both seemed to enjoy displaying their own
cleverness—perhaps she could try that.

'There is something I do not understand,' she announced curiously. As she'd hoped, both George and
Emma looked at her mildly—possibly relieved to break
the tedium of the journey. Carefully cultivating a puzzled
expression, Olivia addressed Emma directly, at the same
time absent-mindedly fiddling with one of the buttons
on the cuff of her riding habit. The matching button on
the other sleeve was missing.

'You say that you have need of money. Yet your
clothes are of the finest quality and are clearly new and
fashionable. This dress, for example—' she indicated
Emma's mauve silk overdress '—I have not seen anything so fine before. That lace trim is exquisite! How
could you possibly afford it?'

'Ah!' said Emma, preening slightly. 'It is rather fetching, is it not?' She smoothed her skirts, gliding her hands lovingly over the fine fabric.

'Indeed, it is the height of fashion,' Olivia agreed, 'and I confess most women I know would not wear something so fine or delicate for a journey. I always wear cotton or wool when travelling, never my finest muslins and certainly not any of my silks! If I were worried about money, I imagine I would be even more concerned about protecting my best dresses by stowing them carefully in a trunk.'

'You have never known hardship,' said Emma, her gaze hardening, 'or known what it is to be short of money.'

Olivia held her breath. She should not have mentioned money!

'But,' Emma continued, 'I shall explain. Yes, we are always in need of money. Both George and I have a fondness for fine clothes, comfortable surroundings and jewels.'

'And I have always admired your eye for fashion,' said Olivia. Was that too much? She wanted to flatter and soothe the woman, but if she was too obvious about it, Emma could turn against her.

Emma smiled serenely. 'I know. I have moved in the finest circles in five countries, yet nowhere have I met anyone with my impeccable taste. That is why I deserve the money to display my talent. I would not have been given such genius simply to spend my life as a seamstress.'

A seamstress—so that was how she had started out! Making fine dresses for wealthy ladies.

'You wanted to wear the dresses, not just make them.' Olivia spoke softly.

'Yes!' Something blazed in Emma's eyes. 'So I found myself a patron. He was old and disgusting—' she made a face '—but it was worth it. I had silks and furs, and a maid to wait on me. And for the first time, I felt as though things were right. Eventually I met George—'

'And I worshipped at your feet!' said George gallantly, on cue, like an actor in a play. Reaching across Olivia, he again lifted Emma's hand, kissed it, then smiled unpleasantly at Olivia. She almost retched. Oh, how had she ever taken this evil man seriously?

'We discovered that we were suited,' Emma continued. 'George and I have made our money in a dozen different ways these past years.' She smiled, a cruel smile. 'We find ourselves with barely a shilling at present and, this time, it is you who will suffer. An Earl's sister, born to wealth and position. We shall enjoy humbling you.'

Olivia shivered. There was, then, no protection to be had from Emma.

'We have used our intelligence and our skill to make a living everywhere we go. We ran a gaming house in Paris for a while and lived off a decrepit count in Italy for a year before that. That was when we first pretended that George was my brother. The old fool had no idea!' She laughed harshly. 'We know exactly the sort of weak-minded people to focus on. Mrs Buxted was ideal. She and her daughter have fed us and housed us for nigh on three months now. They even gave us the opportunity for George to try to seduce one of you into marriage.'

'I should have gone for Miss Ford or Miss Turner instead,' said George sulkily. 'This one is too opinionated.'

This one! It is as though he does not really see me as a person, Olivia thought. The notion repelled her. *Keep them talking!* she told herself.

'But—where did you get the clothes?'

'We ordered them from the finest modistes and tailors in London,' said Emma airily. 'The bills will be

presented to Mrs Buxted. Of course, if George had by
then been engaged to be married to a woman of wealth
and consequence, we would have explained that it was
simply a mistake.'

Olivia gasped at their audacity. 'Mrs Buxted believes
you have betrayed her.'

'Pah!' Emma waved this away. 'Mrs Buxted will recover!'

Olivia glanced out of the window, still fumbling absently at her sleeve. Recognising her surroundings, she
realised they were nearly at the crossroads. Her heart-
beat picked up pace again.

Suddenly, the carriage lurched to the left and they all
grabbed the straps to avoid falling over. Before Olivia
could even work out what was happening, they passed a
lumbering cart, coming from the other direction—Gunn
had clearly only just managed to avoid a collision. The
farm cart, Olivia saw as they flashed past, was teeter-
ing towards the ditch.

'Gunn is as useless a driver as he is a kidnapper!'
Emma snapped.

George was also taking stock of their surroundings.
Using his cane, he rapped the roof of the carriage to draw
Gunn's attention. 'Drive more carefully, man! And at the
crossroads turn left,' he ordered, 'towards Godalming!'

Soon, thought Olivia. *Wait until he has made the
turn…*

She tensed, then, at the right moment, she sprang
for the door. She managed to get the door open before
George, with an expletive, grabbed her from behind.
Emma helped subdue her, slapping her painfully in the
process.

'Idiot girl!' George snarled, when they had forced
her back into her seat. 'You will pay for this stupidity

later, when we have you to ourselves.' His tone changed. 'Emma, please look out of the window for a moment.'

Emma nodded regally and slid to the edge of the seat, staring fixedly out.

Slowly, deliberately, George advanced. Gripping Olivia's chin painfully with one hand, he forced his mouth on to hers. It was a blessedly brief demonstration of anger and power. There was not even, Olivia realised dimly, any lust in it. George simply wanted to punish her. And she felt it. Humiliation. Fear. Powerlessness. And, somewhere deep down, anger.

After only a few seconds he pushed her away, satisfied. Olivia wiped her mouth with a trembling hand, wrapped her arms across her body and cried.

Chapter Twenty-Four

Nearly there! Jem dashed along the road, knowing that the crossroads was very close. He rounded a bend in the road and pulled up with an expression of dismay. A farm cart had overturned and the cart, the horse, the farmer and a large amount of hay was entirely blocking the road. One wheel of the cart was in the ditch and the axle was broken.

'What happened?' he called out.

The farmer, who was still untying his prancing horse, launched into a convoluted explanation, in which 'cow-handed carriage drivers' featured prominently.

'When? When did this happen?' Jem interrupted, tersely. Normally he would have every sympathy for the farmer and would stop to help, but right now he could not.

He must reach Olivia!

'Not more'n two minutes ago,' replied the farmer. 'And what I'm s'posed to do now, I know not! I shall have to ride the horse bareback to Little Norton and fetch someone to take the cart away.'

Jem was no longer listening. Backing up, he spurred the stallion to a full gallop, then leaped over the pile of hay, landing sweetly and safely on the other side.

Just two minutes ago. So close! He pushed his mount harder and, thankfully, the crossroads came into view. Reaching the junction, he pulled up, looking left, then right and straight ahead.

There was no sign of the carriage.

No! This cannot be!

His mind fought the reality. He would have to choose and had only a one-in-three chance of choosing correctly. He looked to the right. That was the most obvious choice. There were any number of towns and villages along the route and plenty of side roads for them to hide themselves in. And yet…he looked left. Past Godalming was the road to Guildford, and beyond that, London. Or Maidstone and Dover.

Olivia! he thought. *Where are you, my love?*

As he spoke the words in his mind, the sun emerged from behind a cloud, glinting on something small and metallic on the Godalming road. Turning the horse, he trotted directly across to it, leaning over to look carefully at it.

It was a small silver button, in the military style. Its twin rested in his pocket.

'Oh, Olivia!' he said aloud. 'You are an absolute genius!' He straightened in the saddle. 'Let's go!'

Foxley's stallion, a gem of a horse, responded instantly. Jem galloped down the Godalming road, constantly scanning the way ahead.

There! In the distance, a lumbering carriage, with two saddle horses tied behind, one a familiar-looking skewbald. Slowing to a canter, Jem opened his saddlebag and took out a pistol.

'Oh, do stop snivelling!' Emma, with no sympathy whatsoever for Olivia's plight, handed her a handkerchief.

'Cry all you like, but do it *quietly*. This confounded snuffling and ragged breathing is irritating my nerves.'

'Well, tell him not to make me cry, then!' Olivia retorted, blowing her nose loudly. She offered the snot-filled linen back to Emma, who looked at it in disgust. Olivia tucked it into her sleeve—which now, like the other one, had a button missing.

She had thrown it out of the door just after they'd turned at the crossroads, in the hope that whoever came after her—Adam, Harry, or possibly Jem—might see it and know her direction. She had known that she couldn't possibly escape that way herself—not with two of them to haul her back—but, she reasoned, throwing the button without them realising might possibly help.

Discreetly, she was already working on loosening another button—this time from the front of her habit. It would be more noticeable once it was gone, but that couldn't be helped. She needed to have it ready to throw out, the moment they left the main road.

Logically, she knew that the buttons might never be seen and might not help her rescuers at all. But it helped *her* to feel better now, to do something which gave her a tiny sense of control over the situation. Remembering how she had rescued herself from the cellar, she made herself feel better by repeating confident words in her mind.

I am strong, she told herself. *I am resourceful. I have family who love me. They are coming for me.*

She refused to listen to the tiny voice inside that told her it would likely be at least another hour before anyone found her. Yet, when she heard the sound of hoof-beats approaching from behind at the gallop, she could not help but hope.

On either side, she felt George and Emma tense. 'If

you say the wrong thing,' hissed Emma, 'we will get Gunn to kill you!'

If I get the chance, Olivia resolved bravely, *I will tell this rider exactly what is going on!*

They all waited, keen to see if the rider would maintain his hurried pace and pass them with a nod, or whether he would slow down for a conversation alongside the carriage.

He was slowing. He was definitely slowing! He was going to pass on George's side of the carriage. George sat up straighter and hummed a little. He looked every inch the gentleman traveller, accompanying two ladies on a journey to Godalming.

'Good morning!' said the rider jovially, as he pulled up alongside.

Olivia's heart leapt—she knew that voice!

'Good mor— *You!*' George replied, with loathing.

'Yes, me,' confirmed Jem. 'Oh, dear, you sound disappointed! Never mind. I am come,' he continued in a pleasant tone, 'to fetch Lady Olivia back to Monkton Park. She has an appointment there, you see.'

Olivia's heart swelled. How had he caught up with them so quickly? His eyes met hers and his softened briefly. She nodded to signal that she was well and ready to do his bidding.

Jem quickened his pace and drew level with Gunn, briefly disappearing from view. A moment later, the carriage slowed, then stopped altogether, in a clatter of heaving wood and jingling reins. Without dismounting, Jem leaned forward and opened the door. 'Olivia,' he said. It was a command.

Olivia rose and climbed out of the carriage. 'Just a moment!' George, following, grabbed her arm. 'I say she stays with us, or I will have Gunn shoot you!' He put his arm around Olivia, then, looking insolently at Jem, he laid a wet kiss on Olivia's cheek.

Jem's eyes blazed. Without even dismounting, he leaned forward in the saddle and swung his fist hard at George.

Olivia distinctly heard the crack as George's nose broke. In the same instant, as he recoiled under Jem's blow, she found herself free to move. George lunged forward towards Jem, then pulled up short.

Jem seemed unperturbed. He held a lethal-looking pistol, now aimed at George. 'Gunn, unfortunately, is no longer in possession of his shotgun. When he saw my pistol just now, he decided to throw his shotgun to the ground, then pull up, at my request. He was sensible. Now, are you equally sensible, or must you go down as the one man in history who is more stupid than Mr Gunn? Hmmm?' He raised the pistol slightly and George, blood flowing freely from his nose, stepped back.

Jem glanced at Olivia. 'Untie your horse.'

He had thought this all through! Relieved, for her mind was almost overcome by her sudden change in fortune, Olivia hurried behind the carriage and liberated Faith's mare. She stroked the horse's face briefly, speaking soothing words to her, then drew her across to the milestone at the side of the road, which she perched on in order to mount.

Returning to Jem's side, she flashed him a brief smile. She was free—and it was Jem who had rescued her!

'It is not for me to tell you what you should do,' said Jem to George, 'but, if it were me, I should be leaving for the Continent before the Earl of Shalford catches up with the people who abducted his sister. Twice.'

Not waiting for a reply, he wished them a polite 'good day' and wheeled around, Olivia by his side. Her last sight of George and Emma was their set faces, grim with anger.

Jem looked over his shoulder as they cantered back down the road towards the crossroads. 'Gunn has jumped down and is searching for his shotgun. Let us make haste, in case he should decide to send a parting blast our way.'

Thy spurred their horses to the gallop and soon the carriage—and its armed driver—were left far behind. 'Was Manning armed?' Jem asked, not slowing his pace.

'I believe not,' Olivia replied. Then the implications of his words dawned on her. 'Do you mean to say you approached the carriage without knowing if he was armed or not?'

Jem grinned. 'Reckless, wasn't it? I do have Foxley's pistols, of course, but, yes, I had no idea what I would find. Will told me that Gunn had a shotgun, but I saw that the carriage driver had been punched, not shot. It gave me hope that they were trying to avoid actually murdering anyone.'

Olivia shuddered. 'Gunn must have hit him. He was threatening to kill George when I arrived. But you should not have taken such a risk!'

What if Jem had been killed? Her blood ran cold at the very thought.

'I had to do it, Olivia. You were in danger.' His tone was compelling. Olivia looked at him and the expression in his eyes was all she could wish.

She smiled shyly, then frowned. 'So—what do you think will happen now? Gunn threatened to turn George and Emma over to the magistrate. He had said he would, if I escaped again.'

'Did he?' Jem frowned. 'I did not anticipate that. I assumed they were all working together on your abduction, like last time.'

Olivia shook her head. 'Gunn was angry that he hadn't been paid. He told George, when they took me, that it was George's last chance.'

'I think their priority now will be to try to escape before Adam and Foxley's men catch up with them.' said Jem. 'I suspect they will aim for the coast. Their best chance will be to work together. The Mannings need a driver, and Gunn needs someone who will plan and make decisions.' He gave a short laugh. 'They are hobbled together in a mess of their own making!'

'Indeed,' Olivia agreed, remembering their cruelty in the carriage. 'I am glad that they are truly gone this time.'

By unspoken consent, they had slowed their horses to a walk, the better to converse.

Jem grimaced. 'Foxley will inform the magistrate, who will send word through his connections. Gunn's strange-looking horse and Manning's broken nose will be noticeable everywhere they go. They will be caught, unless they leave for France immediately.'

'But they have no money for their passage.' Olivia shuddered. 'What will happen to them?'

'Transportation, most likely. A few years' hard labour in New South Wales.'

They had turned at the crossroads and now discovered the road to Monkton Park was blocked by an overturned cart with a broken axle. There was nobody around it, but its cargo of hay was piled all over the road.

'The cart!' Olivia exclaimed. 'I think Gunn ran it off the road.'

'He did,' confirmed Jem. 'The farmer was most discommoded and has had to ride bareback to Little Norton to seek assistance.' He frowned. 'We shall have to go through the field, I think.' He patted his horse's neck. 'This fellow jumped it perfectly on the way out, but he is exhausted now. And I would not ask you to make such a jump side-saddle.'

He jumped down and opened the gate, leading his horse through. Olivia followed. After closing the gate again, Jem turned to catch Olivia as she dismounted.

Although she was a competent horsewoman and had no need of assistance, they both conveniently overlooked this fact. She landed lightly on the springy turf, his arms on hers, and was conscious that they both lingered a little longer than they should before Jem's arms dropped to his side.

Olivia's heart, stomach and gut were being severely tested today. First, the exhilaration of waking up this morning with her thoughts full of Jem, then the fear and distress she had experienced with Gunn and the Mannings. And now, her heart was racing again—this time in excitement. Finally, she was alone with Jem.

They walked towards a small stream running along the edge of the field, allowed the horses to drink a little, then turned and continued through the lush grass, all the while leading their horses and keeping parallel to the road. The scene was idyllic—sunshine on green meadows, a stand of oak trees in the distance and, somewhere close by, a bee humming among flowering hedgerows.

Jem stopped. 'Shall we rest here for a moment?'

Olivia agreed, sat down on the lush grass and arranged her skirts. Jem threw up the reins of both horses and allowed them to graze.

In truth, Olivia was glad of a chance to pause now that the danger was past. She looked up at him. 'That was hideous,' she said frankly, 'but I always knew that you—that someone would come for me and that all I had to do was to stop them from harming me in the meantime.'

He sat down beside her and took her hand, his face anguished. 'And did they harm you?'

She shuddered, remembering Emma's slaps, George's assault on her. 'It was not a pleasant experience,' she said carefully, 'and I promise to tell you later about it. But, would you mind if we do not—? I mean, right now, I am happy to be here in the sunshine, safe.' She eyed him directly. 'Safe with you.'

He caught his breath. 'Olivia, if you only knew how much I wanted to see you safe. I was so angry with Manning—and with myself for my blind stupidity. I should have seen how ruthless he was. But I knew one thing. I would have gladly given up my own life to rescue you.' His deep blue eyes gazed into hers, blazing with sincerity.

'That is—' She swallowed. 'That is the most wonderful thing anyone has ever said to me. And the most terrifying.'

He blinked. 'Terrifying? Why is it terrifying?'

She took a deep breath. *Now is the time*, she thought. *Say it!*

'Because if you were dead, then I might as well be dead, too.'

For an instant, he looked at her blankly, as if doubting her meaning. Then his gaze cleared, a look of wonder replacing the confusion. 'Truly?' He reached towards her, his hands gently sliding up her arms. 'Please tell me now, before my heart explodes in my chest. Is it possible that you feel for me something of what I feel for you?'

She sent him a mischievous smile. 'That depends on what it is that you feel for me. If you are asking if I love you, then, yes. Yes, I do.'

He did not reply with words. He simply took her in his arms and kissed her. And what a kiss! It was as if the danger they had faced, the real fear of losing each other for ever, came through in the hunger and relief with which they kissed each other. Olivia felt as though her body was on fire. *This* was where she was meant to be. In Jem's arms.

'Oh, Olivia, my love!' he murmured against her mouth. He moved back slightly to gaze at her. 'I cannot believe that you love me. I must be the luckiest man in history.'

'It is I who am the lucky one,' she retorted happily. 'Until very recently, I did not know my own heart and I might have lost you.'

He gave her a crooked smile. 'You really wouldn't have, you know.'

'But you might have fallen in love with someone else—Amy Turner, perhaps. My stupidity was so complete that I had told myself that what I had felt for you before was a young girl's infatuation.'

He spoke carefully. 'Miss Turner is a dear, sweet girl, but my heart has been yours ever since you cajoled and bullied me into trying to walk again, in your garden in London.'

Her jaw dropped. 'What? In London? Four years ago?' He nodded. 'But you treated me with such *politeness*! You indulged me as though I were twelve! And then you *left me*!'

He heard the anguish in her tone. 'I did, didn't I? I suspected that you were not indifferent to me. But I assumed you would experience many such infatuations before you were old enough to know your heart. I am so sorry.'

She considered this, trying to be fair. 'It is true that I did not understand then how deeply I loved you. It was after you had gone that I knew it beyond doubt. I was miserable. And even then, I convinced myself last month that it had been a case of an old *tendre* and that I should be friendly towards you, not expecting or seeking anything more.'

'I, too, tried to convince myself that my feelings for you had been a passing fancy. Yet I never forgot you, all those years I was away. And then I came back and your *friendship* almost slayed me,' he growled. 'I was wild trying to get you to truly *see* me—and not just as a friend.'

The irony—both of them had wanted more than friendship, yet had not known how to bring it about.

A new thought struck her. 'But you cannot have *known* back then, four years ago, that you loved me?'

'Oh, I suspected it. But how was I to woo my Captain's younger sister, a girl of only eighteen, whose mind was full of balls and routs and compliments from numerous young men? How could I have spoken? You were a young girl, only just out, and sister to an Earl. And who was I? A humble ensign, crippled, green and unsure. Of good family, but—back then—few prospects. Your guardian would have been an idiot to allow me to court you!'

'I never thought about what Adam might say. It is true that he did not know you then. But he does now.' She shook her head wonderingly. 'All this time and I had no notion… Well, I take it back.' He looked at her quizzically. 'I am not the only stupid one. You were very stupid, too.'

He laughed aloud at this and she watched, enjoying the view of his handsome face, totally relaxed and content. 'Go on,' he said. 'Elucidate. Tell me of my stupidity.'

'Well,' she said primly, 'you cannot complain now that I did not *see* you. You should have *made* me see you. These past weeks, I mean.'

'How?' he asked. 'You are my sister's best friend *and*

you are my best friend's sister. Our two families are so close and so mixed up that I believed you saw me as a brother. Indeed, you told me so. That is why I resisted for so long.'

She was a little chastened by this, but determined to be honest. 'Well, I did give that impression, I suppose. Until I discovered the truth in my own heart. I—' She blushed a little. 'The kisses helped.'

'Sorry? What was that?' He placed a gentle finger under her chin, tilting her head up so he could see into her eyes. 'Something about my kisses?'

Her blush deepened, but she forced herself to be frank with him. 'Your kisses are amazing. I have never experienced anything like them. I—'

Jem had clearly heard enough. His mouth covered hers again and once again they became lost in a sensuous dream.

Some time later—or it might have been just a few minutes—Olivia realised that Jem had suddenly stopped kissing her. Not only that, but he had leapt to his feet and was now standing, with a hand outstretched, offering to help her up. She looked at him in confusion and he groaned.

'Please do not look at me like that, Olivia, or we shall never manage to wait for the wedding.'

'Wedding?' she repeated foolishly, her mind still considering—and rather liking—the physical effect they had on each other.

'Yes. Wedding,' he replied tersely. 'You know, when two people get married.'

She stood, suddenly very interested in the conversation.

'What wedding?' Her hands went to her hips as she glared at him.

'*Our* wedding, of course!'

She arched her brows. 'Well, if that is meant to be a proposal, I must inform you that it is not very romantic!'

He grinned, unperturbed by her feigned outrage. 'Wait a moment.' He took both her hands and gazed at her, his expression suddenly serious. 'Olivia.' Her breath caught in her throat. The entire universe stilled, coalesced around them. Everything else disappeared. Only Jem mattered.

'You are the most beautiful, kind-hearted, loyal woman I know.' His voice shook a little. 'You are also the bravest. These past weeks have confirmed what I always knew. You have an uncommon heart and a capacity for courage that would not shame the greatest of generals. You are in truth my best friend, my favourite companion and my inspiration. I love you. I have loved you since the earliest days of our acquaintance and I shall always love you like this. I have spent years falling ever more deeply in love with you—even when we were apart. I want nothing more than to spend the rest of my life with you.' He took a deep breath. 'Olivia, will you marry me?'

'Yes,' she said, her eyes shining. She was incapable of saying more.

He kissed her sweetly, then they simply stood, arms about each other, resting in each other's embrace. Olivia closed her eyes. She felt it all in that moment. The peace of the countryside, the sun warming her back and the love of her life in her arms.

Happiness, she thought. *This is true happiness.*

* * * * *

COMING NEXT MONTH FROM

⬡ HARLEQUIN®

⬡ ISTORICAL

Available October 16, 2018

All available in print and ebook via Reader Service and online

CONVENIENT CHRISTMAS BRIDES (Regency)
by Carla Kelly, Louise Allen and Laurie Benson
Delve into three convenient Regency arrangements with a captain, a viscount and a lord, all in one festive volume.

A TEXAS CHRISTMAS REUNION (Western)
by Carol Arens
Bad boy Trea Culverson returns, bringing excitement back into widow Juliette Lindor's life. With the town against him, can Juliette show them *and* Trea that love is as powerful as any Christmas gift?

A HEALER FOR THE HIGHLANDER (Medieval)
A Highland Feuding • by Terri Brisbin
Famed healer Anna Mackenzie is moved by Davidh of Clan Cameron's request to help his ailing son. But Anna has a secret that could jeopardize the growing heated passion between them...

A LORD FOR THE WALLFLOWER WIDOW (Regency)
The Widows of Westram • by Ann Lethbridge
When widow Lady Carrie musters the courage to request that charming gadabout Lord Avery Gilmore show her the wifely pleasures she's never had, he takes the challenge *very* seriously!

BEAUTY AND THE BROODING LORD (Regency)
Saved from Disgrace • by Sarah Mallory
Lord Quinn has sworn off romance, but when he happens upon an innocent lady being assaulted, he marries her to protect her reputation. Quinn must help Serena fight her demons, and defeat his own...

THE VISCOUNT'S RUNAWAY WIFE (Regency)
by Laura Martin
After many years, Lord Oliver Sedgewick finally finds his runaway wife, Lucy. The spark between them burns more intensely than ever, but does their marriage have a chance of a happy future?

HOME on the RANCH

HRCBPA18R

Get 4 FREE REWARDS!

We'll send you 2 FREE Books
plus 2 FREE Mystery Gifts.

Harlequin Presents® books feature a sensational and sophisticated world of international romance where sinfully tempting heroes ignite passion.

FREE Value Over $20

READERSERVICE.COM

Manage your account online!

- Review your order history
- Manage your payments
- Update your address

We've designed the Reader Service website just for you.

Enjoy all the features!

- Discover new series available to you, and read excerpts from any series.
- Respond to mailings and special monthly offers.
- Browse the Bonus Bucks catalog and online-only exculsives.
- Share your feedback.

Visit us at:

ReaderService.com

RS16R